SUSAN BARRETT was born in 1938 in Plymouth and was educated at the Royal School, Bath. She spent some years in various London advertising agencies. Since 1962 she has spent most of her time in Greece, at one period teaching English in Athens. She now lives on a Greek island with her husband, Peter, a painter, and her two children. Her first novel, *Jam Today*, was published in 1969 and is also available from Sphere Books.

*Also by Susan Barrett and available
in Sphere Books*

JAM TODAY

Noah's Ark

SUSAN BARRETT

SPHERE BOOKS LIMITED
30/32 Gray's Inn Road, London WC1X 8JL

First published in Great Britain in 1971 by Michael Joseph Ltd
Copyright © Susan Barrett 1971
First Sphere Books edition 1973

Set in Monotype Times

Printed in Great Britain by
Hazell Watson & Viney Ltd
Aylesbury, Bucks

ISBN 0 7221 1454 0

CHAPTER ONE

Timothy Blunden had got into the unpleasant habit of waking up sharply too early in the morning. He swiftly crossed a clear demarcation line between sleep and wakefulness at 6.10 a.m. by the bedside clock. He woke as though pushed from behind into the day, with a feeling of anticipation. It took him until 6.11 to work out if it was a childhood birthday morning feeling or a French examination one. At 6.11 he knew. It was a birthday morning feeling. He would then lie awake looking for its cause. It hardly ever was his birthday, and anyway by the time you've had thirty of those you don't wake up with much excitement. Had anything happened at work which might possibly cause it? A rumoured bonus, perhaps, that would be confirmed today? The sudden grant of a week's holiday? The opportunity to check the mail in the small mail-room with Joyce? Was it Sunday, or even Friday? Was it kippers for breakfast?

By 6.15 he had examined minutely the present circumstances of his life and realised there was no possible reason for waking brightly, early, and excited; and with this realisation, the feeling of happy anticipation would fade rapidly, leaving him gloomily awake.

Timothy Blunden would then settle on his back beside Mrs. Blunden, wait with resigned patience for the alarm to ring at 7.35, and indulge in fantasies.

He had several favourites. There was the one in which he was behind the counter at the travel agency and in walked this willowy black-haired widow. (He made her a widow to give her a substantial legacy from the husband.) He saw the scene from a point a little to the back and right of the window, which gave him a view of himself as well. He looked casually alert, the light of sophisticated amusement and foreknowledge playing in his eyes, and his nose was straight. The widow leant on the counter between them, and asked his advice in a low voice. She wanted to travel, a long way and for a long time, to forget her sorrow. She didn't want to go alone. She couldn't go alone. Did he know anyone trustworthy and capable who might accompany her, all expenses paid, and where might they go? Timothy usually made her visit the agency several times over a matter of weeks, which he skipped, until at last she prevailed on him to accompany her. But in spite of skipping the time element, he often found himself bogged down in working out the details of the trip—two 1st-class tickets to Venice was so much, plus boat to Piraeus, what was seven and eight, he always thought it was 13 but it never was, and had he remembered to send the Two Fabulous Weeks in Wales leaflet? Often the alarm went off before he and his widow had left Dover.

More satisfactory was the Polly Kitchen one. Polly Kitchen was real. She—and her husband Paul, but forget him—ran the antique shop next door but one to the travel agency where he worked. Polly Kitchen was a goddess, larger than life, with fair hair drawn away from her noble brow and caught at the back of her head by an assortment of strange clips, picked from the shop-window tray of murky metal jewellery. From there it cascaded in unstylish ringlets on to her broad shoulders. She padded round the shop in thong sandals, always wore black trousers, but over them a different tent-like garment every day. Timothy, who passed the shop several times a day, often speculated on the origin of these garments. Were they Indian shawls, in which Polly had sewn a few seams in appropriate places? Were they table-cloths? Bedspreads? Did Polly wear one on Tuesday, and sell it on Wednesday as a curtain? The colours and patterns were consistently oriental.

In reality Timothy and Polly had a nodding acquaintance. When he passed the shop—Paul & Polly Kitchen Antiques, each word having equal weight so that one was left in doubt as to whether it was Paul & Polly Kitchen, Antiques, or Paul & Polly, Kitchen Antiques—he nodded hopefully at the window. Sometimes beyond his reflection he saw Polly nodding pleasantly, if vaguely, back. Was she nodding at him as a possible customer, or as the man who worked two doors away? It hardly mattered, because from 6.11 to 7.35 most mornings she and Timothy were at far closer quarters.

Sometimes these fantasies were so vivid that Timothy couldn't bring himself to nod at the window of Paul & Polly Kitchen Antiques when he passed it an hour or two later.

Timothy and Tina had been married for six years. Tina's parents had helped them with the deposit on number Six,

The Grove, and they had lived there for two years having spent the first four years of their marriage in a succession of meagre, ill-furnished flats. Number Six was precious to them; they still discussed paint colours in the evenings, whether they might buy an armchair they had seen or not, if they could yet afford curtains in the third tiny bedroom. Timothy's salary as manager of the branch of the travel agency barely covered the mortgage repayments. Tina did as much typing as she could, in the evenings and while their eighteen-month-old son slept in the afternoons, to earn a bit extra. Occasionally a letter from her parents contained a generous cheque, with a brief message from her father to get herself some little thing. The some little thing was invariably settlement of a two-month-old grocer's bill.

Number Six was theirs, though, which more than made up for infrequent evenings out and in spite of the fact that it was identical to numbers One, Two, Three, Four and Five on their side and to numbers Seven to Fourteen down the other side. One could almost say number Six was exceptional. It was an end house like numbers One, Seven and Fourteen. But numbers One and Fourteen were at the wrong end of the two rows, only separated from the road by a narrow forecourt provided for the temporary parking of Grove cars. (Rule 27 of The Grove Residents Association Regulations: residents with garages must garage their cars for any period longer than one hour.) Numbers Six and Seven lay at the garden end, number Seven gaining slightly in amenity by being the end house of the longer row, and so looking out over the garden. Number Six missed this view, through having no side windows, only the standard front and back windows. But a white-barred gate in the private back garden of the house opened in the yellow-brick walls on to the shrubs of the communal garden, which had been chosen for their hardy resistance to children rather than for delicate beauty. It was possible to slip from the back of number Six through the shrubs that bordered the muddy grass and into the front door of number Seven without being seen. This could be, and was later, most useful for the occupants of numbers Six and Seven.

Timothy had first met Tina at the tennis club. They had paired in mixed doubles and did well as a couple, Tina doing the running around and Tim thudding them back from the serving line. But, although Tim had admired Tina's

7

long plait, and Tina had liked the backs of Tim's legs, no serious romance had developed, which wasn't surprising as they were only twelve at the time. Then Tina's mother had got worried about her daughter's vowel sounds and had persuaded her husband, who was more concerned for his finances, to send Tina to a small private school, which paid far more attention to quiet behaviour and rigid manners than to education. Fortunately, Tina's mother was happy with the results. The vowels that had been stretched sideways at the local school were drastically pulled out the other way at the distant boarding school and Tina lost the friends she'd had at home. When she was eighteen, there was another long talk from her mother to her father—thank God, he thought, I've only one child—and Tina was sent off to be finished in Switzerland. There she acquired a few sophisticated mannerisms, a liking for lemon tea, and an ability to type. Also she became reconciled to her name. In her last year at school, she had been going through a fattish stage and had called herself Antonia to counteract this. But the name Tina in Switzerland made her think of fragile Russian princesses rather than poodles and girls in organza. So she gave up Antonia and creamy cakes. After a year, when presumably she was finished, she returned to England, languid and dangerously thin. Her mother was horrified and planned a domestic science course, after another talk with her husband. But Tina had developed a will of her own, and suddenly and without warning went to Finland as an au pair for a year. She came back with a strong social conscience brought on by a Lapp fitted not only with Finnish health service dentures and spectacles but with a health service nose as well, and enrolled at the London School of Economics. She found herself a flat and some friends from various parts of the world, went home less and less for weekends and, with a deep frown on her forehead, was happier than she had ever been before or was likely to be in the future. By this time she was a girl with a set of firmly-held opinions, none of which would she give up, although she was always ready to gain new ones. She had a consuming interest in other people, and an exaggerated admiration for anything foreign. People, places and objects were better and better the further away from home. So, in her scale, a bun from her home-town bakery would be at the lowest point of the scale and a Japanese rice cracker at the top. She was brisk and bright and completely lacking in a sense of humour. Her friends, and she had many friends, would say dear Tina and I'm so fond of Tina and not see her more often than once a month. She was rather heavy-going, a little too intense. Her pale blue eyes hardly ever blinked in conversation but stared into her companion's. It was noticeable that anyone talking to her became strangely jumpy, glancing up and down, around and away, and hands nervously fiddled with hair.

Only Tim remained calm before Tina's blue eyes. After some years of marriage he had ceased to be conscious of her steady gaze; and at the beginning, when he had been aware of it, he had been thrilled with the attention, convinced that it was adoration.

They had met again in Dillon's second-hand bookshop. They had both reached to pick up the same book, and drawn back when they had noticed the other hand.

'Sorry,' said Tim, looking up at Tina.

'Sorry,' said Tina, looking up at Tim.

They liked to talk about this re-union, they often went over the details. 'It was awfully romantic, wasn't it,' Tina would say, staring into Tim's brown eyes. 'Meeting again over G. M. Trevelyan's *Social History of England*.'

'Yes,' Tim would say, gazing back.

'You know,' Tina would go on, as though she had just thought of it, 'I think it was significant, a kind of symbol. Don't you?'

'Yes,' Tim would reply. He wasn't much of a talker.

The middle child of five, he had missed out on a great deal of the family conversation and attention. To have Tina talking to him alone and looking at him alone was thrilling. For years he had sat almost unnoticed in a row of children at family meals, only remembered when he had failed to pass the salt. 'Salt, Timothy!' they'd shout. '*Salt*. Oh, he's off again.' His mother would then come to his rescue. 'He's in a brown study, don't get him out of it, it's dangerous to jolt a child out of a stare, it damages the brain cells,' So Timothy would be left in his brown study, which he imagined literally as a small cosy den, painted British Railways brown, with chocolate brown walls, the paint peeling slightly in places, and himself seated on the single brown chair at the single brown desk. There were no books. It wasn't that sort of study.

At school he would have done far better had he not hated competition. In the lower forms he got exceptionally high marks at English, History, Science and Mathematics. Then a boy called Blight, E. Arthur Blight or sometimes Edward A. Blight, caught him up and challenged his star position. Blunden T. dropped Science completely, much to the dismay of the Science Master. He ceased to try at Maths and regularly failed the end of term examinations. He still got good marks at English and History, though he made a point of not learning what he should, and knew to his secret satisfaction that if he tried he could beat Blight E. A. By the time the G.C.E. examinations came up and it became necessary to try, he had lost the knack; and though he sat eight subjects, he gained only five. To his intense surprise, he found he had left school. Looking back, Tim often considered that it was at this stage that he had become conscious for the first time. If only it had happened earlier. . . . He would have passed all his subjects, and stayed on to take Advanced Levels, maybe gone to University. As it was, he had left school at sixteen, with five Ordinary Levels and no plans for the future bar a week's hitch-hiking in Devon and Cornwall with three school-friends. He tried to glorify his adult state by smoking and drinking heavily that holdiay, to demonstrate to his friends his superior position. He had left school. They were going back. But his friends smoked and drank too, and besides the hang-overs which they shared with Timothy, they would soon have Advanced Levels and even perhaps degrees.

On his return from Cornwall, his father singled him out from his brothers and sisters. 'Well, Tim,' he said, 'what did you say you were going to do?'

'Nothing, I don't think,' said Tim, opening the front door.

'Nothing? You don't imagine I can support you all for ever.'

You all, thought Tim, never just me. 'I meant, I had said nothing about what I'm going to do.'

'Oh. Ah. Where's Moth-ah?' He always called her Moth-ah, as though it were a joke, and it probably had been the first couple of years of her motherhood.

'In the kitchen, I think.'

His father moved away down the hall. Tim opened the front door wider, and his father turned quickly. 'Don't go out just yet, we're having a chat. Come into the kitchen and tell me your plans.'

So Tim went into the kitchen and joined his father, and

younger brother and sister and his mother at the table. While his mother dealt a series of unanswered questions around the table, and his brother and sister muttered over their homework, he told his father his plans, made up that moment. 'I was thinking of a foreign correspondent,' he began.

'Which one had you in mind?' asked his sister, 'If A is equal to the sum of the oh deary deary me.'

'Shut up for once.'

'What on earth do you mean by that?' asked his mother.

'Is that my tea?' asked his father, looking at the cup before him with misgiving, 'It's blooming worse than the office.'

'I made it fresh just a moment ago.'

'Can we stay up late, it's Dangerman.'

'Certainly not, you were up to all hours last night. Anyway, it's the Circle tonight and I have to go because Mrs. Willis didn't last week and she said it was my turn, not that that has anything to do with it, and Helen's got that dance and will you be in, Tim?'

'Of course I suppose you mean a journalist, you can't be foreign correspondent straight off, and that means a job on the local paper, that's how journalists start, I suppose, a job on the local paper, not a bad idea, I know old Winch, he's an awful old fool at the club but I daresay he's not a bad boss and he might take you on if I had a word with him. Moth-ah make us a fresh pot, I can't drink this.'

So, rather than do this and stay at home, Tim surprised his father and saddened his mother by finding out on his own how to join the Merchant Navy, and joining it.

It was the three years in the Merchant Navy that appealed to Tina when she heard about this stage of Tim's life as they drank coffee together after meeting in Dillon's. There was something tough and threatening about the Merchant Navy; it was totally masculine, a rough cloth contrast to her angora upbringing at boarding and finishing school.

'I suppose you travelled a lot,' she said ingenuously, admiration and awe in her gaze.

'We got around,' said Tim, though he looked as though he had never been further south than Penge or further north than Pinner in his life. At this point he was apprenticed to a firm of chartered accountants and re-sitting his law papers every June. His skin was sallow, which made him look tanned in the orange light of the coffee-shop; his face was still

11

boyish, and so was his light brown hair, which grew in springy curls straight up from his broad forehead. He looked freshly shaven, even when he missed a morning's shave. He gave the impression of being good-looking; he was the same height as Tina but his slimness made him seem taller, he moved gracefully and dressed well, his expression was open and kind. But if you were to look at him more carefully, you would sense petulance in the face, hinted at by the slight droop of his lower lip which gave him the expression of someone who is losing at cards and determined not to cry. His eyes were almost too beautiful for a grown man, large and sometimes the brown of pale ale, but more often veiled through looking inwards. And his nose, that had been his best feature and had drawn a classical line from mid-brow to mid-lip, now led as straight as ever but from mid-brow to right-hand corner of his mouth.

'And what on earth happened to your nose?' asked Tina, not for a moment thinking this might be considered too personal a question. She could be relied on to ask the questions that other people wanted to ask, but were too tactful to do so. But Tim was pleased. The girl he was taking out at the time would never have shown such interest and no doubt thought that his nose was naturally at an angle, although he had made a point of displaying a photograph of himself taken before his nose had been broken.

'Oh, that,' he said, fingering the bridge. 'Happened in the Merchant Navy.' This was true. He had been a merchant seaman when he had run for a number 26 and bumped into the bus stop. How tough, how threatening, thought Tina, and before they had finished their coffee, they were both delightfully in love with each other and with the image of themselves in each other's eyes.

The period of courtship started. They glowed for each other. Tim provided Tina with a comforting part of her background and childhood. Now, instead of listening to fellow-students discussing the problems of the world, she did the talking, to Tim. He listened patiently to her concerned quoting of the statistics of world poverty; though he often tried to balance the picture by slotting into the conversation various affluent acquaintances of his from Merchant Navy days. Tina, in fact, welcomed their appearance; they provided a distinctly refreshing antidote to the great armies of poor and diseased and under-privileged that peopled her set books and lectures. She liked to hear, too, of Tim's plans for his personal wealth. He had hundreds, and she skilfully sorted them into two classes—profiteering, which she discouraged, and socially philanthropic, which she encouraged. Fruit-machine salesman, for instance, she put in the first category and dismissed; but picture gallery on wheels was encouraged for it was Culture for the Masses and decidedly socially philanthropic. Luckily, her second category was elastic in terms; for she didn't want to be the wife of a poor man.

In return, she gave Tim an introduction to another world. At this time, he was paying guest with an aunt in Beckenham. He went up to the City every morning on the 8.5 in the dark, he returned on the 5.55 in the dark, and he escaped from the depressing and almost friendless routine of his life by the most enjoyable fantasies. Now he had met Tina again, he found himself invited to parties, to gatherings at her flat, where he met a refreshing variety of girls. There was Diane, small, blonde, and athletic, who dressed in heather-mixture tweeds and went home to Dorset most weekends to see her horses. She treated Tim like a favourite cousin; using the flirtatious, safely bantering approach which is reserved for boyfriends of girlfriends when the alternative, coolly polite approach is not considered necessary. As a result, Tim often saw himself in hacking jacket, carrying Diane home after a nasty accident on a hedge. Then there was Sumi, who sat cross-legged on the floor at his feet, dark-skinned Sumi, black-ringleted Sumi, from Manchester; and June, who was distinguished by her job, which involved driving Foreign Office cars around at night and not talking about it. They provided Tim with excellent fantasy material. Then there were men around the flat too, of course, coming up the stairs, going down the stairs, waiting outside the kitchen or the lavatory; but Tim never got to know who belonged to whom. He never seemed to meet the same one twice.

One weekend they went to their home town together. Tim stayed with his parents, Tina with hers. A meeting was arranged between the two sets of parents on the Saturday afternoon. Tim's parents went to tea with Tina's. It was not a success.

'I hardly had time to stub out a cigarette, before she whipped the ash-tray away and washed it up.'

'The poor husband, he had to take off his shoes before coming into the porch, did you notice?'

'Seems a nice enough girl though, and I should think there's a bit of money around.'

'She'd bully Timothy—'

'He needs it. Maybe she'd push him through his exams.'

And, on the other side,

'Where can she have met him?'

'At the club.'

'We should never have let her go to that socialist college.'

'But she met him here, at the tennis club.'

'At the tennis club? I wouldn't have thought—'

'I daresay it's only a stage.'

'As long as she grows out of it.'

'He seemed a nice young man though, quite polite.'

'Doesn't seem to have a proper job.'

'He's studying to be an accountant, a chartered accountant.'

'Well, that would be all right, I suppose. But he doesn't seem to be getting on very fast with it.'

'I think we might take Tina abroad with us this spring.'

But, in the spring, Tina announced her engagement to Timothy Blunden, without her parents' approval, even encouraged by her parents' disapproval. She romanticised the situation to her friends till it took on the flavour of elopement. 'Just so long as you're really happy, darling,' wrote her mother, 'we don't expect you to take any notice of what we think.' This worried Tina.

'Might Tim come and stay with us one weekend, so that you can get to know each other?' she wrote back, by return of post.

'So *this* is the fiancé,' said an elderly friend at a cocktail party, held bravely in Tim's honour.

'Well,' said Tina's mother and laughed brightly.

But at the party, an unsuspected quality in Tim emerged. He was almost shockingly attractive to older women, and through no effort on his part. In fact, he seemed quite unconscious of it. He merely stood in front of them, arms folded, one leg crossed over the other, and gave them all his attention, occasionally nodding agreement or smiling sympathy with whatever they happened to be telling him at the time. He handed round drinks and plates of tiny food, fetched extra glasses, opened bottles, found ash-trays, and Tina's mother suddenly saw the assets of a son-in-law. Next day he went with them to church and seemed to know the hymns. He discussed his money-making plans with Tina's father, a retired naval officer who had made in the past many similar plans for execution in retirement. He helped with the washing-up in a willing manner, and by the time they went to the station to catch the train back to London, he was considered a success, qualified only by his parents (and they wouldn't have to meet them often) and his unqualified state.

'Love to Tim,' wrote Tina's mother at the end of her next letter.

'Good luck in your exams,' wrote Tina's father on a card attached to a bottle of whisky.

Tim failed the law papers again.

Tina gained her Social Science Diploma.

Impatient of the narrow bed in Tina's room in the shared flat, they were now anxious to get married.

'Well,' said Tina's mother, struggling to find her hand-kerchief, 'it was a lovly wedding, though I say it myself.'

'Yes,' said Tim's mother, thinking of her daughter's wedding which had been much more fun, 'it was beautiful, and weren't we lucky with the weather.' She handed Tina's mother a Handy Andy. Tina's mother looked at it, and found her own lace-edged handkerchief.

'Let's be realistic, Tim,' said his father-in-law, 'you can't support a wife and maybe children in your present job.' He introduced him to a friend of his who had a travel agency with branches in South London, and Tim was fixed up with better pay, and a small furnished flat in Wandsworth over one of the branches. Tina, instead of joining the Child Care Department of the Borough Council as a trainee officer, as planned, joined it as a typist and so earned more. Both these courses were considered merely temporary. Tim would continue to study in the evenings for his accountancy exams, and Tina would return to her social work as soon as he was qualified.

Five years and several flats later, Tim was still unqualified —he had virtually forgotten all about accountancy—and Tina was a mother and part-time typist, rather than a Child Care Officer and part-time mother.

We were in a bit too much of a hurry to get married, Tim sometimes thought, as he caught sight of Tina's cross face over the typewriter in the evenings. If we'd waited like I said

15

(he forgot that he had been more impatient than Tina), I would be a qualified accountant by now. But of course, if we had waited, I probably wouldn't have married Tina in any case—which might have been a very good thing.

He knew he was unfair in his reasoning. If he hadn't married Tina, he wouldn't have had the deposit on a house like number Six, The Grove, he wouldn't have got into the travel agency, and he might still be trying to pass the accountancy exams. He might have married the watery girl who lived near his Beckenham aunt, and have turned out quite a different person. As it was, he and Tina had developed together and they thought they understood one another perfectly. They knew how much sugar each liked in coffee. He knew that her 'just a moment' meant 'don't talk to me now or I'll scream'; she knew his 'all right' meant he didn't agree at all. They had, in fact, reached the stage—which, dangerously, they did not consider dangerous—when words become unnecessary. Any resentment they felt towards each other was quickly hidden away, to make room for gratitude. For Tina was grateful too. She needed someone to push and pull, manage and comfort; she was a giver and Tim readily accepted her gifts. And when there was a little too much pushing and pulling, or too many demands for thanks, he escaped into the imaginary embrace of Polly Kitchen.

On Friday, 7th May, at 6.10 a.m. Timothy Blunden shot into the day from the blankness of deep sleep. What was so exciting about today? It was Friday, yes, the end of the week, true, but that was hardly enough to cause this tingling anticipation. Oh fuck it, he said to himself, turning over on to his back, this bloody habit I've got into. Here we go again.

Now. This widow comes into the office, no not her again. Somebody new. This girl comes into the office, like that one yesterday but not with her husband, what's happened to her husband, gone on a business trip, good idea, and she's off on her own for a week make it three and she wants to go she wants to go to well I'll leave that for the moment. Immediately there is this great physical attraction between us, there she is standing in front of the counter and there am I standing behind the counter or maybe I was at the leaflet table that's better there I am at the leaflet table bending down looking at the leaflets and I feel her there behind me and I

16

straighten up and we look at each other this great physical attraction she doesn't wear a nightdress in bed but we haven't got there yet Tina always wears a nightdress can't see her in the great rampaging freedom of nudity like this girl. Now. What size are her bosoms? Large, small, medium. The widow has large, Polly Kitchen has large, so let's make this girl have size 36 A cup, or maybe 34 B cup don't say it's raining again I wish we had a car a huge old Bentley convertible is that my style or a small and speedy sports but what we would have of course is the Grove classic, an A40. I'd drive to work instead of getting wet at the bus stop, I'd snarl and hoot to work screech of brakes and this girl with the 34 B cup would jump in, she's small blonde and athletic like Diane. Maybe she is Diane, how about that, meet her again, where though? At a party, we don't seem to go to parties any longer, now why is that, there must be parties going on in London but they're not inviting us, they're inviting beautiful single girls, why don't our friends invite us to parties with beautiful single girls. Maybe our friends don't know any beautiful single girls. We don't know any beautiful single girls. Our friends don't have parties. We don't have parties. We have supper parties, *supper* parties, and we go to them in pairs, married pairs, I'm living in a bloody Noah's Ark. I wonder whether there was rebellion on board.

Once upon a time there was a giraffe called Timothy. He lived on Noah's Ark with his wife. He and his wife were the only giraffes on board. The giraffe called Timothy began to dream of beautiful single giraffes. But there were no beautiful single giraffes on board; only married monkeys, married crocodiles, married bears, married elephants, married iguanas, a pair of every species of bird, beast and fowl of the air or however it goes, each half of the pair linked indissolubly to the other by the laws of nature. The giraffe called Timothy grew tired of his dreams of beautiful single giraffes that did not exist and began to covet the goods of his neighbour, which in this case happened to be a female hamster. Although he had chosen his female giraffe above all other female giraffes he had known at the time, chosen her as Ark's companion, it had been a comparatively hasty decision with Noah waiting there in the pouring rain, and he hadn't fully appreciated at the time that it might go on for ever. The female hamster possessed many charms that were lacking in his wife; she was golden-furred, delicately made, light and

17

quick on her feet, and had the sweetest shortest neck he had seen in his life. He wove fantasies round the female hamster. As they lined up in the meal queue together—for the meal queue was in alphabetical order, elephant, giraffe, hamster—he hankered after her. But without hope, for he knew the union between giraffe and hamster was taboo, socially and biologically impossible. Unfulfilled desire gnawed at his soul, his skin grew itchy, he went off his meals, only joining the queue to help Tina get her quota and to have the opportunity of standing next to the hamster at the bus stop. Better to have stayed outside, drowned in the flood, than to have joined the Ark—

An elbow prodded his ribs. He let out an exclamation of anger. My wretched bony giraffe is at me again, oh for the softness of the hamster. Stroke the golden fur, look into those liquid eyes in all this lashing rain, oh it's gone, got out of bed, let in the chill, it wasn't a hamster at all, it had bones, bloody giraffe again—

Tina ripped back the curtains, making sure that daylight reached Tim's pillow. He'd pulled the covers round him again, and turned over, his face deeper in the pillow. She went and leant over him, quite gently pulling the sheet down till she could see his nose. 'It's a quarter to eight, we slept through the alarm again.'

He groaned, and his mind put out feelers towards reality. It was Friday, it was raining, he'd woken at dawn, he'd just been drifting off again, he was cross. Tina was bright and awake. She said it was late. He'd been late yesterday, he must be on time today. He had to get up. He would wait till Tina had peed and washed.

'Rotten night again,' he mumbled into the pillow. 'Been awake for hours, let me sleep in.'

'Been awake for hours!' Tina snorted, and sat down at the dressing-table. It was a kidney-shaped piece of furniture with an oval mirror edged with pink, green and yellow china flowers and, to match, pink, green and yellow flowered material gathered and flounced from table-top to floor, hiding the neat shelves on both kidney curves. There was something about this dressing-table, not necessarily connected with his wife sitting before it, that gave Tim a feeling of nausea if he looked at it too early in the morning.

Tina had had this dressing-table since she was eight, and she loved it. It was part of the safe mummy and daddy world

18

of childhood. She picked up her hair-brush and started beating her head. Her hair was thick and wiry, only tamed when long enough to plait; this style was no longer suitable, so she wore it short and hoped to brush it into manageable sleekness by unmerciful beating. She longed, as people do, for the impossible—long, thin, straight hair. It was a good thing, as it always is, that she would never have it. It wouldn't have suited her at all. As it was, her busby of wiry curls added height to a narrow forehead and its full curve complemented an oval face. She narrowly missed being pretty. Her eyes were striking, doll's blue and round, her eyebrows grew in natural curves, her nose was short, straight and sparsely freckled, well-defined cheek-bones balanced an equally well-defined jawline. Her head, helped by the hair, was a good shape and balanced nicely on her long neck. Below this line, Tina was never optimum shape, however. She was either too thin, from strenuous slimming, or too plump from equally strenuous eating. She went up and down in size as easily as a balloon. Her face, on the other hand, was perfectly static, and this was why she could never be pretty. She gazed out of her blank blue eyes, and her mouth was set in its narrow line. Even when she was talking with feeling, and she was always talking with feeling, nothing lit up. Her voice was flat, belying the intensity of the emotions it expressed. There was a fault in transmission. She gave the impression of a fake-coal electric fire—turn on the switch to see living flame. Tim, though neither of them realised this, hadn't found the switch.

She sat up straight-backed in her blue brushed nylon nightdress, which wasn't transparent and which covered her from neck to knees and wrists, and thumped her head. 'Been awake for hours indeed! Look at you.' She looked at the reflection of the hump which was Tim in the bed behind her.

'I was just drifting off again nicely.'

'Well, *I* didn't get to sleep for ages, and I was up twice for Ricky in the night, and *I'm* up.'

'Oh poor love,' murmured Tim dutifully, and settled himself for a quick snooze while Tina was in the bathroom. But he was now thoroughly awake. From the other side of the built-in cupboard he could hear the bumps and chants of his son waking up in the next bedroom. Beyond was the lavatory and from that tiny box he could hear with what vigorous relief Tina's kidneys greeted the first visit of the day, accompanied by the brisk spinning of the blue scented

19

paper roll. Then came a metallic bang, as Tina pressed the cistern handle, with no result. Tim waited for the second and third attempts, then he heard the gush of water. She could never get it to work the first time, though he had no trouble, it was only a knack and he kept showing her how. Ricky called out 'Mummy!' in a peremptory way. Tim knew he would say it the second time confidentially, and then in a rising crescendo of urgency while Tina would call back 'Coming, darling,' from the bathroom.

'Coming, darling!' called Tina, from the bathroom. Chuggle, chuggle, chuggle, rinse and spit.

'Mummy, mummy, mummy, mummy, muMMEEEEE!'

'Fuck it,' said Timothy and rolled painfully out of bed. He staggered with exaggerated difficulty to the mirror and, with his hands on his knees, bent down to find himself reflected beneath the china flowers. He did this every morning, in spite of the nausea; it was necessary to see himself first thing in the morning. It was a vital check-up on his identity. 'Yes,' he said to himself with wry depression at the ghastly sight before him. 'I though that was me.' He raised his head slightly, so that the flowers gave him a halo. 'Sweetly pretty,' he said aloud and made a bridesmaid face at the mirror. He heard Tina leaving the bathroom and straightened at once. She wouldn't have time to think that funny. She would say 'Sorry,' meaning 'out of my way', and reach round him for her clothes. She had already begun her day, and Tim should have begun his.

At breakfast, Tim and Tina sat either side of their son, and watched his movements fondly as they drank their coffee.

'Careful, Rick,' said Timothy, and moved the plastic mug of milk a little further from his son's elbow.

'More, darling?' asked Tina, reaching for his empty bowl.

'Moo-er,' said Rick.

'Moo-er,' said Tim, imitating Rick's pronunciation with a proud smile.

'Goodness me,' said Tina, filling the bowl with Rice Krispies for the third time.

Ricky shoved his hands between his knees, thrust his chin to the ceiling and beamed.

The rain slid down the expanse of glass behind them and collected in muddy pools on a level with the polished parquet floor. Tim sat opposite the window and watched the Davis children putting on gumboots in the porch of number Ten. The youngest boy threw a red boot out on to the square of lawn that divided the two rows. Nasty child, thought Tim.

'Butter,' he said, and Tina pushed over the butter-dish.

Singed toast popped out of the toaster. Tina removed it, waved it in the air, and put in two more slices from the wrapped loaf.

'Er-ba, er-ba, er-ba,' said Ricky, beating his mouth with the back of his spoon. Tina looked at him blankly, wondering what time of day it would be best to go to the launderette.

'Er-herrrr,' said Timothy, a loud, long sigh. He'd had a rotten night.

The toaster erupted, to show two underdone slices of toast. Tina handed one to Tim. He looked at it. A wretched woman had said she'd come in today to collect her tickets for the Round Rumania on £30 trip, and he hadn't got them ready. He pushed his chair back from the table.

'Don't you want it?' asked Tina.

'What?'

'The toast.'

'No.'

'But I asked you if you wanted another.'

'You didn't.'

'Well, I can't eat it.'

'Neither can I.'

'It's a waste.'

'Give it to Rick.'

'He doesn't like toast.'

'That's hardly toast.'

The clatter of a milk crate made Tina turn to the window. 'Heavens, just look at it, I'll never get out today, did you put on clean socks?'

She got up from the table, and opened the door into the porch. As she shut it behind her and opened the front door, Ricky screamed, 'Mummeee.'

'She's not going anywhere,' said Timothy.

The milkman passed the window and banged his crate down at Tina's feet.

'Mull,' said Ricky.

'Mull,' said Timothy. 'It's the mullman.' He poured himself another cup of coffee. Buses got delayed in the rain, there would be an excuse for lateness.

'And could we have some butter today please? A half.

Thanks very much.' Tina backed into the house holding three pints of milk, using her hip to open the porch door. The milkman passed the window on his way to fetch the butter from the van on the road.

'What about some yoghourt for a change?' said Timothy.

'Oh, that's a good idea. Ricky loves yoghourt, don't you, darling? Yoggi?' she asked her son, leaning over the high chair. She rubbed her nose in the back of his neck with a humming sound, and then gave him an exaggerated kiss on his ear, mmmschmutt. Ricky liked it, and laughed. 'Gain,' he said.

Mmmmschmutt, went Tina.

The milkman, back with the butter, looked balefully through the rain at the window.

Tina went to the door. 'And I'm terribly sorry,' she said, giving the dripping man her sweet, rueful smile, 'could we possibly have two raspberry-flavoured yoghourts too, I forgot?'

'Anything else?' asked the milkman, who could do without the rueful smile.

'No. I don't think so. Thanks very much.' She felt a little guilty so she waited at the open door until he returned with the yoghourt. Then she smiled again and said that it was awfully wet today, wasn't it. The milkman didn't answer. She shut the door with a snap, now brisk and cross. She whipped Ricky from his chair, and started piling up the plates with a great deal of noise.

'Do you know what time it is?' she asked Timothy. This was a statement of lateness.

Timothy deflected the sarcasm by treating it as a question. 'No? What time is it?'

'I don't know,' she said in a tone which implied she was far too rushed and busy to know, and put her empty cup into Tim's half-full one. 'It must be almost nine.'

'Hey, I was drinking that.'

'Oh, I am sorry,' said Tina, and made a business of retrieving his cup of coffee.

But Tim had given up. He wouldn't get a quiet read of the paper at home, unless he went to the lavatory, the coldest room in the house. So he might as well get off to work. He went to the porch for his raincoat, Ricky following, holding his father's legs in close embrace as Tim put on the coat. They shuffled back into the room together, Ricky still locked round

Tim's knees. 'Well, I'm off,' he said towards the kitchen. Tina appeared, putting on her rubber gloves. Her mood had changed again, now she had got Tim nearly off to work. There was time for a kiss. 'Bye, my love,' she said, lifting up her face. 'Got your umbrella?'

'Bye-bye,' he said, fond of her again. 'Prettiness,' he added. They leaned towards each other, but Tim, hampered by the way Ricky had locked his knees together, lost his balance and the child fell down with a howl. Tina bent to pick him up and Tim backed to the door. By the time Tina had Ricky yowling on her shoulder, Tim was the other side of the glass porch door. They gesticulated at each other as the wails increased in pitch, Tim waving with a sympathetic expression on his face, Tina, nodding, smiling and raising her eyes to heaven. The front door shut.

'Oh! heavens!' said Tina, and put down Ricky, whose howls grew louder at this fresh insult. She ran to the porch door, and pulled it open. Then she opened the front door and leant out. 'Tim! I forgot!'

Tim was ten yards away, crouched defensively under his umbrella. He felt resentful, as though, having shut the front door on his home life, it should stay there and not jump out after him. 'What?' he shouted.

Tina beckoned him, glancing at the eyes of the group of houses.

'What is it?' Tim wondered why she wouldn't call to him.

She beckoned again and made a few indecipherable motions with lips, hands and head.

He sighed, and turned back to the house.

'Sorry,' said Tina in a low voice, 'I forgot to tell you, the Frises are coming in for drinks tonight, so don't be late.'

'The Frises? Who are the Frises?'

'New number Seven.'

Tim's morning changed, his expression hardly at all. 'Oh yes,' he said, casually. 'Them.'

'I said about 8.30 so that we can eat first. So hurry home, won't you.'

'Right-ho.' He rarely said right-oh.

He turned and walked down the path again, waving a hand.

Tina shut the front door and paused in the porch. The sound of Rick's crying was muffled slightly by the glass door, but she could tell by the colour of his face that this was a major tantrum. What a way to start the day. She took a deep breath, and opened the door.

Tim walked buoyantly down the path, and through the parking space. The Swedish sex-pot! Coming to drinks! Oh Helga, Helga. Helga is my hamster.

He swung briskly out of The Grove, and into tree-lined Beechley Avenue, with the tune of 'Charlie is my darling' running through his head.

> Helga is my hamster, hamster, hamster,
> Helga is is my hamster, my Swedish cavalier.

That's why he'd been waking early in the mornings, why hadn't he realised before. Couldn't possibly be cavalier though. My Swedish what? A three-syllable what? Helga is my hamster, hamster, hamster, Helga is my hamster, my Swedish clair-de-lune? Apple-pie? Valentine?

CHAPTER TWO

Timothy hadn't met Helga yet. Nor did he realise that he had seen her. But he had learnt something about her a day or two after she and her husband had moved to The Grove. He had been walking down Beechley Avenue to the bus stop with number Three, a sympathetic man called George, who was one of the bowler-hatted Grove and under the impression that Timothy shared his passion for racing.

'Any ideas for the 2.30 at Newmarket?' he asked Timothy as they crossed the road diagonally. On his own, Timothy walked down The Grove side of the road because there was some kind of hostel on that side, for girls. But, whenever his departure time coincided with number Three's, they crossed together to the other side, which cut the time to the bus stop by ten seconds. (George, on his own, walked down the hostel side, too.)

'No,' said Timothy, thoughtfully. 'No, I haven't.'

'Fancy Lazy Daisy myself. Out of Popsy by Easily Does It, trained by Williams, second in the 1000 Guineas, first, first, third and fourth this season.'

24

'Mm,' said Timothy, even more thoughtfully.

'But, on the other hand, I have a hunch about Swedish Cream,' said George, using his umbrella as a walking stick. He walked faster than Tim, who found himself having to take an occasional skip to keep in step.

'Oh. A hunch,' said Tim, with a skip which got him back in step. They swung along together, at a pace which was soothingly rhythmical for this early hour of the day.

George laughed. 'Oh, I know what you think of hunches,' he said, and Tim looked surprised, for he didn't know himself. George went on, 'but you've got to follow them sometimes if only to renew faith in form.'

They were opposite the hostel and Tim stole a glance across the road. Faith in form, he thought, yes I'm in good time, she's just got up. A girl at an open upper window raised her arms above her head, held her hands together, and then slowly, inch by inch, dropped out of sight, as though she were in a lift.

'You know why?' asked George, turning on Timothy who quickly looked up at a tree.

'No I don't.'

George whirled his umbrella in a circle. 'Because of Seven. New number Seven.'

'Seven's, er, good?' asked Timothy, thinking that you can't have faith in form if you don't know anything about it.

'Good!' George laughed. 'I should say. The legs on her, what lines, I saw her running my God, what a sight.' He lapsed into momentary silence at the recollection, then added, 'And you know what they're like in Scandinavia.'

Helsinki, Copenhagen, Stockholm, the fjords in a fortnight, all the delights of the north with the warmth of the south, there and back for £65, get in touch with your local travel agent now, thought Timothy.

'Mm,' he said.

They had reached the bus stop which, by tacit agreement, usually meant the end of their conversation. They both produced their papers, Tim with some relief. Three minutes of racing tips were enough; enough to provide him with fantasy material to last the short bus ride to the High Street.

'What was the name did you say?' he asked after some minutes, during which time he had decided how to spend his colossal win.

George looked up from his *Financial Times*, puzzled. 'Whose?'

'Seven's'

George laughed. 'Rogue! Thinking of placing a bet?'

Tim smiled. 'I might yet, you never know.'

'Name's Helga.'

'Helga? I thought you said Swedish something, Swedish Cake or pudding or something.'

'Oh you mean the *horse*!' George laughed loudly this time, and the queue summed him up with cold eyes. 'I thought you meant our new neighbour . . .'

Their bus approached, joining the end of the stream of cars some thirty yards from the stop. The queue became tense, its members glancing surreptitiously at each other and the now stationary bus. A thin, jumpy girl, obviously late for work, suddenly left the stop and darted up the road towards the bus. The queue watched with interest. The traffic started moving, and the girl stopped, glancing back at the queue which had now sealed ranks and was watching the approaching bus smugly. She turned and started walking back to join the queue. But the bus behind her had stopped again. This was the moment, Tim decided, and ran. At his approach, the girl understood what had happened, swung round and darted back. They arrived at the bus together, panting. They were lucky. The conductor leant out, decided to call this the stop, ushered them on, and rang the bell. 'One inside, one up top,' he said.

'Lucky,' said Tim and turned with a team smile to the girl. She was already on her way up the stairs. Tim thought she had the best pair of legs he had ever seen outside the pages of *Playboy*.

The bus moved off, then came to a stop opposite the queue. Tim, from his warm sitting position, looked for George, almost feeling guilty. George gesticulated, grimaced, smiled, pointed at the top deck, held thumb and finger of one hand in a circle, nodded again, counted on some of his fingers, mouthed, nodded again, pursed his lips, smiled, grimaced, pretended to turn up his coat collar, stamped his feet, grimaced, smiled, and waved as the bus moved off. Tim didn't understand from this that the girl on the top deck was Helga. But she joined the ranks all the same, on the strength of George's description, and took turns with the widow and Polly Kitchen in Tim's imaginary sexual forays. However, till now, she hadn't been very satisfactory fantasy material. She was neither wholly imaginary—after all, she did exist, in number Seven, The Grove. But neither was she wholly real, for all he knew was what George had said. She was Swedish with legs.

However, in spite of being unsatisfactory fantasy material, she had—he now realised—provided him with something: the feeling of anticipation that had lately been waking him at dawn. For it was probable, possible, unavoidable even, that he and Helga would meet.

Now Tina had told him they were to meet today! This injected a great deal of energy into his step, as he started off down Beechley Avenue. This morning he didn't spare a glance at the hostel, he had better things on his mind. The Swedish sex-pot coming to drinks! Should he wear his polo-neck? It suited him. Or open collar and new mustard-coloured V-neck? It suited him. Or stay in his suit? It suited him.

Hello, he said sexily, answering the front door bell. He gave her a slow smile, as she came into the house. You must be Swedish Pudding—

Damn, can't concentrate this morning, thought Tim and he crossed the road.

Hello, he said sexily, answering the front door bell. He gave the girl a slow smile, as she came into the house. You must be Helga—

Now should he know her name or not? Try again.

Hello, he said rararadiddlediddle as she came into the house. You must be our new neighbour—s.

Oh God, neighbours, the wretched husband, there he was standing at her side, and Tina was at his, had even answered the door because she usually did. Never mind, never mind, he was sitting in the G-plan rocker, wearing his polo-neck (or his open collar and V-neck? Suit? Respectable, City-man impression? Rugged, outdoor, in his fisherman's knit? Anyway, leave that, on we go). He rose to his feet and gave the girl, and her husband, a slow smile as she, as they, came into the house. He shook her hand, warmly, confidently. Her hand was small-boned, fragile. Did it return his pressure, ever so slightly? Yes it did. But there was the husband's hand too, ready to shake. Probably a threatening grip. Let's make the husband's hand small-boned and fragile, but of course he couldn't make the husband's hand anything

27

because it already was, and would be coming to drinks this evening. Oh, things weren't going at all well this morning, and it was raining. But this evening . . .

He turned into the main road and joined the long, sodden queue at the bus stop. George was two in front, without an umbrella.

'Morning,' said Timothy.

'Morning,' said George.

They waited, not even able to read their papers in the rain.

'Share my brolly?' suggested Tim

This meant that George had to sacrifice two places in the queue. 'Oh well,' he said with despair, and joined Tim. 'Left mine at the office. Bloody awful isn't it. Late too.'

Tim agreed but looked quite happy. He was in the porch greeting Helga again.

'Four gone by, full up,' said George after a while.

'Might walk, then,' said Tim.

'Not me, mate, this morning. Head's full of hammers.'

Hello, he said sexily, helping her off with her coat. Her back was bare.

'Party last night,' said George.

Her back wouldn't be bare, that was ridiculous. She wouldn't wear a coat, to pop across from number Seven. Hello, he said sexily, not helping her off with her—'Party?' he repeated, suddenly interested. So there were parties still. 'Good?' he asked.

'So-so,' said George. He leant out from the shelter of the umbrella to look down the road. 'They'll cancel today in all this rain.'

'Cancel? Surely not,' said Tim, looking amazed.

'Can't race in this, bloody mud-bath today.'

'Ah.' Her fair hair hung down between her white shoulder-blades. Chilly? he asked, and put his arm round her. Now he was getting somewhere, although rather wildly—this was unlikely to happen in the porch on their first meeting.

'Number Seven was there,' said George.

'Where?' asked Tim, leaping swiftly back to the bus stop.

'At the party.'

Who can have given the party? Had it been a Grove party? Were he and Tina missing out on Grove social life?

George was amused by Timothy's sudden expression of interest and anxiety. He cheered up. He made a few sideways movements with his chin and screwed up one half of his mouth. This upset the angle of his bowler, which he corrected. 'Some legs,' he said.

Tim felt a surge of jealousy. George was forgetting that number Seven was a married couple. 'Are they nice?' he asked, to remind him.

'Nice!' George exclaimed. 'They're splendid, quite splendid. Best pair I've seen in a long while.'

'I didn't mean the legs,' said Tim sternly. Then he laughed.

'Oh!' George laughed too. 'Seems nice enough, hard to say.'

'Was it a Grove do?'

'The party, no. Turns out we have mutual friends with number Seven. You know that junk shop in the High Street, Paul and Polly Kitchen Antiques? They gave it.'

Tim wondered if he had gone pale. George, wretched George, had met Helga *and* knew Polly Kitchen! 'Oh yes, I know,' he managed to say.

'Actually,' said George, peeping out at the road again, 'you know the legs too. Remember last time I saw you, some weeks back, you sneaked on the bus, you unprincipled queue-jumper you, well, that girl you were chasing was none other than our Swedish dream-boat.'

'No!' Another surprise for Timothy, and still not nine o'clock.

'Yes. She, I discovered, works for an air-line and leaves—' George was about to give away the information that Helga always caught a bus about eight twenty-five in the morning, but decided against this. If Tim learnt this, he would be infected with his own sudden and surprising desire to get to work early. He didn't want competition. '—leaves for work by bus,' he finished lamely.

There was a lull in their conversation.

'I think I'll walk it today,' said Tim at last.

'I'll stick it out,' said George. 'See you.'

Tim nodded, and walked off down the road, leaving George to regret the loss of the umbrella.

It wasn't hard for him to work out why he hadn't coincided with George lately on the walk to the bus. George had been leaving earlier than normal to coincide with Helga. He remembered that the day he had seen her had been one of his earlier mornings—the hostel girl had been doing the arms-above-the-head exercise, which meant, thanks to his

29

careful research, 8.15 a.m. Timothy resolved to get up much earlier in the mornings.

Hello, he said sexily. They were alone at the bus stop. If it were raining, she could share his umbrella, that was a good idea. It was raining, and he held his umbrella over her head. Come under, he told her with a slow smile. She came under. Her head reached his shoulder. She looked up at him trustingly and whispered thanks. Mm, this was a good one, he liked this one. Maybe she slips as she gets on the bus, breaks her ankle? No, just a slight strain, and he supports her. His strong hands grasped her waist as she collapsed against him with a sobbing cry of pain. Hello, can I help? asked George, arriving at the bus stop at that moment. Go away, George, damn you, you've overslept, you went to a party last night with Polly Kitchen (that was generous) and you have a hang-over and you've missed the bus.

A large removal van spun through a deep puddle in the road and whooshed a sheet of milky-coffee-coloured water at Timothy's legs. He cursed at its rear, and moved away from the kerb. The bus, which he might have caught, passed with George waving happily at a window. Timothy pretended not to notice, and walked on more quickly. Further along, the bus had stopped again in a long pile-up before traffic lights, and Timothy overtook it, this time turning to wave at George. But George was reading his paper. Five minutes more of this shuttling, and the bus and Timothy reached the High Street cross-roads. George jumped off at the lights and joined Timothy on the kerb waiting to cross the road.

'Got a bit wet, haven't you?' said George, looking at Timothy's trousers.

'I like to keep fit,' said Timothy, looking at George's stomach. They laughed, and galloped across the road against the lights, trying not to pant. George called good-bye and disappeared in the crowd entering the tube station. Timothy hurried down the High Street, forgot to look in at the window of Kitchen Antiques, and burst into the office. He stood on the mat inside the door, shaking a shower of water from himself like a wet spaniel.

'Do you *mind*,' said a large grey-haired woman, sitting on a stool just inside the door.

'Hell,' said Timothy, looking at her, 'you must be Round Rumania on £30.'

The working day had started before he'd even got his feet dry.

It was a busy time of year. People who had planned their holidays in a dream-like state during the winter were now growing anxious about the forthcoming reality, and were constantly on the telephone checking dates, prices, connections, bookings. Plans were changed too. Holidays that had sounded romantic in January seemed more likely to be three weeks' hell when considered in May. Gipsy caravans in Eire were cancelled, and bookings in Majorca stepped up.

Timothy had a busy morning, a hasty sandwich and beer lunch, and hiccups at three o'clock. Business slackened after this and, as the afternoon dragged on, he had time to look forward to the evening. But, like his clients, he was growing anxious about forthcoming reality. When he met Helga, he must try hard to remember he hadn't met her, hadn't shared his umbrella with her, hadn't saved her from drowning in the Thames, hadn't held her in his arms when she twisted her ankle.

Hello, he said sexily, now stop that. The phone rang.

'Dolphin Travel,' he said sexily. 'Good afternoon,' briskly.

'You sound odd. Beery lunch?' It was Tina. 'You haven't forgotten about this evening, have you?'

'No,' he said at once. But this was out of character. Normally, he would have forgotten. 'Yes,' he said. 'I mean, what about this evening?'

'There, you have. I knew it. The Frises are coming in for drinks, and I've asked Jake and Margaret too, they'll help things along. Can you call in at the delicatessen and get some cheese-cake on your way home?'

'O.K. Anything else?'

'No. Busy?'

'Terrific today. How's Rick?'

'Fine. How're you? Did you get awfully wet this morning?'

The pace of the conversation, Tim noticed, was slowing down for a long session, so he rattled his chair on the floor, rustled papers near the receiver and said, in urgent, low tones, 'Must go now. See you later darling.'

'Don't be late, will you?'

'No, bye love.'

'Bye.'

He replaced the phone as Joyce brought him a cup of tea. 'Sugar in?' he asked her.

'You always ask me that, and I always put it in.' She was wearing a dress that Tina would wear as a blouse. Her thighs were perhaps a little thick for such a short skirt, but Tim had no strong objections to this as he watched her cross them and then hook one heel over the top rung of the stool. She would be nineteen the following week. She looked about fifteen. She thought Timothy was probably the same age as her father, and certainly as boring. She didn't class him as a male. Timothy did nothing to correct this, except in his mind.

'You forgot once,' he told her.

'I never,' said Joyce. She sipped her tea and gazed dully out of the window. If this rain kept up till going-home time, her lashes would come off.

'We must get that Rumanian Tourist Office letter off tonight, I'll dictate it when you've finished your tea.'

'Oh no!' she wailed. 'I got to leave sharp on tonight.' She looked at her watch which seemed to Timothy to be in competition with Big Ben in size. 'It's all of 4.30.'

'It'll only take five minutes to dictate.'

'Yes, but half an hour to decipher, and another to type at least. I'll do it in the morning.'

'No, it must catch the post tonight.'

'But I haven't done the stamps on all the others yet.'

'What have you been doing all afternoon, then?'

Combing her hair. 'Filing,' she answered promptly.

'Your nails,' he said.

In the end, Timothy wrote the letter out in long-hand, as usual, and stamped the rest of the mail, as he often did, while Joyce typed it out, with a lot of sighing and swearing and blowing at eraser dust on the carbon paper, and starting again. At half past five she had reached Yours faithfully on a copy which had only one mistake. This was Dear Sris and she didn't think Timothy would notice this. She held her breath and typed with agonised care Yuors fiath—'Waa,' she began on a rising scale. She felt she might cry with rage and that would be fatal for her lashes, let alone what damage the rain might do. She backspaced rapidly and stopped the waa, hoping Timothy, who was in the lavatory, hadn't heard. She typed over the top, smacking down the keys, Yours faithfully. It looked a mess. She went back and did it again. Yours faith was now very black, fully rather pale.

32

She whipped the letter out of the typewriter, removed the carbon paper, put it on Timothy's desk, and rushed to the cloakroom for her coat and boots.

By the time she was dressed and ready to leave, Timothy had come out of the lavatory and was at his desk. 'Well done, Joyce,' he said and picked the letter up.

She reached the door without turning. 'Bye then,' she called and opened it.

'Hey, what's this, you've left out the bit I wrote on the back, you dolt! "We would therefore be most grateful if you could be Yours faithfully." I ask you.' He looked up as the door closed. He saw Joyce scampering past the window.

Swearing in a resigned and feeble way, he sat down at the typewriter. 'Dear Sris,' he typed.

Half an hour later, he was home.

'Did you get the cheese-cake?' called Tina from the bathroom where she was scrubbing Ricky.

Timothy put on his wet raincoat and shoes once more and went out, without answering.

At half past eight they had eaten supper, washed up, Tina was percolating coffee and plumping up cushions, and Timothy was in the bedroom struggling out of his fisherman's knit. He pulled on his office shirt again, so that it looked as though he hadn't gone to the extent of a full-scale change of clothing, and looked around for his pullover. He couldn't find it. The door bell rang. He hurried on to the landing and shouted down to Tina. 'My pullover, where's my pullover?'

'They're here!' she called back. 'For goodness' sake hurry up, you can't still be changing, can you?'

'MY PULLOVER!'

'In the wash,' shouted Tina.

Timothy listened on the landing as Tina opened the front door. It was Jake and Margaret Davies from number Four. He went back to the bedroom. It would have to be the polo-neck, which would show he'd made a special effort, but there was no help for it.

'Oh that is pretty,' said Margaret as Timothy came down the stairs into the open-plan living room. 'Hello Timothy, I'd love one like that myself.'

'Hello, Margaret,' said Timothy. 'Hello Jake.'

'Thoroughly unisex,' said Margaret with a laugh. Her laughter was warmly suggestive, no matter what remark it punctuated. She could laugh at 'Isn't it cold?' and make one look for its hidden meaning.

Tina regarded her with round eyes and smiled politely. Was Margaret suggesting that Tim was queer? 'He got very wet today,' she said.

'I'm afraid I haven't changed,' said Jake, rocking the G-plan gently. They laughed at his jeans and loose sweater. He was an illustrator and worked at home.

'So did I,' said Margaret to Timothy 'wasn't it quite dreadful!'

'Well, what about a warming drink,' said Tina. The front door bell rang and they all looked towards the door tensely. 'There they are!' said Tina and went to the door, her hands patting the back of her head with upward movements. Margaret sat down on the sofa and crossed her legs. Jake stood up and examined the ornaments on the carved wooden mantelpiece. He was fascinated by the way the Blundens felt the need of a mantelpiece, even though there was no fireplace.

Tim began to follow Tina to the door, decided not to, turned to the drinks cabinet, opened it, shut it and then, with sudden haste, slipped into the kitchen saying Coffee.

Margaret watched the arrival in the porch. Tina had closed the glass inner door, to keep the room warm, which meant the porch was more crowded than it usually was with its large pram, coats, mackintoshes, umbrella stand, and shelf with cactus. She could see the male half of number Seven shaking something out of the front door—an umbrella no doubt. He looked large and promising. His wife looked small and nervous. She had her face turned to Tina who was talking, but her eyes kept glancing into the room.

'Well, here they are,' said Tina brightly. 'Do come in.' They followed her with shuffling hesitation, giving the impression of members of an audience being led on to the stage. Tina, as compère, clasped her hands and looked from one couple to the other, urging them into contact. 'Let me introduce you,' she said, as though they might protest. 'Margaret Davies and Jake from number Four, and this is Alexander and, and oh dear.'

'Helga,' said Alexander.

'Oh yes, Helga, I'm so sorry, Helga Frise, from number Seven. Now where's Timothy?'

'Are we going to play oranges and lemons?' said Jake. 'We ought to have our names pinned to our lapels.'

Tina looked at him doubtfully, as Timothy's foot appeared at the bottom of the sliding kitchen door and pushed it open. The door had, some months before, come off its bottom runner and swung dangerously from the top. The frosted glass panels banged and shook. The Frises watched with alarm.

'Here he is,' said Tina, and slid the door right back. Timothy stood there holding the coffee-pot and looking hard at Alexander. Alexander's hand came forward. Tim tried to change the coffee-pot into his left hand, found it too hot, retreated into the kitchen, put it down, picked it up with his left hand, and came back into the room. He shook Alexander's hand, which he found was not small-boned and fragile. Nothing was fragile about Alexander Frise. Tim bent his neck back and looked up. He saw an exceptionally large man, broad, strong, fit, tanned, blond—a formidable husband. He turned to Helga, still trying to disengage his hand. Yes, what a relief, he was looking down on her. Oh God, this is Helga, he thought, confusion covering him, Helga, Helga. He examined her feet, shook her hand briefly, and said 'Coffee'. He made a business of indicating that the coffee-pot was heavy, and hurried over to put it down on a low teak table at the far end of the room.

Tina chivvied them over to the group of chairs round the table and, after some fussing, they were settled down with cups of coffee and brandy. Margaret was still on the sofa, set well back in a corner and wedged in comfortably with cushions. She was a heavy woman of about thirty-eight with short curly hair, not unlike Tina's in texture and style, but greying. She had a friendly open face and always seemed at her ease; an earth-mother type, except that her three children were all over eleven and no longer needed much earth-mothering. She was an editor of a Sunday paper's women's page, and employed a French au pair to speak French with the children in the afternoons and to give Jake his lunch. She was always careful to choose exceptionally plain girls.

Balancing Margaret, in the other corner of the sofa, sat Alexander. He looked relaxed too, almost bovine. He had one leg hooked over the knee of the other, and was lighting a pipe. The match flicked shadows on his face, accentuating an overhanging brow, a high-bridged beaked nose, jutting cheekbones. He looked like a blond Red Indian. The carefully veiled interrogation had started, the home team bowling and he, batting for the visitors, was providing the answers. They learnt quickly that he was in marketing, working for a firm that made soap and toothpaste (how appropriate, thought Tina, he's a very clean-looking man and has good teeth); he had met Helga on a business trip to Sweden, and they had been married a year. He played rugger on Saturday afternoons.

'Do you play?' he asked Jake, hoping it was the visitors' turn to ask questions.

Jake shuddered.

'Go on, darling,' protested Margaret from her corner. 'You used to. When I first met you, you did. I had to go and shiver on the touch-line and cheer when you got the ball.'

'That was years ago. I was young then.' He was thirty-five now, his eldest son was thirteen, he had been married fourteen years. He felt much older, especially when he looked across at Helga. She was sitting on the edge of her chair, holding her cup of coffee a foot above her knees and away from her body as though it might spill at any moment. She hadn't said anything yet, except to murmur agreement when her husband spoke, and to send a quick occasional smile around the group—a smile which seemed to be only on loan. It went out, nearly reached someone, and then was retrieved and hidden behind her face.

'Do you watch your husband?' Jake asked her, with a smile he tried to make gentle, not to frighten her away.

She looked up at him, startled, and placed her cup of coffee on the table carefully. 'Please?'

'Do you watch your husband playing?'

'Playing?'

'Rugger,' he said, and then began again, enunciating carefully, 'Doo eeou watch eeour—'

'Oh rugger,' she said. 'No.'

Jake tried to conceal a sigh. They were going to be a dead loss, number Seven. Then, as Helga picked up her coffee again and settled further back in the chair, he noticed her legs. They made him check her face again, which he hadn't yet registered. It wasn't the sort of face one does register, he thought—pale, long, expressionless. Two ropes of pale-brown hair hung either side of it. He decided it looked like a plate set between knife and fork, and dinner hadn't come.

But why worry when it walked around on a pair of legs like that.

He felt Margaret watching him, looked up, and they exchanged a hint at a smile. Tina, next to him, was leaning forward. Good old Tina, he thought, as he heard her ask Helga where she'd learnt her excellent English.

'We learn in school,' said Helga.

'We learn in school, too,' said Jake. 'But then we forget. Ich und Du, Mullers Kuh, Mullers Esel, Das bist Du.'

'I am from Sweden,' said Helga. 'In any case, I left school recently last year.' Jake felt very old.

Tim now had control of himself, and felt he might be able to take part in the conversation. He leaned forward, his hands on his knees.

'It must be lovely,' he said to the coffee-pot. 'Sweden.'

Margaret laughed. 'Why must it, Tim?'

The sexual freedom, he thought, all those Swedish girls lying around in bikinis, waiting for you. 'Oh,' he said, 'one hears such a lot about their cakes, or is it puddings?'

'Are you thinking of smorgasbrød?' asked Tina. 'I thought that was only in Denmark, though I may be wrong.'

'Yes,' said Helga.

After all, Tina thought, she was an authority on Scandinavia. 'I spent a year in Finland actually,' she said to Helga.

'Oh yes?' said Helga.

'Yes,' said Tina.

Alexander had lit his pipe now, and removed it. 'Helga is Swedish,' he said.

Margaret thought it was time to get things going. She turned to Alexander. 'Do you know many Grove yet?'

'Erm,' said Alexander, and put the pipe back in his mouth.

Jake said, 'Grove has become a generic term. You are Grove. We are Grove. Not to be confused with groovy. To be Grove is the very opposite of being groovy. To be Grove, you not only have to live here, you should also have one pram in the porch, one television set (which you *wouldn't* have but for the children—and it does keep them quiet), one washing-machine, and this can be dish-washer or clothes-washer, but both is not pure Grove; one car, and ideally it should be an A for—'

Margaret cut in quickly. 'A station-waggonny car.' The Blundens had had an A40 once, and might not like this. 'This is changing though. Now the standard to aim for is

37

two-car: a mini for the wife, and something sporting and fast for the weekends.'

'Mm.' Jake was doubtful. 'Not pure Grove yet. Give it a few more years.' He paused. 'Also, I rather think, it would be a mini for the man, and something sporting and fast for the wife.'

Margaret laughed. 'And what else?' she asked generally.

Tim thought he must say something. They probably thought the Blundens were thoroughly Grove. He had noticed Jake sneering at the mantelpiece—which had been Tina's idea, nothing to do with him, he thought it ridiculous without a fireplace underneath. '—and a bowler?' he suggested. He didn't have a bowler.

'Yes,' said Jake sadly. 'I'm afraid nowadays a bowler is *de rigueur.*'

Alexander decided to carry his bowler in a paper-bag in future, and put it on when he reached the station. 'Ha, ha, ha!' he laughed. 'Well,' he went on, when he had finished, 'we know the people who live in number Twelve, George and Judith something, we met them last night in fact, at a party.'

'Oh yes, the party given by the Kitchens,' said Tim.

'The kitchens?' asked Tina.

'Oh, I know who you mean,' said Margaret, 'Paul and Polly. Yes, they told us they knew you. They're *great* friends of ours.'

'Oh,' said Alexander, 'I see. You must be, er, Jake and Margaret Davies. Yes.' He looked at Margaret more carefully.

'Oh dear!' cried Tina. 'Don't tell me I forgot to introduce you.'

'Don't worry, you did,' said Jake. 'One just never gets names first throw of the dice.'

Tim finished his coffee with a gulp. Everyone seemed to know Polly Kitchen, except himself.

'Who are these Kitchens in any case?' asked Tina.

'You know,' said Jake. 'Paul and Polly Kitchen Antiques, in the High Street.'

'Oh yes, very near Dolphin.' She suddenly became suspicious, and turned on Timothy. 'Is that how you know them, darling?'

'I don't know them,' he replied.

'It sounded as though you did.'

'No, it was just that George mentioned something about their party at the bus stop.'

'Was it good?' Margaret asked Helga.

'Yes,' she said. She had, in fact, found it a middle-aged gathering, and been bored. 'You couldn't come?'

'Well,' said Margaret, 'we don't usually go to their parties.' She turned to Jake. 'Do we, darling.'

'No,' said Jake.

Though their faces were expressionless, Tim got the impression they were laughing, as though a private joke lurked beneath the words somewhere. Maybe the Davieses didn't like Paul and Polly at all. Maybe Paul and Polly were awful people. It didn't matter, for now there was Helga, with her legs about nine inches from his. He changed position, and now they were fourteen inches away, which he found more relaxing.

Tina brought out her bright, conversational voice. 'And how do you know these people?' she asked Helga.

'It is Alexander really, He, we, bought a lamp from them, and it needed a new flask—'

'Mantle,' put in Alexander.

'Glass?' suggested Tim.

'Funnel?' suggested Tina.

'Mantle,' said Alexander again.

'Mantle,' said Helga, 'and Polly said she would get one, and Alexander went in again, but it was the wrong size, so Alexander went in again, and it was still wrong, so Polly looked for another—'

'Oh yes,' said Jake, 'I know the sort of thing.'

'It *is* hard to find mantles for these old lamps,' said Margaret.

'—and the end of this story is that he, we, knew them well by now and she said come to the party we are giving. So that's how it happened.' Helga looked flushed and exhausted after this long explanation, and reached for her brandy. Her glass was empty. Tim looked for the bottle, and Tina discreetly tugged the back of his sweater. So he didn't offer more.

'So that's how it was,' said Jake as though he was thinking of something else. He was. He was thinking it was time they could decently leave. A Grove meet-the-new-neighbours evening was not meant to go on long. He rocked his chair forward, and kept it forward by concentrating his weight

39

over his knees. 'Well—' he said, and looked across at his wife.

She sighed as though she were reluctant to move from her cushioned corner, and repeated the same sort of sad 'well'. 'Please don't let us disrupt things,' she said, heaving herself to her feet. 'But we'll slip away now. Must be up early in the morning.'

So must I, thought Tim, to catch Helga's bus. But of course, if Helga stays late, she might miss it too. Maybe they'll stay very late, friendship will blossom, I'll put on a record, we might dance. Tina might show Alexander something. What? Rick, perhaps, he's quite sweet when he's asleep, or should I show him to Helga, that's better, the dark room, lit only by the Noddy lamp, pink halo round her hair, she leans over the cot, stumbles, breaks her ankle, I put my arm round her . . .

He felt an arm around him. He jumped. Jake's face was close to his. He seemed to be saying good-bye. Tim struggled to his feet.

'Don't get up, boy,' said Jake, patting his shoulder. 'Thanks so much.' He moved away. Tim followed, and joined the huddle at the door. Tina and Margaret were arranging something about milk. He hung around waiting for it to finish, then decided he must get back to Alexander, Helga and his chair, otherwise they'd get up to leave too. He murmured something and backed away, but too late. Alexander and Helga were already on their feet, Alexander had his hand on her shoulder and was absent-mindedly tidying her hair. Now if that were me, thought Timothy, I wouldn't be absent-minded about it.

'No need to go yet,' he said, sitting down. They didn't hear him, as they were exchanging a few words of Swedish. They moved towards the door and joined in the good-byes and thank-yous. Jake and Margaret left, waving vaguely back at the room.

Tina handed Alexander his umbrella. 'If there's anything we can do for you, please let us help. I know moving is a ghastly job.'

Helga said, 'We've been here a month.'

Alexander smiled down at Tina. 'Thanks a lot,' he said. He then gave Helga a prompting look.

Helga dutifully said her piece. 'We would like it if you would come and eat dinner with us one evening—'

Tim left his chair at the far end of the room and hurried

to join them. He knew Tina would receive this vague invitation in an equally vague way.

'That's very kind of you,' said Tina, 'we'd love to.'

'Yes,' said Timothy, smiling eagerly over her shoulder. How was he to get a definite date out of them? 'We'd love to. Not a Friday, though.' That was clever. He avoided Tina's puzzled glance. 'Nor a Wednesday.'

'And Saturday's no good for me, it's my rugger day. So let's say Thursday. Thursday of next week?'

Tim pulled a diary out of his hip pocket and flicked through the pages rapidly. Quite blank. 'Yes, that's all right. Next Thursday then.' He scribbled in the air, supporting the diary in his left hand. *Dinner*, he wrote, *Helga*—candlelight, soft music, starched white napkins, crystal glass, ornate silver, he led her out to the moonlit terrace to dance amidst the jasmine—*and Alexander*. 'What sort of time?'

'Please?'

'Seven-thirtyish suit you?'

'Lovely, we'll slip along then.'

Later, as Tim climbed into bed feet first like a small boy, and Tina thumped her head at the dressing-table, they exchanged opinions of the new people.

'She's sweet, isn't she?' said Tina, thinking of the strange effect Alexander had had on her. She realised she had never felt this overpowering attraction before. Going to bed with Tim had simply been a necessary part of the whole business of marrying him. Sometimes she enjoyed it, more often she merely put up with it. Never before had her first thought on meeting a man been bed. An internal shiver went through her, and she thumped her head harder. 'And hasn't she got marvellous hair!' she said.

Tim made a business of tucking in the sheet. 'And he's quite a nice, straightforward sort of chap, isn't he. A good player I should imagine. I wonder who he plays for?' Every Saturday afternoon Helga would be on her own. Now there was an opportunity; he must work on that. Not just one opportunity, either. An endless chain of opportunities, recurring every week. He closed his eyes.

Tina climbed into bed beside him, leaned over and kissed his cheek. 'Night-night then, can you switch off?'

Tim reached for the bedside lamp. 'Night-night.' He turned off the light, and they lay back in their private dreams.

41

CHAPTER THREE

The sun outlined the mane of the plaster lion that strode the roof of the pub opposite, and poked a tube of dust through the flimsy curtains and on to the bed. In the bed, a rickety iron four-poster with three cracked gilt knobs and patches of white paint, lay Paul and Polly. Polly was asleep. Paul was awake.

Polly lay on her stomach, her hair flowing over the pillow as though she was slipping down through water. Her broad white shoulders were hunched, her arms flung out—one stuffing the pillow to her face, the other across Paul's neck. He lay captive, like a diminutive effigy of a medieval knight beside a Victorian figure of victory.

There was little else in the room, except one chest of drawers, which was on its way to the shop downstairs, and clocks. There were clocks on every inch of floor. It looked as though Paul and Polly must have leapt into bed with a giant bound from the doorway, or else they had been there long before the clocks. There were clocks under the bed, and clocks on the temporary chest of drawers. Some were ticking, most were silent; marble, mahogany, gilt, brass, grandfather, carriage, skeleton, as diverse in style as in opinion of the time. Each clock showed a different hour, minute, second of the day. The faces passed urgent messages to the two in bed: five minutes past twelve! A quarter to eight! Three-thirty! But Paul and Polly had lived with clocks for so long, they no longer wanted to know the time.

Paul knew, however, from the sun's progress over the pub's lion that it was late enough. Red mane, yellow body, it would look good in the window, he thought, how much would he offer for it? But Jenkins wouldn't sell, he'd say it wasn't his responsibility, ask the brewers. He would have to get up now, otherwise his bladder would burst.

Carefully, not to wake her, he removed Polly's arm from his neck, and laid it above her head. It had made him hot and sweaty. He jutted his chin and scratched his fringe of black beard. He felt tired. The association was getting him down. Margaret made him work so hard. They needed new members. He would suggest it. Tactfully, of course.

He pulled back a small triangle of the patchwork quilt (ordered by a Canadian and never collected), and inched his legs out into the day. Pressing down with his hands on the edge of the bed, he stood up, his feet either side of an antique French skeleton clock. It seemed to echo his unclothed bony figure. He made his way to the door, a path made easy by familiarity—right foot on to a clock with a flat wooden case, left foot slotted on to the marble base of another, right foot under the grandfather by the wall, left foot back into a minute space between two chimers (ding, ding, boing, boing) and out of the door. If you foolishly began with the wrong foot, you got stuck with a foot under the grandfather and the other in the air, and there you stayed till someone came to move several clocks and let you out.

Paul barely had time to go to the lavatory and turn on his bath when the phone rang. He hurried downstairs, not wanting to lose any business. He hated to oversleep like this. It was the damn association, sapping his strength. Halfway down, he recalled his nude state and seized a piece of material hanging over the banisters, a length of blue velvet which he wrapped around his shoulders like a bathtowel.

He unbolted the door that led into the back of the shop, and squeezed in past a heavily-carved bookcase. The phone wasn't in its usual place on the desk. All the rest of the usual stuff was there, the ledger, the Toby Jug of biros (the biros were not for sale, but the Toby Jug was), the dirty coffee cups, the pile of ancient comics with the label 'Collector's Items', and today an ornamented commode that Polly had bought yesterday. The phone was in it.

'Merrivale double two seven eight, Kitchen Antiques, good *morn*ing.'

'Good *morn*ing. I love your shop voice.' Soft laughter.

'Oh you. I thought you meant business.'

'But I do, I do,' More soft laughter.

'I'm not up yet.'

'All the better.'

'Aren't you at work?'

'Yes. Unfortunately. It's late, you know.'

'I know. My bath's running.'

'Shall I come and scrub your back?'

'Please.'

'Wish I could.'

There was a pause. Paul gazed out of the window to the

street. Polly's nodder was crossing the street, dangerously, in front of a baker's van. He made it to the pavement with a skip, and walked past the window. Funny, thought Paul, that's the second morning running that he's failed to look in. Maybe the shoe shop next door has a new assistant.

'Well,' came the soft voice in his ear, 'when's the next meeting?'

'Soon, I hope,' said Paul, trying to make it sound enthusiastic.

'We'll ring this evening.'

'Good. Must go now. My bath'll come to me, if I don't go to it right away.'

'Wash behind your ears.' Then, in a swift change of tone, prompted no doubt by the approaching footsteps which echoed down the receiver, 'We'll be in, er, touch then.'

'Mmm,' said Paul. 'Close touch. Bye, sexy.' He felt more awake now.

'Good-bye.' Briskly.

Paul replaced the receiver, lifted the phone out of the pot, looked around for a place to put it, and then put it back in the pot. The shop door rattled, and he went to open it. He had pulled up the blind, and unlocked the door, before he remembered he hadn't dressed yet. He pulled the blind down again, but the door had opened and someone peered in. The head withdrew, then appeared again.

'So sorry, you're not open.'

'Not quite, I'm afraid.'

The young man looked doubtfully at Paul's blue velvet. He rubbed his nose which Paul noticed was set at a curious slant.

'Perhaps you can call back? In about ten minutes or so?' Paul didn't want to lose a possible sale.

'Er yes. Yes, I'll do that.' He backed away.

Paul shut the door and bolted it again. He smiled to himself. That was Polly's nodder. Nerved himself to come in. He would be buying something next.

Tina had spent half an hour cleaning Ricky's bedroom. She seldom did it so thoroughly. It faced front, across the communal lawn to the row of houses opposite. When she polished the chest of drawers in one corner by the window, she could see number Seven. She had been polishing the chest of drawers for a long while now, Ricky was whining to go downstairs, and it was nearly nine. Surely he didn't leave for work as late as this. Tim had left half an hour before. She was just about to give up, when Alexander appeared. He was carrying a paper bag. She backed into the room, feeling weak.

Alexander strode down the path with his nose in the air, forgot the shallow step opposite number Six, tripped and dropped the paper bag. A bowler hat rolled out. He looked round guiltily, picked up the hat, stuffed it back in the bag, and straightened. He looked up at the front window of number Six and saw Tina.

Tina, who had been leaning forward, curious to know the contents of the bag, backed into the room. He's seen me, she thought with horror. Then—why not? She waved her duster at him in a friendly way. He raised his hand in a half-salute, showed a flash of teeth, and hurried on down the path.

Tina closed her eyes. She had the sensation of going up or maybe down in an express lift.

Helga left her desk to go to the Ladies. Her heels rang on the tiled floor and echoed from the high ceiling. Tap tap tap, such a long way to go, she thought, right down the length of the counter, heads of the male clerks lifting down the line like knobs on a machine. These Englishmen, starved, starved —small thin men like Timothy Blunden, Paul, and Jake Davies, who, though tall, was not fat. And their wives were so big. Big Margaret, big Polly, bossy Tina. What a bunch. She would shop in Soho at lunchtime, cook a large filling meal; Alexander needed a great deal of food. He was big.

Jake leant over his desk and pulled down the blind to cut out the sun. He rubbed his eyes. He must have been working in strong light and shadow for several minutes without realising it. He was tired. The association was so demanding, taking a lot out of him. So to speak. He laughed aloud, and pulled a piece of paper towards him. Last night Margaret had suggested they increased membership. She had said what about the Blundens. He knew she fancied Tim, however hard that was to believe; but she liked that shy, young, boyish type, he had noticed before. But he had objected strongly too. He didn't want the Blundens in. Tim was all right, but Tina— no. He must think of some other names. Anyway, leave that for the moment, he must get on with this job, a jacket for a book on bridge, now what *could* he do for that?

45

He stared at the paper in front of him, and saw he had drawn a pair of exaggeratedly long legs. He knew at once where they belonged. Well, it wasn't such a bad idea, they might approach the Frises. He'd talk it over with Margaret.

He leant back in his chair and swivelled it so that one hand reached the door. This was one advantage of working in a room the size of a layout pad. 'Marrrrice!' he called, rolling the 'r' like a wine gum in his throat. This was his chief (if not only) pleasure in having a French au pair, and he always insisted on girls with 'r's' in their names. 'If you're making coffee, make me one too please.' A democratically phrased command.

Polly stumbled into the bathroom, still wrapped in sleep as though it were a blanket. She sat down heavily on the lavatory, her eyes still closed, and rested her chin on her cupped hands, and her elbows on her lap.

Paul lay in the bath looking more like a medieval effigy than ever. His hands were folded on his black-haired stomach, his feet were crossed at the ankles, and his eyes were closed. The cold tap dripped.

He moved his feet a fraction to the left, to avoid the drip.

Polly breathed in slowly through her mouth, held it a second, then expelled the air loudly through her nose.

The hot tap dripped. Paul moved his feet back to the right.

Tim wondered if he might not take up smoking a pipe. He thought it might suit him. It might give a pleasing, tweedy, Englishman appeal to his image for Helga. 'That letter to the Rumanian Tourist Office,' he said to Joyce, who was raising her eyebrows at her reflection in a tiny mirror propped against the typewriter. 'We must get it off today.' Alexander Frise smoked a pipe. He might get one this morning and practise in the pub at lunchtime.

There's a soothing, uncle touch to a pipe, he thought, a satisfactory popping sound you make with your mouth as you suck it. Definitely an attractive accessory, and exclusively masculine. Hard to find things exclusively masculine, really. Had women got on to pipes yet? He wasn't sure. She watched him light his pipe. How masculine, she thought. Hello, he said sexily, between puffs. She slipped, stumbled, he put his arm round her . . . 'Come on, Joyce, we haven't got all day. You made a right hash of it yesterday. I've put it on your desk

46

and for heaven's sake don't forget the last paragraph this time.'

In a few minutes' time he could slip out and see if Paul and Polly were open yet. I just want to have a look around, he would say. They must often get people just looking around. They wouldn't expect every customer to buy something. It wasn't a tobacconist. Then, after a moment or two, he'd say casually, I believe you know some neighbours of ours— and then they'd talk about George, and then the Davieses, and then the Frises. And then they'd say, after a certain amount of friendly chit-chat, of course, when they'd *warmed* to him, that they were having a party, why didn't he come along, drop in, meet their friends? Helga would be there, a dark candle-lit party, smoochy background music, and in the smoochy background himself and Helga . . .

'And don't forget to change the date.' If he had a pipe, he would now light it. It would give him an air of authority. Joyce might start doing what he asked her. She was now pencilling a black and hideous line along her left eye-lid. He stood up abruptly. 'This isn't the Ladies, Joyce.' He had intended biting sarcasm but his voice made it sound like a good-humoured joke.

Joyce looked up surprised, sensing real anger behind the words. She immediately regretted her casual treatment of him, and the way she had slid away yesterday evening, knowing she had got the letter wrong. Leaving one eye unlined, she hurriedly stuffed her make-up and mirror into her bag, and opened the drawer of her desk for paper; blue copy paper for the office file, carbon, and a sheet of paper headed Dolphin Travel bearing a grotesque emblem of a dolphin in a bikini. She fitted the sheets together with hurried care, and slotted them into her typewriter. 8th May 1969, she typed, far too rapidly for her skill, Dear Sisr.

Two doors away, and one floor up, the cold tap dripped on to Paul's toes. Enough torture, he thought and with a tidal wave of bath water, climbed out.

'How much did you pay for that chamber-pot thing?' he asked Polly, who woke with a start. She yawned widely. 'Oh, ah, ah.'

Paul, watching her, yawned too, but got over it more quickly. He rubbed himself dry with a dressing-gown which a visitor had left behind some years before.

'Not awake yet,' Polly mumbled, 'tell you in a moment.' She reached blindly for the roll of paper. Paul bent to pick it up and put it in her hand.

'You know, your nodder came in this morning,' he told her, squeezing an already flattened tube of toothpaste. He tore the tube open with his teeth, peeled the sides apart and scrubbed at the inside with his brush. 'He's going to call back later. Getting very daring.'

'Who's this?' Polly stood up, pulled the chain and reached for her toothbrush. 'After you.' Paul handed her the tooth-paste. 'This is finished.'

'No it isn't.'

'It's empty.'

'Lots there. Is it late?' She was waking up.

'Yes.'

'Must get some more. Who called?'

'No need. How much did you pay for the pot?'

'What pot?'

'The pot the phone's in.'

'Which phone?'

'Our phone.'

'Oh that. We really must get some more toothpaste. This is finished. Ladbroke Grove yesterday, a job lot of two to-pees, *Encyclopaedia Britannica E-H*, a spoon and the pot. Four quid, no, three fifteen we ended at, I think.'

'Polly!' Paul spat into the bath water. 'That's junk. You really shouldn't go wild. We are trying to upgrade this thing, and you bring in pots and topees.'

'But, my little love,' she said, behind her toothbrush, 'the spoon is 1832.' She smiled her slow, bland, secret smile that made her look like the Virgin Mary, as Botticelli might have painted her for the scene after the Annunciation.

'Sure?' asked Paul, doubtfully.

'Course I'm sure.'

'Better check. And we'll price the pot at thirty-five bob in any case. It looks good on the desk. People love that sort of thing.'

'Mm, for putting plants in. Or punch.'

'Anything that begins with a p, you might say.'

Polly gave this an approach to a laugh, as Paul left the room. He came in again a few moments later, now dressed, and stood behind Polly who was brushing her hair in front of the mirror.

'Morning, my love,' he said at their reflection. He could see a sinister-looking black-haired man peeping over the shoulder of a mermaid. He made a variety of faces to make her laugh, pretended to eat her shoulder, continued munching down her spine, kissed her bottom, and left.

As he entered the shop, the door was rattling. He opened it, and Timothy walked in.

'You did say ten minutes,' said Timothy.

'Have you been waiting? Apologies. Overslept this morning.'

Overslept with Polly, thought Tim, with remembered greed. But he mustn't be unfaithful to Helga. It was Helga all the way now. He was glad it was Paul in the shop; he didn't want to be distracted by Polly.

'Might I just look round?'

'Certainly, certainly.' Paul moved away to the desk and busied himself there. He wrote 35/- (1873?) on a gummed label and, while Timothy's back was turned, he stuck it on the pot. The phone rang, as though in response.

'Merrivale double two seven eight, Kitchen Antiques, good-*morn*ing.'

'Hi, Jake here.'

'Hi there,' said Paul. It was not one of his words, but he often found himself repeating Jake's hi.

'Just rang to suggest a meeting tonight.'

'Oh, er—' said Paul, feeling tired immediately.

'Not a full-scale meeting, just a casual chat at our house. We've one or two points we'd like to bring up. About the association.'

'Ah,' said Paul, relieved. 'I see.'

'Can you make it?'

'For this evening? I'll ask Polly. I think we can.'

Bet that's an invitation to a party, thought Timothy looking mournfully at a dusty cherub.

'Met our new neighbours last night. You know them. Frise,' said Jake.

'Oh yes, Alexander and Helga.'

Timothy grew rigid. Oh this whole new world, he must get into it. Parties, Helga, Polly, Timothy Blunden and the Merrivale set . . . he held his breath, to hear more.

'Might do as new members, I was thinking,' said Jake cautiously.

'Mm,' said Paul doodling with his biro on the back of

gummed labels. '*She* might . . . not so sure about him, though.'

She might what? thought Tim horrified. He examined a cameo brooch with minute attention.

'Get the girls' opinion any rate.'

'Good idea. We'll drop in this evening, what time? Nine-ish?' asked Paul.

Party time, thought Timothy.

'Right, see you.'

'Bye.'

Tim turned to see Paul replacing the receiver. It was an old-fashioned brass phone. He'd like it. Just the sort of thing to have, not in the least Grove. (Or *was* it? What would Jake think?) But it would be expensive, they couldn't afford luxuries like that. On the other hand, it worked. So it might be called a necessity. Phones are a necessity. And, if he bought something, Paul was much more likely to be friendly. No, he mustn't be extravagant, he would just ask the price. Out of curiosity.

He wandered casually towards the desk, and looked into the pot at the phone. 'Mm, that's awfully nice,' he said. 'What sort of price might that be?'

Paul never gave away prices so early in the game. 'It is a lovely thing isn't it. Victorian of course.'

'Really?' said Tim. 'You wouldn't know the date, would you?'

'Yes, it has a label somewhere, 1880's I think,' he said vaguely, in spite of having written the label not five minutes before. Now, when the customer read 1873, it would seem that much more valuable than an 1880's pot, and he wouldn't worry about the question mark.

Fantastic, thought Timothy. It would be way beyond his means. 'How much are you asking for it?'

Paul disregarded this again. 'Funnily enough, they are very hard to find nowadays.' He summed Timothy up. 'They are *just* starting to become fashionable,' he said, having decided that Timothy wouldn't risk anything that wasn't yet fashionable; but neither would he want something that everyone else had.

It certainly sounded safe to Timothy. It would be one step, but not two, ahead of Grove. 'It's very pretty,' he said cautiously. 'And you can use it too.'

There was a second's silence. Then Paul laughed. 'Yes, of

course you can use it if you want to. Or need to.' This was the moment to say the price, before the customer asked again. 'It's thirty-five shillings as it's very slightly chipped. Not noticeably of course.'

'But it works though? I mean, it's reliable?'

My God, thought Paul, I think he seriously intends to pee in this thing, keep it under his bed? Maybe he has a long cold walk to his loo. 'Oh, quite watertight. I've used it myself.'

'So I noticed,' said Timothy.

Paul looked into the pot with some alarm.

'Thirty-five bob you said?' checked Timothy. It sounded a strangely reasonable price. He had expected it to be ten pounds at least. Tina would be thrilled. 'I'll have it.'

'Excellent,' said Paul and removed the phone from the pot. He looked around for wrapping paper.

There was the thumping creaking sound of someone large coming down the stairs. Polly, thought Tim, now quickly get it in before she arrives and puts me off. 'I believe-youknowsomeneighboursofours,' he said.

'Do we?' said Paul, finding a pile of old newspapers.

'Yes, we live in The Grove, Beechley Avenue—'

The door behind the desk opened a foot, and Polly squeezed in. 'Not those!' she said sharply to Paul's back. 'Those are Of Interest, Suez Crisis, Five Guineas!'

'But we've had them since the Suez Crisis too.'

'No matter, they'll come in yet. The wrapping paper is on the lectern.' She glanced at Timothy, who was crouching to look at a china dog. 'Morning.'

'Good morning,' said Tim, turning his head slightly. Polly moved over to the door and looked out at the street. Tim straightened and said rapidly in a low voice. 'Jake and Margaret Davies. George and Judith Toms. Alexander and Helga Frise.'

'But this is tissue paper,' said Paul.

Polly watched a traffic warden watch a woman park a car on a double yellow line. 'Well, there's some brown in the bottom drawer then,' she said, and wondered how Paul would manage without her.

'We know them, the Frises,' said Timothy. 'They came in to drinks last night.'

Paul was on the floor behind the desk, getting brown

51

paper out of a bottom drawer, and probably hadn't heard. But Polly turned.

'Oh you're Grove too, are you?' she asked, looking interested. 'We used to live there at one time. When it was first built. It was quite—' She was going to say 'lively then' but tailed off, not intending to be rude. 'New then,' she said instead.

'It must have been,' said Timothy, trying to help. 'If it had just been built.'

Polly looked at him carefully and wondered if he was teasing her. But he looked earnest.

'What a coincidence,' said Paul, coming over with the parcel, which was large and round. 'I was just talking to Jake on the phone.'

'Oh *were* you?' said Polly.

Tim brought out his wallet and found a pound note. He felt in his pocket for change. This was certainly a rash impulse buy. He would have nothing left to pay for lunch. Laying his silver on a table, he counted reluctantly towards thirty-five shillings. Paul waited.

'. . . thirty-*four* . . .' tried Timothy hopefully, and put his hand half-way into his pocket.

'Well,' said Paul, 'I daresay we'll meet one of these days at The Grove.'

Tim's hand went right into his pocket and produced a shilling.

'Don't worry,' said Paul, relenting, and pushed the shilling back.

'Oh thanks,' said Timothy, taking the shilling and the parcel quickly. 'Yes, we're bound to,' he said, and moved towards the door. Polly opened it for him. 'Thanks very much,' he said to her with a nod and a smile. 'Thanks,' he said to Paul. And out he went, with a large parcel but no invitations. But maybe he, like Alexander, would find a reason to return again and again to the shop, and they would get to know him well. Here comes Tim again, hello *Tim*, they'd call cheerfully, glad to see him. Doing anything tonight? Come to a party with us, you'll know lots of people there—

'Oh Mr. Blunden,' said Joyce, as he arrived back in the office, 'there's someone here waiting to see you.'

Tim moved behind the counter, put his parcel under it, and looked expectantly towards the waiting client, like a doctor bracing himself to hear yet another patient describe flu symptoms. His expression melted to an encouraging smile as the client rose to her feet. 'Good-morning,' he said, 'I'm sorry to keep you waiting.'

'Good morning,' she said huskily and approached the counter. Tim noted with appreciation the fluid movement of her hips. 'I've got up a party—' she began. Tim looked startled—an invitation! She was going to invite him to a party, she had admired him from afar, maybe from the boutique on the opposite side of the High Street, she looked as though she might possibly come from a dark, red, glittering, pop-musical background like the boutique, and he would—but he killed the foolish hope at once. The only parties he heard about were group travel parties. '—and we want to find a villa to rent in Greece somewhere,' she continued. 'Can you help us?'

Tim hesitated. This was not the sort of job Dolphin usually undertook. He would refer her to some organisation that did this sort of thing. The client noticed his hesitation, rested her arms on the counter, and looked up at him anxiously. 'There *are* villas in Greece, aren't there?'

'Oh yes, yes,' said Tim, noticing the colour of her coat. It was black. Was she a widow? Perhaps one member of her party would drop out, and she would ask him to join them? 'Certainly we'll help,' he said, 'it shouldn't be difficult to arrange.'

He did help. He enjoyed helping. It wasn't difficult to arrange; though he managed to find several small complications which made it necessary for her to call in frequently. All the same, some months later, he was to wish that she and her wretched villa had never entered his life.

That evening, Tim gave Tina her present. 'But it's not my birthday!' she said and began unwrapping it, excited.

'Oh well, you deserve a present,' he said and, to justify the extravagance, he added, 'and you can use it too.'

'I don't think that's funny,' said Tina looking at the pot.

Tim was rather pleased at the mistake. It gave him an excuse to return to the shop.

Paul and Polly arrived at the Davies house at about half past ten. Jake and Margaret had given them up and were getting ready for bed. 'Shall we pretend to be asleep?' suggested Jake.

'No, better go down. It's not that late,' said Margaret. So they pulled on dressing-gowns and went downstairs.

'I hope we're not late,' said Polly.

'It depends what for,' said Jake, taking her coat. 'You're frightfully late for a social visit.'

She moved into the room, put her hands on Margaret's shoulders and patted her dressing-gown, and kissed her cheek. 'Look darling!' she said, turning to Paul. 'They were in bed! We are naughty.'

Paul hung his coat in the porch, and followed her into the room. ''Umble apologies,' he said, 'but you don't mind *really*, do you.'

'We do in fact. We're dead. Let's have some strong coffee.'

'So are we!' They all laughed, and went to sit down at the far end of the room.

'Incredible,' said Paul, trying to find a comfortable way to sit on a coffin-shaped toy-box covered by a red and orange rug, 'how every Grove house, though identical in design, looks different.'

'Oh don't say that,' said Jake, 'people are always saying that. It's one of Grove's opening conversational gambits.'

'It's not true, in fact, any longer,' said Margaret, spreading herself over several enormous cushions on the floor. 'Quite changed since your day.'

'Yes, that's true,' said Jake. 'They go in for green a lot nowadays. Ranging from sage?' he checked with his wife, 'to a very daring Thames.'

'Careful, sweetie, we used to have a Thames Green kitchen,' said Polly.

'True, true. But there's a world of difference between a Thames Green kitchen 1960 and a Thames Green kitchen 1970.'

'I suppose we all want coffee?' said Margaret, not getting up.

They agreed they all wanted coffee.

'We peered into number Two on our way past. They have a gnome in the porch!'

'I know!' Margaret, Jake and Polly fell about at this, but Paul jutted his chin and scratched his beard. 'I'm not so sure,' he said, when the laughter had subsided, 'that we might not take up gnomes.'

Polly looked aghast. 'I'm not having any gnomes in my shop.'

54

Paul disregarded this. 'I think they might have a comeback soon. After all, the great mass of the population have gone beyond gnomes now. So gnomes could safely become pop material.'

'You haven't been out in the country lately. Drive down to Cornwall—they line the route.'

'But the shop isn't on the A3. It's in Merrivale High Street, S.W. Light years away.'

'And Merrivale High Street is light years away from London.'

'Did someone say something about coffee?'

'I did, but I don't think I have the energy.'

'Paul will make it, won't you darling?' said Polly.

'*Thank* you Paul my own sweet love,' said Margaret.

Jake got to his feet. 'Watch it now. Don't forget the rules. Can I take some paper from your desk?'

'Oh, business now, is it? Can't we have coffee first?' asked Polly.

Paul got up. 'You can tell who holds this group together. It's only the men who do the work.' He went into the kitchen as they laughed at this. 'Me making coffee, and Jake making lists,' he added.

'Oo,' said Polly, 'I love lists. What are we making lists about?'

Jake sat on the floor, so that he could use the low table as a desk. 'Well,' he said, his voice taking on the tone of an agenda, 'I think we all feel the need to expand.'

'Ha!'

'Ah!'

'Oh dear!' This was Margaret. 'New members, I feel so frightfully conservative.'

'Flattered, I'm sure,' said Paul from the kitchen.

'Well, it could be interesting,' said Polly, closing her eyes. 'If we all agree. We'd have to be careful though. In choosing.'

'Yes,' said Jake, 'extreme caution is called for. We must first of all unanimously agree to expansion—a vote, I think—'

'—secret ballot—?'

'Should be.'

'—and when, that is, *if* we all agree, we must then make a list of all our friends, not necessarily mutual, pool our circles bearing in mind, er, suitability, adaptability, er—'

'Ability, pure and simple!'

'Ha!'

55

'Ah!'

'—and then arrange a few meetings . . .' continued Jake.

Polly opened her eyes. 'Before mentioning the, erm, function of the association, or after?'

'Before, before, surely.'

'I say, isn't that one of your children?' Polly was looking at the stairs where the youngest Davies child had been sitting unnoticed for some time.

'Oh heavens!' said Margaret, pulling herself into a sitting position. 'Benjamin, what are you doing?'

'Sitting on the stairs.'

'You should be asleep!'

'I wasn't sleepy. I wanted to see who it was.'

'Well, go back to bed at once.'

'But I'm not sleepy. Can't I stay here?'

'Certainly not,' said Jake. 'Do what your mother tells you.'

The boy looked from face to face for a moment, decided the odds were against him, and said, 'Oh all right.' He got to his feet, and went upstairs.

'Night, darling,' called his mother.

'Night,' he said, padded across the landing, shut his bedroom door, and crept back to the top of the stairs. By the guilty expressions on their faces, that dull conversation must have been about something adult, forbidden and exciting.

There was a short silence downstairs. Then Margaret said, 'What had we been saying? Nothing awful, I hope?'

'I don't think so.'

Paul brought in the coffee and, while Margaret stirred from her cushions sufficiently to pour it out, he found a bottle of whisky and glasses, and Jake began to write down a list of names. This took a very long time. Each of them would suggest a name, the other half of the couple would object, 'Oh no, not *them*.' The other couple would ask details of the proposed pair, and when, after a great deal of discussion, it would be finally decided to omit the name, Jake would write it down. 'We can't be selective at this stage. We need quantity not quality. We'll grade them later.'

Benjamin stayed at the top of the stairs for some time, hoping it might get interesting; but it didn't. He went to bed.

Eventually, after one hour's hard labour which pulled to shreds two substantial circles of acquaintances, they had achieved a short list of ten couples which read:

		A	S of H	C
Orr-Brown	Michael	3	5	1
	Jane	4	2	1
Toms	George	1	3	5
	Judith	3	5	5
Blunden	Timothy	3	3	5
	Tina	3	0	5
Frise	Alexander	5	2	5
	Helga	3	?	5
Lefevre	Pierre	5	5	0
	Janet	4	5	0

and so on.

'There,' said Jake, laying down his biro. 'We might open the discussion now.'

Polly held out her hand for the list. 'Pity we can't fill in Helga's S of H,' she said, and passed it on to Paul.

And a pity the Lefevres rate so low on C,' he said. 'Otherwise they have the highest aggregate, don't they? Shall I work out aggregates?'

'Do that,' said Jake, yawning as he poured more Scotch.

Paul, with remarkable swiftness, jotted down the total scores for each couple. 'Oh, that's funny. The Toms come out top!'

'The *Toms*, my God. He wears a bowler.'

'How on earth did they score so well?'

'*I* like them very much.'

'How do the Frises rate?'

Paul checked the list. 'Quite well, too. Twenty with one score missing. That's Helga's S of H'.

'We must fill that in,' said Polly, who was lobbying for the Frises. 'I rather got the impression she might be high on that count, though it is hard to tell. I think she's probably rather shrewd and no doubt laughing at *us* all the time.'

'Do you think so?' Paul looked put out at this thought. 'I wouldn't classify that Sense of Humour.'

Margaret had the list now. 'The Blundens have nineteen, that's not bad.'

'Which ones are they?' asked Polly. 'Oh yes I remember, you described them. They're Grove, too, that's how they've got five for convenience. And we worked out it must have been Timothy who bought the pot this morning.'

'If you ask me,' said Paul, 'he'd be thrilled to join. He has his eyes on Poll,'

'And Margaret has her eye on *him*, haven't you darling,' said Jake.

'Only very lightly,' said Margaret. She yawned. 'Right then. Next stage is to arrange a few casual meetings. Shall we have the same system as we did when we considered expansion before?'

'What, dictionary evenings again? But that was total failure, we didn't expand then.'

'No, but we had a lot of fun, even if we didn't get new members.'

Polly said, 'I'd love to play Dictionary again, we haven't for ages. And it is a good proving ground.'

Jake was worried for Helga's chances. 'But Dictionary is hardly fair on the non-English and we have two on our list.'

'Pierre read English at Oxford though. And Helga—well —in any case, we are not worried about how they score at the game, only about how they score on the, er, other counts.'

Finally, it was agreed that a series of Dictionary evenings should be arranged. The first would be held at the Davies house and would include the Lefevres and the Frises.

'That's fair,' agreed Jake. 'Pierre and Helga will cancel each other out.'

'In a manner of speaking,' said Margaret.

CHAPTER FOUR

Timothy Blunden still woke up sharply too early in the morning, but the habit was no longer unpleasant.

At 6.10 a.m. he was awake, keyed up and ready for ninety minutes delicious dreaming. His life was full of reasons for his feeling of anticipation. There was the possibility of seeing Helga on the way to the bus, and on the bus. There was the exciting prospect of dinner with her (and Alexander and Tina) the following Thursday. There were plans to make for chance meetings on Saturday afternoons, when Alexander was away playing rugger in a muddy field somewhere—or had the season stopped? Perhaps Alexander played cricket in the summer. Surely.

And, when he was bored with Helga, he resorted to the widow who wanted to rent a villa in Greece. Or to Polly, who, although demoted to second place since Helga's arrival on the scene, was still active in his fantasy life whenever he gave her the chance. An hour and a half before the alarm was barely long enough.

So when he woke at half past five on the Thursday of the dinner with the Frises, he was relieved rather than dismayed. He had a lot of ground to cover before the alarm; so much indeed, that he would have to go about it systematically.

First of all, and lowest in the anticipation stakes, there was the widow. She had come in the previous day, but with a husband. That had been a blow. On the other hand, they had told him that two members of their party had fallen out. Instead of a villa for ten, they wanted one for eight. Timothy had found a villa for ten. He told them he would try to cancel it, and find a smaller villa, but he thought it might be difficult. Could they perhaps find another couple? He had been so busy in the office, he hadn't had time to work this one through, so he would do it now.

Well. The widow and her husband have had great difficulty in finding another couple. They, no, she, pleads with him—after several meetings, and maybe a friendly lunch or two, discussing villa details and discovering their mutual attraction (he could do this another morning, when he had more time)—she pleads with him to join their party. Her hand rests on his arm, and she looks up at him with promise in her eyes. 'It would be such fun,' she says in a low lingering voice. No, no, he had a better idea. They've been unable to find another couple, but they have a friend, a single, beautiful girl, who wants to join them. So it's necessary for Tim to go on his own. In the course of duty, really. Like a courier, he'd tell Tina, just a fortnight. What should he take? No, he mustn't get side-tracked by clothes, they are already on their way. On a coach. What a pity he'd arranged for them to go by coach, that was a frightful way to get to Greece, maybe he could make a better arrangement, part of a charter flight. That's it, so off they fly. On the plane, he sits next to the widow. She is, after all, the organiser of the party, and he the courier. They have a lot of details to talk over, so it's quite reasonable for him to be sitting next to her. She is frightened by the take-off, she closes her eyes, he holds her hand, she leans her head against his shoulder, he puts his arm around her, or would the safety belt be in the way? The lights go off—do lights go off in planes, like in trains

59

going through tunnels? He couldn't remember. Anyway, the lights go off. It's a night flight, much cheaper, cheap night tourist return. She goes to sleep, her head still on his shoulder. When she wakes, they kiss in the darkness.

But Timothy was too worried by the darkness to really enjoy the kiss. He didn't think it would be dark on a plane. Lights don't go off on planes. So suddenly they were in a train, but then of course there would be others in the carriage and it would take three days and two nights, or was it two days and three nights, and it would be hell. Back to the plane. What a business travel is, he would skip the journey and there they were lying on a beach, much more promising. He knew that the villa he had found for them was one kilometre from a shingle beach, but he hadn't passed this information on to his client, naturally. Now if he was joining the party, he had better change this, find a villa near a stretch of golden sand.

Where?

He must look into this when he got to the office.

Time slipping past, he wasn't doing too well. *Concentrate.*

There they are, lying on the golden sand, her body tanned dusky brown his body tanned dusky brown, two bodies tanned dusky brown, lying side by side. This was good. No one else in sight. Fingers touching. What next? She has sand in her eye. He leans over to help her get it out. She grips his shoulders, in pain. In passion. Oh, oh, said Timothy in bed, and rolled over on to his back. Polly now.

Polly.

He had an uncomfortable feeling that Polly found him a joke. He had another uncomfortable feeling that he disliked Polly.

Never mind. She rings him up. Tim darling, can you pop in for a second, I think I've found exactly what you're looking for. Yourself? he jokes, gay, debonair Timothy. He leaves the office, steps briskly down the street, heads turn to watch his handsome figure, and into Kitchen Antiques. No, in fact, he would leave in half an hour. I've been *waiting* for you! cries Polly in anguish. Sorry, my love, casually, pressure of work, y'know. She leads him upstairs to show him, ostensibly, an antique telephone. It's in their, her, bedroom. A palatial room, quite unlike a Grove bedroom, deep-pile carpet, white of course. The bed, a four-poster, richly hung with velvet curtains. She is wearing a floating white? black? purple? negligée, her hair a cascade of gold down her back.

And the phone, where might that be? he asks her, teasingly sophisticated, tall, cool, devastatingly attractive. I'm not going to show you a phone, she says and pulls him down (and into, as it's curtained) the soft bed. Oh, oh, thought Timothy, and rolled over on to his side. Helga now.

He felt much more in control with Helga. Polly often manhandled him. But he manhandled Helga. There was the Saturday afternoon when they went punting on the river. This was a good one. He didn't get bogged down with paltry details like where was Tina? Which river? Was Alexander playing rugger or cricket? They were simply punting on a river, just the two of them. Weeping willows, high summer, rather a 1920's feel to the whole scene, boaters, and Helga in a fringey sort of dress, probably muslin, buttercups on her lap, in her hair, trailing her hand in the water, gazing adoringly up at him as he deftly propels the punt along the cool river, between lush banks. Placid cows regard them. They are silent, but together in their silence. Suddenly Helga slips, stumbles, he catches her around the waist, they fall into the water—no, that has gone wrong this morning, they're covered in green weed and muddy slime, that's not how it's supposed to go at all. Obviously it is altogether too idealistic a dream, too absurd and unlikely. He would do the bus one.

This was a very likely one. Helga is waiting at the bus stop. He comes round the Beechley Avenue corner, and along the main road, a dashingly handsome figure, swirling his umbrella rather like George. Her heart misses a beat. She has loved him long and hopelessly. And he doesn't know it. Good-morning, she says timidly. Hi, he says, rather like Jake. I come from haunts of coot and tern, I make a sudden sally and I love Sally but not so much as *you*. . . . He is witty, speedy, the daring glitter of his conversation fascinates her. . . . And sparkle out among the fern to bicker down the Merrivalley. Any buses to bicker on? he asks her.

(He really should have persisted with the punt one long enough to see them out of the river. The image of himself and Helga struggling and splashing in the slime and weed is worrying him.)

A 216 went past, full, and two 87s, says Helga.

He grasps her round the waist and strikes out for the bank in a strong (one-armed) crawl.

Let us bicker on our feet, then, he says, and off they go along the main road. It's very wet, the pavements are treacherous, Helga slips, stumbles. They are lying on the bank gasping, soaked, muddy, they kiss feverishly, a bus speeds past, the alarm rings.

The alarm! Time up already, and still hardly begun on Helga. Tina was not beside him. He got up quickly, feeling wide awake, looked in at Ricky's bedroom and saw an empty cot. He could hear sounds of breakfast from downstairs.

'Well, you are sleeping well,' said Tina, when he appeared.

'I had a rotten night actually,' said Tim crossly. 'I nearly got up at half past five, I couldn't sleep, but then I suppose I must have drifted off again.'

'So it seems,' said Tina. 'Shall I put some in for you?' she asked, holding a piece of sliced white above the toaster.

'Yes please,' said Tim and looked at the kitchen clock. 'But it's only a quarter to eight for heaven's sake.'

'Ricky's been awake since half past six. I got him up at seven. He was screaming.'

'Oh,' said Tim, and picked up the paper.

'Dadadadada,' said Ricky.

'And dadadadada to you too,' said Timothy. He was in excellent time for once, and might easily coincide with Helga at the bus stop. Hi there, Helga. A sunny morning, too, and even if he didn't see her at the bus stop he would see her tonight.

'You sound cheerful,' said Tina, who was hugging her cup of coffee, with her elbows propped on the table, and looking haggard.

'Do I?' said Tim, guiltily.

'Yes. You were whistling.'

'Was I?'

'I hope I can get a little shut-eye this afternoon when Rick has his rest. I feel dead and we're going out tonight.'

'Oh yes, so we are,' said Timothy as though he'd just remembered.

It wasn't a quiet breakfast. Tina was full of questions which she had been collecting since half past six. Where were they going for their holiday? Had he decided yet? They—that is, he—mustn't leave it too late, like they—that is, he—had done last year. Was there still the possibility of the cheap trip to Morocco? Yes, but Tim's idea of a holiday was two weeks in Wales, Scotland or Cornwall. He had loathed travelling since his Merchant Navy days, though he squeezed a certain amount of pleasure out of sending other people off to loathsome parts of the world. Tina wouldn't dream of a holiday in the British Isles, she was a continental at heart, she said, a true European. She would dearly love to show Tim Finland or Switzerland and guide them nimbly through their holiday in Finnish or French. Their planned holiday last year had been three weeks touring the Swiss and Italian lakes, at a remarkably low price through Dolphin. But Tim had delayed making the arrangements, and finally they had spent two weeks in Pembrokeshire, a reluctant and amazed addition to a group of bird-watchers. Tina had made the best of this by borrowing her father's binoculars. The previous year there had been the idyllic possibility of a trip to the West Indies. This had fallen through at the last moment and they had found themselves on a leaking barge on an unidentified canal, again in South Wales. And the year before that, they hadn't been able to afford even the cut-rate of a Dolphin arranged holiday. They had been saving up for the deposit on number Six.

'If we find ourselves in South Wales again . . .' muttered Tina threatening her toast.

'I'll look into Morocco this morning, I promise darling,' said Tim and braced himself for the next question.

'Right. Now where did you put the button that came off your blue shirt?'

'Ah. Um. In the bedro—' he checked himself. Tina was always irritated by vague answers. 'In the bedroom, on your dressing-table, a little to the right of your hair brush, to the left of your hand-mirror and very near your jar of crepey-neck cream.'

'Oh. O.K. Have you taken that thing back yet?

'What thing?'

'To Kitchen Antiques. Because if you don't take it back soon, they'll refuse to change it. In any case, they have such a load of old rubbish in that place, I just hope you'll be able to find something to change it with.'

'But I'm going to get the telephone—'

'An antique telephone, darling, would cost thirty-five pounds not shillings.'

'But it can't be all that antique. Telephones weren't invented till, till, till—'

'Bell patented his telephone system in 1876,' said Tina,

pouring herself more coffee. 'Finished darling?' she asked Ricky. 'Down, down?'

'Dow dow dow dow dow,' said Ricky.

Typical Tina, she had looked it up.

'Next question?' he asked.

'Well, I just wanted to ask you—' began Tina and paused while she disentangled Ricky from his bib and high chair. 'Ooooooooo,' went Ricky, chuntering off in search of toys.

'Careful!' she shouted in warning. He had narrowly missed waddling into a chair. 'Now, the other thing I wanted to say was. I had a letter from Mummy yesterday, and she wants to know when we're going up there again.' She watched Tim's change of expression and added, 'We haven't been for ages, you know.'

'It seems like the other day.'

'February in fact. We should go soon.'

Now, what about Tina going on her own, with Rick? There's an idea. He's all alone at Grove, Helga takes pity on his grass-widowhood, brings along pies and cakes, he kisses her lightly in thanks, the kiss turns passionate in midstream . . .

'I suppose so,' he said. He considered the best way to engineer this situation was to make it seem as though he would go too, fix the weekend, and then at the last moment fabricate a foolproof reason why he couldn't get away. 'Of course, it's a hectic time of year now at the agency, but I'll see if I can't get a Saturday off soon.'

'We should take the Friday evening train, oh dear, how I wish we had the car still.'

'But we only had it a month or two and it wasn't ours then.'

'Maybe your brother'll go abroad again.'

'Unlikely.'

'Will we ever have a car of our own?' Tina drooped, and Tim got up, went round the table, and kissed her. He was often affected by Tina's regret at his lack of ambition; and sometimes he was infected by it too. 'Cheer up love. Fogle rang me the other day and as good as promised a rise in the near future. He sounded pretty doddery too.'

'But he's only the same age as Daddy! He won't give up for years.'

'You never know.' He went to the porch. 'Do I need a mac today?'

'Heavens no, it's lovely. I'll take Rick to the river to feed the swans. You're terribly early you know. I'm sure there was one more thing I had to say . . .'

'No, I must get off. I've got a woman,' (not a girl) 'coming in early about a villa in Greece—'

'Oh! A villa in Greece, that would be heaven,' said Tina bitterly.

'Dream of Morocco,' said Tim, at the front door.

'Huh.'

'See you then.'

She joined him at the door and gave him a kiss. 'Don't be late.' She paused at the door, and waved at Tim walked away. Sometimes Grove looked happy, pleasant, quiet, rural. At this time of year, there was blossom, the grass was young and green, sun exploded on the glass of the trim box-like houses. A good place to live, thought Tina, with a warm surge of satisfaction. The Davies children came out of the house opposite, not quite dressed as always. They ran down the path, still pulling on coats. The last one, Benjamin, smiled politely across the lawn at her. She hoped Ricky would look something like him when he was that age. 'Hello Ben!' she called, but she realised the boy had been looking at a cat. His mother called to him to hurry from the car park, and he responded by slowing to a shuffle. Beyond, in Beechley Avenue, the milkman's trolley appeared. She would order cream, they hadn't had cream lately, but silly though as they were eating out tonight, good, so she wouldn't order cream. She must wash her hair, wear her petunia-pink, the neckline suited her, was he attracted to her? As though in reply to this thought, the door of number Seven opened, and she backed into the porch. But it was Helga. Lucky, lucky Helga, in a gorgeous white spring coat, going off to work. Oh the freedom, the independence of going off to work, and mornings only; and the coats she could afford; and Alexander in the evenings. Tina could hardly bring herself to return Helga's wave, but she managed it, with a smile, too.

Helga paused opposite number Six and outside the open front door of number Nine, the Davies's house. Jake appeared behind her wearing, Tina saw—and rebuked herself for feeling shocked—only a skimpy bath towel tucked around her waist and nowhere near to his knees.

Helga called to Tina, 'This evening, yes?'

Jake looked down the path at the approaching milkman.

Tina called back, 'Lovely, looking forward to it!'

Jake noted this exchange with ironical appreciation. Here were two pairs of candidates getting together. He wondered how they would rate each other. He waved to Tina, who waved back and Helga turned to see him.

'Oh!' said Helga. She tried not to look at his legs.

'Hello,' said Jake. 'Five today please.'

'Very fine,' said Helga and then saw the milkman. 'Oh I thought you said fine.'

'He did say five,' said the milkman.

Jake bent to pick up two pints and his towel began to slip. Helga said good-bye hurriedly, and walked off down the path, leaving Jake clutching two bottles of milk and a small bath towel to his stomach as he backed into the house. Now a likely candidate for the association, thought Jake, as he kicked the door shut with his foot, would have stayed to watch that. Maybe Helga was not as promising as he had thought. On the other hand, if she *were* a member of the association she would have stayed to watch and to help. The only way to test a member's suitability is after that member has joined, he decided, and made a mental note to repeat this to the group. They would appreciate its subtlety.

Meanwhile Tim had reached the hostel. He glanced up at the first floor window. There she was, hands above the head and . . . d o w n . . . good, he was in excellent time. This morning he had a good chance of reaching the stop before Helga got on a bus. He walked on briskly.

Fifty yards behind him, Helga turned out of The Grove into Beechley Avenue. Early sun splattered patterns through the trees. No doubt they were beeches, considering the name of the road, though they bore pink blossom, and Helga wasn't convinced that beeches had blossom.

The bright quality of the morning helped her recapture the atmosphere of quaint foreignness that the road had held for her when they had first moved to Merrivale, but which had been well dissolved by familiarity and a succession of damp grey morning walks to the bus stop. She looked again with tourist interest at each house she passed. The tall red-brick one, with wisteria over the porch; the long low white one, with the neat circle of shaven lawn,

66

another circle of earth in the centre making it look like a monk's head; then the block of flats, stony-faced, forbidding, tasteless in design; the strange red pillar box; the boarded-up gap where one of the large old houses had been knocked down and where she had once seen a bulldozer and two workmen. There was a notice on the road, something something something 24 Luxury Houses in loopy script, 1, 2, and 3 bedrooms—but she had always passed before she had read all the details. Another Grove, it would be.

Beechley Avenue was always quiet, the block of flats seemed tenantless, the big houses deserted. Yet there was evidence that people did live there, the click of a door shutting somewhere behind her, a car coming out of a garage ahead. Milk bottles stood on doorsteps, papers hung in the mouths of doors. When she returned in the early afternoon, the milk bottles stood empty and rinsed on doorsteps, and the papers had been taken in. There must be people living in Beechley Avenue who were human and alive enough to drink milk and read the news, yet the only section of the road which showed more tangible evidence of habitation was The Grove.

Helga, with an industry which puzzled Alexander and which she considered natural, had looked into the history of the area in the local library. Some time ago there had been a large old house somewhere behind the present hostel. Its grounds had stretched as far as the Southern Region station to the east, the hospital to the west, and the river to the north. A few magnificent oaks and an ornamental pond that had once graced the park were still preserved incongruously somewhere in south-east Merrivale. The house had been knocked down, probably about the time of the First World War, the land sold and divided out among private developers and the local council. Rows of red-brick houses appeared over the years, and council flats, and nearer the site of the old house itself, a network of wide tree-lined roads provided spacious homes for dentists, doctors, bankers, stockbrokers. Beechley Avenue was one of these roads. Now the individually-designed and generous houses of the doctors, dentists and stockbrokers were being knocked down in their turn, and on the site of a single home, Grove, a development of fourteen houses, had been built in 1960. On the site of another, in 1970, twenty-four houses were to be built. This progression, in spite of an automatic nod to the socialist principles involved, filled Helga with horror. Where one family had lived, now lived perhaps 2,000. And soon, where 2,000 had lived, would live 4,000 She thought nuclear warfare unlikely; but an explosion of human atoms highly probable. A human being, she considered, needs a minimum of x cubic feet in which to live equably. If more than one human being is confined within that minimum, an explosion will occur.

She rather hoped that the explosion in England would be delayed until she had persuaded Alexander to live in Sweden. In Sweden the population of 8 million shared an area of something like 173,000 square miles. In England 53 million juggled with only 93,000 square miles. Helga had an almost American love of statistics.

She wondered if the bus would be crowded this morning. Small explosions often occurred on buses between 8 and 8.30 in the morning on the way to Merrivale High Street; and more on the tube up to Piccadilly. She envied Tina Blunden, who stayed at home and shared the Grove minimum of cubic feet with one small child who couldn't be much more than thirty inches long. Ahead of her, she could see Timothy. That was when the trouble started—when the husbands returned to the Grove. The people who lived next door in number Eight, she couldn't remember their name, were constantly exploding, and the dividing walls were thin. She wondered how the Davies family managed, with three large children and an au pair. They were always being quoted in conversations with non-Grove to prove how well-designed and roomy Grove houses really were—'do you know, there's a family of six in one of these houses!' Strangely enough, she had never heard a Davies explosion. Perhaps the children let off their energy in the communal garden, the parents theirs—at work, no doubt.

Timothy seemed to be expending his energy on the walk to the bus this morning. He was practically running. Maybe he had seen her and wanted to get away. She thought this likely. It seemed he had taken an aversion to her. She remembered one morning, a little while ago, when she had been rather late for the bus. Just as she had turned out of Beechley Avenue and into the main road, Timothy had left the queue and shot off down the road. It had been pouring with rain, not at all a pleasant morning for a walk. The only reason for his abrupt departure that she could think of was her approach. Then, the other evening, when they had visited the Blundens, he had acted as though she had an infectious disease, edging away from her, avoiding her eyes, snatching his hand away from her handshake. It was almost as though he thought she was pursuing him. This amused her. She decided she mustn't worry him unduly this morning, and slowed down.

Tim had reached the end of the Avenue, a bus passed on the main road, and he broke into a gallop. Helga laughed quietly. He was determined to get away!

Or maybe he was merely late for work? But at eight fifteen? Or could it be he was desperately in love with her?

She remembered Alexander's strangled and embarrassed silence when they had first met. She had come home from school, in a hurry to change and go out with friends, and had burst into the living room to find her father discussing a contract with a tall, fair-haired English businessman. Her father had asked her to stay and help translate. Helga hadn't been unwilling. Her friends could wait; she met them most days, but rarely did she meet such good-looking older men. Alexander was twenty-eight. She sat down at the table with them and panted over the contract '. . . . providing approximately one and a half thousand holes . . .'

'Holes?' repeated her father doubtfully.

'No, no, sorry, *drains*,' said Helga.

'*Drains?*' repeated Alexander.

'Gaps?' asked Helga.

Her father leant forward and took the paper. 'Where are we? Oh yes, "one and a half thousand" well, shops, er, like shops—'

'Outlets!' said Alexander, beaming at Helga.

'Outlets then,' she said, irritated at her failure. Alexander had then said how well she was doing, she had smiled at him gratefully, and he had seized up utterly. He had blushed. They had gone out to dinner the following evening, her father, herself and Alexander; and Alexander spent most of the evening in pink and silent agony, and left next day for London. A month later he was back, took her out without her father, and didn't blush so often. Everyone and everything conspired to make it a romance and they themselves unconsciously aided the conspiracy, fitting each other into chosen roles. The summer light of Stockholm was kind; Helga's father approved of Alexander; Alexander was the perfect Englishman; Helga was the Swedish girlfriend—and very soon his wife.

Helga didn't discover that Alexander was stupid until much later, when they had been married some months and her English had improved. She now realised she had married him for the glamour of it. One up on her friends. She hadn't married him for love—she had known that, basically, at the time. But she had liked him. Now she didn't really like him, but she did love him. He was like a helpless bear, good-intentioned but blundering. He bought her presents— scent, which she never used; stockings, and she only wore tights; necklaces, and she liked rings. She never told him his mistakes, for he would consider it criticism and be deeply hurt. She felt protective towards him, and adult. She liked to cook him large meals, and choose his clothes. She loved his parents who lived not far away in a small red-brick house near the railway, an elderly pair wrapped in the cosy comfort of each other, sharing their wonder at the way they had produced a son of Alexander's brains and stature. Alexander was ashamed of his parents. Helga visited them often, and on her own. They were the sort of parents she wished her own had been. But her mother had left her father, and herself, when she was a child, and had lived since then with a series of different men, a series that Helga had ceased to tabulate. By contrast her in-laws were totally a couple, inseparable in attitude rather than action. So, if one were missing, the remaining one became both. If both were present, together they became one. This gave Helga a sense of inherited security for her own marriage. In the evenings, Alexander (looking amazingly like his father, though on a different scale) would sit in a deep armchair, smoking a pipe and watching television from supper-time to close down, and Helga would read, reassured by the picture of the elder Frises reflected in her own home. It was only occasionally that her mouth looked a little sullen, as she read against the glare of the screen. They seldom talked. Alexander adored her, she knew that. She knew he required nothing more from her. And she had accepted the fact that he could give nothing more to her. Alexander thought they were a perfect and happy couple. Helga thought they were as happy as they could be, but by no means perfect. Something was missing, and she didn't know what. Her mouth drooped whenever she puzzled over this.

She had now reached the main road and the bus that Timothy had run for was still waiting in the traffic a few yards down the road. She got on it, and went upstairs. There were two empty seats, one near the back next to Timothy, and one in the front. Without a pause she chose the one at the front and hurried to it, with her eyes straight ahead. Whether Timothy liked her or disliked her, she would avoid him. Hate and love were equally dangerous, she had decided at an early age.

At the back of the bus, Tim stared morosely over his paper at Helga's left ankle, just visible as it swayed and jerked above a brief case in the aisle. If only he hadn't run, if only he'd had a second cup of coffee, Helga would have been sitting, perhaps, in his seat; and he would have climbed the steps to join her. Hi, Helga.

Twelve hours later, Timothy's right ankle was seven inches away from Helga's left ankle. It was agony. All he had to do—and all he could think of doing at the moment—was lift his foot, and move it seven inches to the right, to run the toe of his shoe up the inside of her leg.

The table above the ankles was round and teak, laid with grey-tinted glass, and straight-limbed cutlery that turned the transfer of food from plate to mouth into a kind of Chinese puzzle. An orange globe hung low over the table, like a punchball, and the four had to dodge their heads this way and that to communicate with each other.

Tim, though, wasn't doing much communicating. His mind, his being, had sunk to his right ankle and was concentrated there, itching painfully. Alexander's head appeared around the rim of the globe. 'What do you think, Timothy?' he asked, as though he expected Timothy's opinion to round off a long discussion.

Tim dragged his concentration to the surface with a long sigh that sounded more like a groan. He changed it to yes. 'Yes,' he said again, this time with crisp decision.

There was silence. Then Helga said really? and Tina said rubbish! Tim delved back to reformulate the sounds of the last five minutes. What had they been talking about? Vietnam? Social welfare? No, that had been earlier.

'Well—' he said and paused.

Tina leant forward and helped herself to more cheese.

'But darling, you know that's the only thing that makes Sunday mornings bearable.'

Tim quickly ran through a list of things that might make Sunday mornings bearable; the long lie-in (when Tina let him), kippers, the newspapers, the brief reprieve from work? Still, she had told him that he knew it was the only thing, so he would be safe to agree. 'True,' he said, nodding his head sadly.

'Well, we haven't any children—' began Helga.

'—yet,' put in Alexander, with a smile round the orange lamp.

'—yet,' she said, 'so of course we agree with Timothy. If he really means he agrees himself.'

With what? Oh dear, he ought to concentrate more.

'Has the association made it a rule yet?' Alexander asked Tina.

Timothy grasped at this clue. Grove housing association was unlikely to make kippers for Sunday breakfast a rule.

'Yes, they passed it at the last meeting, and it will come into force this Sunday. Hell for us!'

'But I must admit good for *us*,' said Alexander.

'Just you wait till you have kids,' said Tina and they exchanged smiles on their side of the lamp.

Thank heaven, thought Tim, that seemed to be the end of that conversation. Helga was asking if they all wanted coffee. 'Yes please,' he said with an excess of enthusiasm, so relieved he was at the change of subject.

Alexander suggested that they should sit down in more comfortable chairs, and waved to the sitting end of the room as though it were the remote end of a baronial hall. Helga went into the kitchen to make coffee, and Tina dragged out the yard or two between table and sofa, by admiring for the second time the various bits and pieces arranged on open box-like shelves along the wall. Tim, however, made straight for the sofa. He had worked out that Tina wouldn't sit beside him as it would look too much like couple versus couple; Alexander would probably sit in the deep armchair, as it seemed to be his usual place; so that left Helga, on the sofa beside him.

'Oh!' exclaimed Tina, bending down to look at a shelf. 'What are these?'

'Oh those,' said Alexander, joining her, 'those are geological specimens Helga collected on our hon— on holiday.'

He picked one up and so did Tina. 'That one,' he said, pointing at hers, 'is an ammonite, a prehistoric shellfish thing. This one is a belemnite, same sort of thing, but a different shape.'

'How fascinating,' said Tina, wondering if Alexander could smell her new scent, which she thought should be intoxicating, 'Isn't it pretty! All sort of wiggly.'

'Mm,' said Alexander, 'a spiral.'

'And that one?' asked Tina, holding out her hand.

'That's a nice one too, feel it,' said Alexander and gave her the belemnite. It lay heavy and solid in her hand, a smooth cone shape. She looked up at Alexander in alarm. Did he realise what a significant shape it was? Had he given it to her to hold, as a—as—what, she hardly dared think. She put it back quickly on the shelf, as though it had burnt her, and turned away. 'How terribly interesting,' she said in the voice her mother used to cover awkward moments, and hurried to sit down on the sofa by Tim. He looked at her crossly, she noticed. Had he seen what Alexander had given her? She hoped someone else would say something, while she cooled down. But there was a long silence.

Silences were like holes in socks to Tina, and needed immediate filling. 'Have you been to a meeting here yet?' she asked Alexander with an urgency unsuited to the question.

'A meeting?' How did she know his parents were Congregational? 'No, I'm afraid I've rather given it up, I mean I don't go to church,' he said and then, not satisfied with the weak apology of his reply, he added firmly, 'I'm agnostic.' Or did he mean atheist? He really must look it up.

'Ah,' said Tina, looking puzzled. 'I see.'

There was a pause, while they thought this over. Then Tina bravely tried again. 'Actually,' she said, 'I meant a meeting of the association, the Grove Residents Association.'

'Oh. Ah. I see. I'm sorry,' said Alexander, and before he lapsed into silence again, Tina swiftly prompted, 'And have you been yet? To a meeting?'

'Er no, we haven't. I think there was one just before we moved here.'

'Yes, that must have been the March one, when we ruled about no children on the lawn on Sunday mornings. There'll be one in June. You'll have to come.'

73

'*Have* to?' Alexander looked alarmed.

'Good lord, no,' said Timothy, who had been listening with admirable attention. 'They're a terrible bore.'

'Tim darling! They aren't! Anyway, I think everyone *should* attend—otherwise it loses its point.'

'Well,' said Tim, watching Alexander fill his pipe with professional interest, 'I have to admit, the last meeting was almost fun. Jake Davies is chairman this year—and he does liven it up.'

Helga came in with coffee, and Tim, who had been about to recount an anecdote to illustrate the liveliness of Grove Association meetings under Jake Davies, said no more. Helga moved beautifully, he considered as he watched her, an air hostess swaying down the aisle, bringing him his airline lunch, leaning over to check his safety belt. Hello, he said sexily, as she— 'Two please,' he said with a start, in reply to Helga's question about sugar. Here he was, in the same room as Helga (and Alexander and Tina), having eaten at the same table, with his foot near her foot (candle-light, jasmine) and all he could do was to dream of her as an air-hostess, frittering away the precious reality of the moment. He should stay alert, extract full enjoyment from the evening, and if possible manipulate the movements of the dramatis personae to create a situation in which he and Helga were alone. The stage is dimly lit, Alexander and Tina have rushed out of the french windows, back left, and he and Helga, front stage right, face each other across a chaise-longue, both tensely conscious that they are, at last, alone. My love! cries Helga with a passionate sob, stretching her arms towards him. He moves forward to take her in his arms, trips over the chaise-longue, Alexander and Tina come thundering back through the french windows . . .

Timothy checked himself with irritation. There he was, off again, while he should be concentrating on the problem of where in this house, and when in this evening, he and Helga might be momentarily alone. He looked feverishly around the room. Grove houses weren't constructed to give many opportunities for illicit contact. What he should have done, of course, was to have gone into the kitchen a few moments ago, and offered to carry the tray of coffee. Maybe, later on, as they were leaving, he could follow Helga into the kitchen on some pretext or other. He must stay alert. Let me help wash up, he could say, sexily.

'Timothy!' Tina was shouting. 'Helga is asking if you want milk!'

'Oh, I am sorry, yes please, oh no! Is it cream?'

'Yes,' said Helga crisply. She had been holding the cream jug poised over his cup of coffee for what seemed a very long time.

'No, no, sorry, not cream, well just a little,' he added when he realised he was being difficult.

'If you'd prefer milk, I can get some.'

'No, no, cream is lovely.'

When they were all settled with their coffee, Helga looked around for a place to sit. The choice was between a singularly uncomfortable stool and the most comfortable chair in the room, a softly-padded swivel. She eyed the Blundens on the sofa. 'You shouldn't sit together,' she said. 'Come and sit here, Tim,' He looked frightened, but stayed where he was. Tina obligingly created the necessary gap, by getting up and saying she should go and listen, the Grove expression for darting home from a neighbouring house to check the children were alseep. When she returned, she found Helga on the sofa, so she sat in the swivel chair, diagonally opposite Alexander, a position she preferred.

Alexander, with his head tilted wistfully towards the blank television screen, was talking about a new serial. 'It's just coming on now,' he said, but with little hope in his voice. Helga wouldn't allow him to switch on. As he described it, Tina studied him, thinking how her parents would have approved if it had been he she had married. He looked naval for a start. He played rugger. He had a bowler, even if he did keep it in a paper-bag. His parents probably lived in Hampshire, retired army maybe, Colonel and Mrs. Frise. Or, better still, Captain and Mrs. Frise, Haslemere, Surrey, She liked the way his mouth turned down when he smiled.

' . . . and then this man, that is, the first man with the wife who's seeing the other man and he doesn't know, at least she doesn't think he knows, and he thinks he knows but he doesn't in fact because it's the other one she's seeing in fact . . .'

'Alexander, I think perhaps this is not so interesting,' said Helga.

'But I'm just coming to the interesting bit—'.

'Do tell us,' said Tina, 'which man was it?'

Helga turned to Tim. 'Do you find television boring?'

Timothy jumped. He'd been taking a heavy tray from her in the kitchen and she had slipped, stumbled . . . 'No!' he said loudly. 'Oh no, not at all.' He got himself further into the corner of his end of the sofa, and gazed intently at Alexander like a front-row pupil.

While both the Blundens paid close attention to Alexander's tangled account of the already complex plot, Helga paid close attention to Tim's face. He had been, when they had first met, the shadowed facet that, with the brighter, more noticeable Tina, made up the Blundens. Yet, during that first meeting, she had occasionally caught sight of a flicker around his mouth and eyes, the beginnings of an expression, quickly concealed, that might be a hint at an interesting personality. The Timothy that gazed glumly at a wall, or cringed or jumped or blushed when addressed could be reassured and laid aside; to reveal a Timothy that would be good to know.

Alexander and Tina were now on to the exchange of titles of favourite programmes, and Timothy had withdrawn behind his eyes. This was the moment when she would have liked to have taken a short cut and asked him what he was thinking about. But she suspected that such a direct question would produce a bad attack of apologies, blushes, politeness and retreat.

She smiled.

Tim, who had been conscious of her scrutiny, turned and looked at her. He smiled too. 'What are you thinking about?' he asked.

There was a momentary hesitation while she recuperated, and then she laughed, pleased at meeting him at last. But Tim had gone again; shocked by his attack, which had taken him by surprise when he'd heard his own voice, and hurt by the laughter it had caused.

'And I was wondering what you were thinking about,' said Helga, hoping to delay the withdrawal.

'How strange,' said Timothy politely, and fixed his eyes on Alexander while he retired to mull over this surprising exchange. It had the quality of secret contact, carried out as it had been under the cover of the others' discussion; a shared and low-voiced parenthesis on the sofa, to dissect and analyse and elaborate one morning before the alarm. She had been wondering what *he* had been thinking of . . . He should have told her. You! he said sexily and stop this.

'Did you see the—did you see the—' he asked Alexander suddenly in an abnormally loud voice, '—the news? Last night?'

Alexander and Tina stopped talking in mid-sentence, and turned to look at Timothy.

'Yes,' said Alexander doubtfully, 'yes, I think so.'

Now what on earth could he say about the News. 'They have an interesting new technique, don't you think,' he said, 'in their presentation.' And before he could be asked to describe it, he went on, 'Oh by the way, darling, before I forget—would you like to go to Greece for our holiday?' He looked as surprised at this as Tina did.

'What's this all about?'

She might well ask.

Turning to Alexander, she went on, 'Please excuse us, I must hear about this. I thought we were going to Morocco!' She laughed in a way that seemed to depreciate the madly gay way the Blundens sped around the globe.

'Well,' said Timothy, wishing he had a pipe, 'remember I was telling you about a client who wanted me to fix a villa for her. She had a party of ten made up. Today she came in to tell me four had dropped out.'

His three listeners registered the 'four'. They avoided each other's eyes, not wanting the others to guess the bold picture of the Frises and the Blundens making up the villa party.

Tim carried on bravely. 'Well, I'd done all the booking. It's fixed for August and there's no possibility of cancelling the villa for ten and finding a smaller one at this stage. She said er . . .' He could see he was growing wild, maybe dangerously so. '. . . she would try and find some people to make up the numbers, but all her friends have already made their plans, and so what about our joining them sort of thing.'

This unlikely proposal hung on the air for a while. The only reason for its likelihood would be if Tim and his client had got on together unusually well.

'How very generous of her,' said Tina eventually, with only the slightest accent on the last word.

Tim started talking about 'they' now. 'Of course, I didn't *commit* ourselves. But they do seem a nice couple, and if we were to consider it, we'd meet them and talk it over and see what they're like and so on—'

Alexander reached for his coffee cup and found it empty.

'Well, that would be rather nice for you,' he said, and the 'you' came out strongly, to compensate for his immediate idea that he and Helga could join the party.

'Well I don't know,' said Tina, looking at her empty coffee cup. 'We'll see. Where are you thinking of going this year?'

Alexander looked at Helga. 'Sweden. Any more in the pot?'

'I'll make some,' said Helga and got up.

Coffee, coffee, coffee, thought Tim, opportunity. He watched Helga go into the kitchen, and lapsed into silence on the sofa, plotting, while Alexander and Tina returned to television.

Can I help? he asked sexily, appearing in the kitchen doorway. She looked at him over her shoulder, her eyes inviting. Please do, she murmured, and he approached her. What can I do? he asked and she said kiss me, lifting her face to his. The Virginian, Eamonn Andrews, David Frost, said Alexander. Come dancing, wrestling, Rowan and Martin, said Tina. It was hopeless, and when Helga came back with the coffee, Timothy hadn't stirred from the sofa.

But, incredibly, an hour later there was an opportunity. They had stayed later than they had dreamt they would; and for the last half-hour, all four had been thrashing over the eternally fascinating subject of Grove. It had culminated in a discussion of paint colours; and Alexander had led Tina upstairs to show the nasturtium of the bathroom walls.

Timothy was alone with Helga.

He braced himself. 'Helga—' he gulped. God, he'd said it aloud! Had she heard?

'Yes?'

She had! She'd heard him say her name. They were off, they were started, they were away, what came next? He leapt to his feet and staggered to the table where he looked at the remains of the meal.

'I'll wash up,' he said. 'Let me help wash up. Can I wash up?'

'Oh no! Tim!' she called.

'Ssshhhh . . .' He wheeled round, shoulders hunched, finger to his lips, his eyes towards the ceiling. 'I mean,' he said, straightening, 'of course I'll do it.' He picked up a plate.

She came towards him. 'Please stop it. Timothy, I'll do it tomorrow.'

'But you'll be on the bus tomorrow morning, I mean, you go to work. Let's do it now.' He spoke in an urgent whisper. Putting down one plate with his left hand, he picked up another in his right. She reached for it, her hand touched his, and he let go at once. The plate fell to the floor. There were voices on the landing above, bright loud voices. Tim stood paralysed.

'It doesn't matter,' said Helga, and bent to pick up the pieces. 'It's only a plate.'

But he had hardly noticed the plate had broken. He was still standing there in a state of shock when Alexander and Tina came down the stairs.

'What on earth's happened to you?' asked Tina.

'Oh nothing!' said Helga. 'Only a plate. Timothy wants to wash up. Tell him not to,' she said to Alexander.

'You're not to,' he said, 'she'll do it in the morning.' And he smacked Helga's bottom as she went into the kitchen with the broken plate. He seemed in a jovial mood, she thought, and glanced at him curiously over her shoulder.

The Blundens took their leave. 'A nice evening,' said Tina when they were out of earshot, 'enjoy it?' Tim made a mumbling agreeing sound. 'And we didn't need a baby-sitter either,' added Tina. She seemed satisfied.

Alexander shut the front door and put his arm around Helga. 'Well done, sweetie. A splendid meal.'

'Mm. Good.'

'Lovely meringue,' said Alexander and turned the key in the porch door. He removed the key from the lock, a nightly ritual to fool burglars, threw it in the air and caught it with a tennis overarm smash. 'Delicious,' he said, and led Helga upstairs to bed.

CHAPTER FIVE

On a Tuesday morning some weeks later, Timothy woke at his usual hour but more excited than normal. That evening they were to go to the Davies house with George and Judith Toms and play a game.

George had told him the day before, as they walked to the bus together, that he wasn't too sure but he had his suspicions. 'Rather a sophisticated sort of game, if you ask me,' he had said, so Tim had duly asked him. 'What sort of game? I've heard of people having crazes for poker, or monopoly. Are we going to play monopoly?'

'Polopoly, more like,' said George and before Tim had worked this out, he had told him to be prepared for anything.

So Tim spent the hour and a half before the alarm busily preparing himself for anything.

When the alarm went off, he woke up. There were sounds of a bath running. Was it number Five's or their own? He felt for Tina beside him, and discovered she was up. Now why was Tina having a bath in the morning? She always had her baths at night. Had she come to the same conclusion as he had about tonight's game, and was having a thorough wash in preparation for strip poker? But, when Tim had got out of bed and checked his identity in the mirror, he saw the absurdity of this pre-alarm idea. Strip poker just didn't belong to the same world as Grove and the Blundens.

He joined Tina in the bathroom. She certainly was having a good clean-up. She sat in the bath, wearing her strange plastic mob-cap, shaving under her arms. Obviously she had already done her legs, because little soapy globs of black hair circled idly on the surface of the water.

'Oh. Hullo,' said Tim with only the slightest hint at a question mark in his voice.

Tina rapidly produced her explanation. 'It's Tuesday,' she said.

Timothy brushed his teeth, trying to remember why Tina had to have clean armpits on Tuesdays.

'Rick's awake,' said Tina, running his razor under the bath tap. 'I won't be long now, but could you get him up.'

'I suppose I'll have to shave after breakfast. Did you put in a new blade?'

'Yes.'

'Hell. That was my last one.'

'Do get Rick up, darling. He has to have his rest early today.'

'Ah, play group.' That was it. Tina, or rather Ricky, had joined a rudimentary play group. Five mothers took it in turns to look after their combined children for three hours every Tuesday afternoon; which meant that every four Tuesday afternoons out of five, Tina was free. She went up to

London to look round the shops. (Hence the clean armpits for trying on clothes.) Timothy had been nervous of this idea at first, thinking it might lead Tina into unnecessary extravagance. But, in fact, she had been most restrained, and all she had brought home from her expeditions so far had been one pair of socks for him, a scarf for herself and two vests for Ricky; although she also brought home excited descriptions of clothes she had tried on and stoically denied herself.

So Timothy was in favour of the arrangement. It seemed to be doing Tina a lot of good. She had acquired a freshness, like a rug that has been given a thorough shake in the spring air.

There was another reason why Timothy was in favour of the arrangement. It meant that Tina was out on Tuesday afternoons; whereas Helga was at home. He hadn't taken advantage of this yet. But he had planned ways that he could. As he rinsed his mouth and cleaned his toothbrush, he wondered if he might not put one of his plans into effect that very day.

Breakfast that morning held an undercurrent of contained excitement beneath the usual more toast careful Rick clean socks chat.

At three o'clock in the afternoon, Timothy recovered from a smokey cough and carefully tapped the ash out of his new pipe on to a piece of Dolphin headed paper. He screwed the paper into a parcel and aimed it at the waste-paper basket. He stood up.

'Got to go out for a while, Joyce,' he said efficiently. He gave no reason; he couldn't think of any reason but his real one, and he could hardly say he had to go and waylay and with luck, seduce, his next-door neighbour. He leant over nonchalantly and retrieved the screw of paper from the floor, one leg swinging out behind him. He dropped the paper into the basket. 'Take the names of any callers. If Round Rumania rings, tell her it was the Tourist Board's fault. If Villa in Greece rings, tell her to ring back. I'll be here at five-ish.'

'It's all right for some,' said Joyce. 'Before you go, what's this word here, I can't make it out.' She held up a letter he had written in long-hand for her. He stared at it.

'Er-rer-rer,' he said, reading through it quickly. 'We must

81

apologise for any—any—conveyance can't be inconvenience that's it. Inconvenience caused. No, let's cross that out.' He picked up a biro, and altered the letter. 'That's all out now. Put in "assuring you of our best attention at all times". Then "yours sincerely" not faithfully. O.K?'

'Shouldn't we apologise? After all, they thought they were on the Down the Rhine and they landed up with the Blue Danube lot.'

'Oh, one river's much like any other, I expect they quite enjoyed it. They might not even have found out, if they hadn't come back Calais-Dover instead of Hook-Harwich. Anyway, I'm off now.'

He polished his pipe on his handkerchief and tucked them both into his jacket pocket. Joyce gazed distrustfully at the altered letter. 'Well, I don't know,' she said. 'If our best attention gets them to the Blue Danube, where would our worst get them, I don't like to think.' She started typing again as Timothy left. Neither of them noticed that the letter was eventually sent off assuring the client of Dolphin's worst attention at all times.

Half an hour later, Timothy was lying on the sofa at number Six the Grove, puffing experimentally at his pipe, with a cup of Ricky's vitamin enriched hot chocolate beside him. He felt like a burglar. It was deliciously illicit, but at the same time soothing and comfortable to be lying there in the deserted house, with Helga unsuspectingly waiting for him not twenty yards away.

He imagined how it would be. I feel rather ill, he said, leaning against the front door. You haven't got an aspirin have you? He fainted at her feet. When he recovered consciousness, he was lying on a bed—no, Helga wasn't muscular enough to carry him upstairs, what a pity—sofa, and Helga was bending over him, stroking his fevered brow with a cool sponge, loving concern shining in her eyes. His eyes flickered to life. Tears of relief welled in hers. Oh, she sobbed, I thought you'd . . . I thought you'd . . . She buried her face on his chest. His arms closed round her. No my love, he said, teasingly sophisticated. I'm alive all right, let me prove it.

He took a sip of hot chocolate. Rather wild, that one. How about—

Hi there, Helga, he called through the open door. A lovely

early summer afternoon. Care for a spin in the motor? They run down the path together, leap into the Aston Martin, hood down, bright yellow red? blue? green? *white*, snarling, they're off, wind in her hair.

Hopeless. Far too much like a commercial for petrol or shampoo.

Back to reality. Now what might, what could possibly, happen? Helga is married to Alexander. He is married to Tina. To create the right opportunities, he really ought to look after Alexander and Tina. What about letting them have an affair? Now that would be an ideal situation. Hi there Alexander, what about this weekend? It's all fixed, they go off to an oak-beamed hostelry in Oxfordshire, Ricky to his grandmother, granny would be pleased. Helga lies in the deep white bed, hair spread on the pillows, she is watching him draw the curtains, muscles rippling his back. *But*.

But next door lie Tina and Alexander.

This is out of the question. A monstrous thought. In any case, Tina wouldn't look at Alexander twice. Or would she? No, and Alexander certainly wouldn't find Tina attractive. Or would he? No, they weren't each other's types at all. It would be unfair on them. A much better arrangement would be to fix Alexander up elsewhere, and leave Tina at home. After all, she wasn't enthusiastic about this sort of thing, she'd be far happier at home with Ricky, and that would save the fare to granny's.

So, what happens is this. Alexander arranges a weekend away with Polly Kitchen! Brilliant. Polly of course. Alexander and Polly were a perfect pair, he should have thought of this before. It was even possible they were a pair already. There had been that business about a lamp. Yes, it was easy to seem them as a pair, and it only gave him the slightest twinge to hand Polly over to Alexander.

Helga calls him at the office. Hello, my love, she says, can you make it tonight—Alexander is with Polly, so I'm all on my lonesome onesome. We can't have that, he breathes down the phone sexily, and jumps into the Aston Martin. He screams through the traffic of the High Street, beats the lights, and roars down the main road in the thunder of his exhaust. Maybe he takes her out to dinner first. Lights, night, speed, reflections on the river, a table for two, obsequious waiters, wine, Helga rests her elbows on the table and leans towards him, promise and impatience in her eyes.

Ready to go, he asks her. Mmm, she says. But what about Paul?

What about Paul indeed. He ought to be catered for. He wouldn't want to let Polly go off with Alexander, if he hadn't anyone to go off with himself. So.

Paul and—Margaret. Timothy felt a little uncertain about this, and finished his chocolate, which had got cold. Paul and Margaret made rather a grotesque couple. If only Paul were not so small and Margaret not so large. Still, he couldn't expect to have ideal couples all along the line. There was himself and Helga; Alexander and Polly; then Paul and Margaret, Which left out Jake. He couldn't really bring in anyone else, the thing was getting unwieldy enough as it was and would need a great deal of arrangement and telephoning. Jake would have to be left out. Timothy regretted this, as he liked Jake and would have liked to fix him up. But, if he was going to keep it to a manageable size, in a group of four families, Jake would have to be left out or paired with Tina; and he felt sure that neither of them would agree to the latter course.

While Timothy lay on the sofa stage-managing his group, Tina stood indecisively among the people waiting by the row of hooded telephones at Oxford Circus underground station. She held a sixpence tightly in her pocket. If there wasn't a free phone by the time she had counted a minute, she wouldn't do it. She counted sixty, and there wasn't. But she had counted unfairly fast. She would count another twenty slowly. As she reached eighteen, the man at the telephone in front of her straightened. She moved forward, but he began to dial again.

She should now turn and leave, go and look at an exhibition or Hamleys or something. But before she could do this, another telephone became free and she was there, under the hot plastic-smelling hood, with the sticky receiver in her hand.

She wouldn't look up his number. She thought she could remember it, and if it were wrong, that would be a Sign and she wouldn't try again.

But the number was right. The firm's switchboard operator told her he was on the other line, could she hold on? Yes, she could, until the pips. Fate, or virtue, had one more chance.

84

While she waited, she struggled to get her purse out of her handbag. She should have another sixpence ready, just in case he got on to the phone before the pips but without enough time to talk. She strongly resolved not to use it if the pips went before he answered. That was fair. And, if she hadn't another sixpence, well, that would be a Sign too, and she would go to an exhibition. Or Hamleys.

Her purse held one more sixpence, however, so she held it ready, and waited, straining to disentangle the secret whirrings of the receiver from the noise of the station around her. Another time (if there was to be another time) she would phone from a proper call-box. She suddenly needed to pee; yet she had been to the Ladies' cloakroom in John Lewis's not half an hour before. In a moment, all would be settled by her having to drop the phone and make fast for the nearest Ladies.

'Putting you through now,' she heard and then his voice, sounding distant and formal.

Any casual openings she had prepared were lost. 'You said to phone,' she managed, in a tight defensive voice.

There was a pause long enough to make Tina think she was speaking to the wrong man. Then he said, 'Oh yes, hello, well, good. Um.'

No doubt there were others in his room, so she would have to make it easy for him. 'I am ringing,' she said carefully, 'about the meeting with Blunden & Co.' She suddenly felt like giggling foolishly, but restrained the impulse, 'Not so much the co. though, just the one-man firm.' Would the switchboard girl be plugged in? 'Would you be able to make it this afternoon? Mr. Blu—Mrs.—er we, they, I am free,'

'Er, good, yes. Um.'

He wasn't doing very well.

'Are you free?'

'Er.'

He must have several directors hanging on his every word.

'Oh, come along, for heaven's sake,' she began, briskly, expecting to hear the pips any moment.

'The response to the coupon offer has been tremendous,' he said, very fast.

'Ah,' said Tina. 'Say about a—'

'The figures show a marked increase in sales in East Anglia.'

'Good. About a mee—'

'You're right. It should be discussed, this afternoon. Should I come along to your er office?'

'Please do,' said Tina, smiling into the receiver. *Beep* . . . 'Help, where is it?' *Beep*.

'What?'

'My office.'

Beep.

'Same place as last time?'

'Yes, when?'

'Half an hour.'

'Sooner?'

The line went dead.

Tina hurried back to Lewis's, no longer needing to pee, but to powder her nose and calm down.

Timothy woke with a guilty start as the clock struck five. A whole afternoon wasted—he hadn't even begun on the initial stage of the group formation, his approach to Helga. And Tina would be home any moment.

He leapt off the sofa, and hurried to the door, then back to the sofa for his cup. He mustn't leave any trace of his presence. He plumped up cushions, and took the cup and ashtray to the kitchen where he washed them. Then he opened the door into the garden and swung it rhythmically to air the room. He tiptoed back across the room, into the porch and opened the front door a fraction. He peeped out. He shouldn't be seen leaving the house. Outside, there was no sign of activity. He gently closed the door behind him and, trying to muffle his footsteps without appearing to, he sneaked off with long strides. Just as he reached the parking space, a woman popped out from behind a bush. But she hadn't seen him. She crouched sideways to him and looking straight ahead at some more bushes. She was wearing a nappy tied in a band around her forehead, a feather stuck behind it, and she had a finger in her mouth. Timothy stopped dead, and watched her. She looked like, but was she really, Judith Toms?

Judith Toms shook her finger in her mouth. 'Awoo-awoo-awoo-awoo.' She paused. 'Awoo-awoo-awoo-awoo?' There was a movement from the bushes, and the flash of a red sweater. Judith began running, still crouched and still, awoo-ing. She saw Timothy, looked momentarily abashed. smiled, waved and disappeared up the garden at a fast lope.

Her awoo was now a little self-conscious and quiet.

Timothy followed her at incredible speed. He had seen Tina and Rick in Beechley Avenue. He joined Judith behind a bush at the far end of the communal garden, a few yards away from Helga's front door, but well behind and out of view of his own. Judith looked with some surprise at the panting figure beside her. Timothy pressed his finger to his mouth feverishly, and then did some hectic nodding and smiling to make it seem like a game.

Through their bush, they could see the rectangular lawn between the two rows of houses. Bernard Toms appeared from the porch of number Twelve just as Tina and Rick came up the path.

'Waa—' he began, uncertainly and then the wail rose in pitch and volume.

Tina bent down and talked to him, while Ricky looked at him with the expression of an enquiring anthropologist. Bernard's mother began to rise in response, but Timothy pulled her down roughly, and she sat with a thump on the grass. Her expression changed from surprise to anger.

'Mummee!' screamed Bernard Toms.

'I'm here!' called Judith, and got to her feet. She brushed down the back of her skirt. '*Honestly*!' she said to Timothy. 'What *are* you doing?' And she left the bush to meet the approaching party. Timothy pressed himself closer to the earth.

'There's your mummy,' came Tina's soothing voice.

'Here I am, darling,' said Judith. She picked up Bernard. 'We were playing Red Indians,' she told Tina, removing her headdress.

'Man,' said Bernard pointing at the bush.

Ricky waddled to the bush. 'Ul-lo Dadee,' he said cheerfully, not finding it at all unusual for his father to be bent double behind a bush. Tim got stiffly to his feet, and said Boo! without much heart.

'Well!' said Tina. 'What a surprise.'

Timothy brushed himself down. 'Er, yes,' he said and attempted a gay laugh. 'I thought I'd give you a surprise.' He picked Ricky up and started towards number Six, talking to Tina over his shoulder. 'Nothing doing at the office, came home early, did you have a good time?'

Tina followed him, beginning to tell him about clothes. She waved to Judith and called 'See you this evening,' but Judith was away down the path, trying to stop the wails of Bernard. When at last she had calmed him down with a biscuit, she recalled Tina's face on discovering that Timothy had been crouching behind a bush with her. It must have seemed peculiar, even suspicious. She must make it clear that evening that she had been playing Red Indians with Bernard, not with Timothy.

But that evening, half-way through her detailed account of the game, she stopped. It was sounding like a pathetically weak story to cover nefarious activities. Margaret helped. 'Oh I know just how you feel, Judith. I remember last holidays I was lying bound and gagged in the porch when the man came to read the meter. I felt extraordinarily foolish— he had to help me to my feet. He was about to call the police, but I managed to get the gag off in time and explain it was a children's game.' They laughed at this, except Tina who was still looking thoughtful.

Jake suggested that, if they all had got something to drink, they might begin their game. The visitors looked apprehensive, so Jake went on reassuringly, 'Now don't be alarmed, it's quite simple, our children play it sometimes.'

Timothy wondered if children played strip poker. George looked shocked, Tina, keen. Judith, sensibly, asked what the game was called.

'Dictionary,' said Margaret. 'Have you got it, Jake? And paper and pencils?'

'Oh a paper game,' said Judith. 'I hope it isn't too frightfully intellectual,'

'What fun,' said Tina politely.

'Jake'll explain,' said Margaret, and handed out pencils.

'Well, now,' said Jake and sat down with his drink. 'What happens is this. We all take it in turns to choose a word from the dictionary—'

'It has to be one none of us knows—' put in Margaret.

'Yes, and the person who has chosen the word—'

'No,' said Margaret. 'Better to say first that we all have to write down our definitions of—'

'Darling,' said Jake, using the word as a threat more than endearment.

'Sorry,' said Margaret, and sat back.

'Well, the others write down their own definitions of the word, and the idea is to make it sound as like the true dictionary definition as possible. We hand them in to the person who chose the word, who then reads them out plus the real definition. Therefore, there'll be let me see, how many are we, six, there'll be six definitions, ABCDEF. We then award marks—we have a total of six to award. You can give six to B, for instance, if you think that is obviously the dictionary's—'

'I might say, this hardly ever—'

'Sshh. Or you can give two to A, three to D and one to B, if you want to hedge your bets.'

'The scoring,' said Margaret, finding it hard to keep silent, 'is a bit complicated, but if we have a trial go, it will all become clear.'

'I hope so,' said Timothy.

'Oh yes, and keep straight faces—you don't want to give away which is your own definition—'

'Oh dear,' said Judith. 'It sounds awfully hard.'

'It isn't, really. Let's have a trial.' Margaret picked up the dictionary. 'I'll choose a word to begin with.' She started leafing through the thick volume. 'This is the hardest part, really,' she said after a while, to fill the apprehensive silence.

'Oh dear,' said Judith again, picking up her piece of paper. 'Can we have something to lean on?'

Jake distributed paperbacks and they waited for the first word.

'Um,' said Margaret at last. 'Kerion? Anyone know kerion?'

They each tried out the sound, and agreed none of them knew it.

'Right. Kerion it is.' She spelt it out, and gradually they lapsed into silence, after a little grumbling and murmuring and arranging of their paper and pencils and books on their knees. After a while, Judith began giggling quietly to herself, then stopped and began writing again. Tina hadn't begun to write anything yet. Tim looked worried, because he had done his a long time ago, and was now thinking the others must be producing far wittier definitions. He considered again, and came up with an alternative definition, but he found it hard to decide which was the better. Jake had handed his folded paper to Margaret, who was copying it down on another piece of paper on which she had already written the dictionary definition.

At last, they had all finished and Margaret read them out. 'A,' she said. 'I'll read them twice by the way. You have six marks to give, remember. Right. A. Kerion. A leather strap, usually with the end cut into thin strips, used as an instrument of punishment, a lash.

'B. A bastard, a fool, the sixth son of a Saxon liege-lord, born out of wedlock.'

Judith let out a crow of laughter. The others looked at her suspiciously. Did her laughter mean that wasn't her definition? Or was she laughing to make the others think that wasn't her definition, while it *was*?

'Sshh!' said George.

'C. Greek derivation. Keri, wax. On, on. An excessive deposit of wax in the inner ear.'

'Eeugh,' said Judith.

'Darling, do be quiet,' said George. 'You'll give it all away.'

'D,' said Margaret, firmly. 'An ox-like creature of the bison genus from the plains of Afghanistan.

'E. An inflammation of the hair-follicles of the scalp, causing baldness.'

Judith pressed her hand to her mouth, and George frowned at her.

'F,' said Margaret. 'See korion.'

They all laughed and Margaret said sternly that she would read them again. Then they sighed and grumbled and murmured some more as they awarded marks. 'Ready?' she asked, and went round the group collecting the scores. 'Now Jake was A, the leather strap, sadistic creature, and gets four from George—'

'Good lord,' said George, amazed. 'I was convinced that was the dictionary.'

'—George was B, the bastard, fool etc. and gets four from Tim.'

'Thanks, man,' said George. Tim looked peeved.

'C was Judith—'

'All that nasty wax?' said George.

'Bother! I gave you three!' said Tina.

'Yes,' said Margaret. 'She gets three. Then Tina was D, the ox, and gets um one from Jake. E was the right one, the dictionary—'

'No! Was it really?'

'Heavens!'

'Jake scores five, because he gave it five you see, and Tim scores two.'

'Clever old thing,' said his wife.

'And F was Timothy, and he's done very well, got two from George, six from Judith—'

'I *know*!' cried Judith in anguish. 'It sounded just like the dictionary!'

'—and three from Tina. So Jake scores five and four, nine. George, four. Judith, three Tina, one. Tim, two and eleven, *thirteen*!'

They looked at Tim in awe. 'Well, let's pretend that wasn't a trial,' he said optimistically. But they didn't let him get away with this, and started to play in earnest. They each had a turn at choosing a word, and spent the rest of the evening tussling with oddities of the dictionary, among them kiang— a Tibetan wild ass, variously described as a Chinese dynasty, a metal pot used in glue-making, a sedan chair made of bamboo and rushes, now defunct, a small beetle found in swampy plains, and a winter sport of the Eskimo people.

By arrangement, Paul and Polly dropped in about half past ten. They had organised the Lefevre-Frise evening and had agreed with Jake and Margaret that there was no need for them all to play again.

Polly's arrival had an adverse effect on Timothy's creative powers, and in the last round—jacana, (ah), n. small tropical wading bird with disproportionately large straight claws (enabling it to walk on floating leaves)—he scored nil. Judith began to make going-home movements but was prevailed upon to stay while Jake calculated the final scores. He had difficulty, and Paul took over.

'Well,' he said, finally. 'T has won hands down. Who is T?'

'Timothy.'

Paul turned to Tim and smiled. 'Oh yes, of course. You want to exchange that pot—'

'A pity, you know,' said Polly, 'everyone has pots.'

Timothy wondered if he could carry off his pipe-lighting business in public yet, and decided he wouldn't risk it. 'Er yes, well,' he said, 'I think Tina will appreciate ornamental pots more when our son isn't using one any longer.'

'Good reason,' said Paul and laughed. 'Well, you have the noble score of thirty-two—fantastic,' he glanced at Jake with a quick smile of surprised approval. Margaret looked pleased too, he noticed. 'Then comes Judith with twenty-two, Jake with nineteen, oh, sorry, Margaret has twenty-two too—George twelve and Tina seven.'

91

Tina experienced the feeling that she had when she failed Ordinary Level Geography. But she was relieved that one half of the Blundens had done so well. 'That *was* fun,' she said brightly. 'We had some lovely words.' She reached towards the table for the discarded scraps of paper.

Judith rose. 'We really must get back now—Bernard doesn't sleep too well, and last time I listened he was tossing rather . . .' She gave George a piercing look, and he duly rose to his feet. With a little laughing chat about the game, they moved gradually to the door with Margaret, said their good-byes and thank-yous, like well brought-up children, and left.

Margaret joined the others who were laughing over their definitions. 'What about some coffee now?' she suggested, and went to make it. Tina asked if she might pop upstairs, and Tim, realising he would be left alone with Jake, Paul and Polly, said he would nip along and listen.

'Nip, pop and listen, what's all this?' asked Paul in a low voice after Tim and Tina had left the room.

'You remember, love,' said Polly, stretching herself languidly, and yawning. 'A Grove gathering is riddled with people nipping off and listening. You see them in bovies—'

'Bovies?'

'Yes. Bovies of Grove standing motionless on the communal lawn, ears cocked, chins raised to the stars, listening for the thin cries of their young—'

'You wait till you have young with thin cries, you'll be listening too,' said Margaret from the kitchen. There was always the faint background of jealousy between the couples; for the others' children or lack of them.

'Anyway,' said Jake, 'quick now. Decisions. Put the test into action on these?' They could hear the cistern upstairs.

They knew each other well enough to know they were in agreement before they had even discussed it. Paul said rapidly and quietly, 'Certainly. Though the others did well on paper, I can see their reaction if approached. They'd have reached the end of Beechley Avenue before we'd even started . . . .'

Both Blundens returned. Tina asked Tim if all was quiet. As Margaret poured coffee, there was an oppressive silence; though the only person who found it so was Tina. She racked her brain for conversation.

'Do you know,' she said gazing intently at Margaret. 'We've got landed with a villa in Greece.'

This was one way of expressing it, thought Timothy. As they had entered number Six, after the business behind the bush, the phone had been ringing. It was Joyce. The widow's party had fallen through, and would Tim please ring her. When he talked to the widow on the phone, he found himself saying he was only too happy to take over the villa himself, and there was no need at all for her to worry about forfeiting her deposit. She had overflowed with gratitude, which had made this easy at the time. But now he was full of misgiving. He had acquired a villa for ten in Greece; and, even if they managed to find eight others to join them it would be a far more expensive holiday than planned.

'It's rather a bore,' went on Tina, 'as we were going to Morocco.'

'Doesn't sound a bore to me,' said Polly. 'Where is it?'

'On one of the islands, I think,' said Timothy. 'It's for ten, a group.' And he blushed vividly. A *group*. His afternoon fantasies paraded colourfully before his eyes; Helga and Polly and himself swimming in the blue Aegean, the two girls splashing, laughing, admiring, as his tanned and muscular arms cleave the water in a fast crawl. They come out of the sea and fling themselves down on the hot sand . . . 'It is a bit of a problem,' he said and, without thinking, got out his pipe, 'as all our friends have long since made their plans—'

'What efficient friends you must have,' said Polly. 'We haven't planned ours. We'll come!' She said it lightly, as though it were a joke; but she had exchanged a rapid glance with Paul and Margaret. Jake was watching her.

'What a good idea,' said Jake slowly, making it sound more possible.

Timothy concentrated on stuffing tobacco into his pipe with trembling fingers.

'Are you serious?' said Tina. Utterly serious herself, she always suspected others of joking, except when they really were joking.

'Of course,' said Jake. 'Except it's probably impossible. I can take time off whenever I want to, up to a point, but Margaret's tied down by the paper. When have you fixed your holiday love?'

93

'August,' said Margaret.

'The villa's booked for August,' said Timothy, aghast at the way his fantasies seemed to be turning into reality.

'Marvellous!' cried Polly. 'Let's do it.'

'Why not,' said Paul. 'How many more do we need?'

The Frises, shouted Timothy silently. 'Four, I suppose,' he said aloud.

'Well,' said Tina cautiously, 'we had mentioned something about it to Alexander and Helga . . .'

'Oh but that was a long time ago before it was—' As Tim was almost holding his breath, he stopped.

'The Frises!' said Margaret, and began laughing uncontrollably. Jake looked at her sternly.

'We might ask them,' said Paul, 'though they're probably going to Sweden.'

They began to talk about cost, Greece, holidays in general and grandmothers. Under cover of this, Paul and Margaret had a quick muffled exchange of words, and soon afterwards Paul and Polly got up to leave, swiftly followed by Tina.

'Oh Tina,' said Jake, 'don't go quite yet. There's something I want to ask you.'

Tina looked alarmed.

'You were connected in some way with the local council, weren't you? Child Care or something?'

'Yes,' said Tina hesitantly. 'I still do a little work for them now and again.' She didn't say typing.

'I've got involved in designing some of their literature, and there's one particular leaflet I don't quite understand —if you could possibly have a look at it—' He got up and led the way to the stairs. Tina followed.

Timothy hoped Paul and Polly would linger, but they didn't. The house seemed suddenly deserted, save for himself and Margaret. Empty coffee cups, glasses, full ash-trays, the jumble of paper on the table, gave the room an after the party atmosphere which turned Tim into a resident rather than guest. He sucked feverishly on his pipe, as though he could turn it into a chaperone. For he had the sudden conviction that Margaret was stalking him. Yet he must be mistaken. This was a ridiculous, unreal, unpremeditated situation.

'It's gone out, Tim,' said Margaret and started towards him.

'What?' he gulped, nearly leaping from his corner of the sofa.

'Your pipe,' she said and sat down beside him. He saw amusement in her face and, although it was gentle, it provoked him. He would show her. He would lean over, and pin her to the sofa with a hard and violent kiss, and—but then, maybe she wasn't after him at all. She had simply chosen to sit on the sofa as the most comfortable place. She would tell Jake later that he had attacked her; and they would laugh. Oh, the embarrassment of it.

'You look tired,' she said and there was her hand over his. This was shattering. She shouldn't have said that. That was what his fantasy girls said to him as they soothed his brow. But here and now, it was actually said aloud to him by a real live woman, by Margaret.

He looked up at her, and their eyes met. Margaret's were warm, brown, lit with a kind, slightly amused encouragement, and a little surprise; for she saw his were not full of fright as she had expected, but conveyed an acquiescence and a command. And she realised, with some surprise, that he would be in control of any situation that might develop. He squeezed her hand briefly and released it. Then they waited in easy silence for Jake and Tina to come downstairs.

'Well?' asked Margaret, when the Blundens had left.

'Oh, nothing in my quarter,' said Jake. 'I just kept her out of the way. And you?'

'Um. *Interesting*,' said Margaret. 'Shall we go to Greece?'

'Yes, why not.'

'Good,' said Margaret.

Whereas the Blundens went to bed without exchanging a word.

CHAPTER SIX

'His face looks so purple though,' said Tina.

'You're probably not adjusted right,' said Alexander.

'Oh heavens, *we* don't have colour, couldn't possibly afford it. No, I saw it at a friend's.'

'Well, they don't have it adjusted right,' said Alexander.

'Maybe that's what it is,' said Tina, not convinced. 'Any-

95

way,' she went on, after a pause, 'he's always so angry, I'm not surprised he's purple.'

There was another pause.

'Colour needs very fine adjusting,' said Alexander.

It was their third meeting and they were in bed.

'How's Helga?' enquired Tina.

'Oh, she's fine, how's Timothy?'

'He's all right, I suppose.' She moved her head on his shoulder. 'Oh dear,' she said, 'I feel awful. And happy.' She spread her fingers under the ginger-coloured hair on his chest; then, closing her fingers, raised her hand to feel the hair pulled straight. 'Very happy and very awful. Don't you?'

Alexander rubbed her shoulder and managed to look at his watch at the same time. He would have to hurry.

'Er, yes,' he said because he couldn't answer this truthfully. He didn't feel awful. Helga wouldn't mind his infidelity, though she would mind being told of his infidelity. When they had been married only a few months, Alexander had been sent to Doncaster on a business trip. He had made, what had seemed at the time, the mistake of a full confession of his brief lapse with a travelling beautician, who had been staying at the same hotel. In fact, this had turned out not to be a mistake at all, for it had set the rules of their marriage for the future. They had reached the understanding that each could support occasional infidelity on the other's part, so long as it were not a lengthy relationship, nor serious, nor recounted. This he could hardly explain to Tina, so he agreed he felt guilty; though at the moment it was towards Tina rather than towards his wife.

Tina sighed. 'Oh dear, what are we to do—'

Alexander didn't like the turn the conversation was taking, and looked openly at his watch. 'I must get back,' he said.

'It's so *sor*did,' said Tina, looking round the room, which was as it happened, a neat, clean and plain, room, belonging to someone who worked with Alexander.

'Never mind,' said Alexander, 'we'll be in Greece soon.'

'Do you think it will be easier there?'

He doubted it. 'Surely,' he said.

'I don't suppose so,' said Tina, thinking that it probably would be. She lay back on the pillow and pulled him towards her.

'I have to go,' he said, looking down at her.

'Just a kiss.'

'Dangerous,' he said, thinking he was safe, as he would

surely be unable to make love again so soon. He leant down and kissed her, his body tensed for the next planned move which was to get up, dressed and away. But her mouth opened and their tongues met and the strength of his body turned to Tina instead of the day.

'I should go,' he said, and her legs opened. 'Beast,' he said.

'Not quite yet,' she said.

'No, not quite yet,' he said.

As they made love—and it took ages as he tried to hurry, and didn't think he could make it, but neither could he give up—he compared Helga and Tina. He decided that Helga was like a marshmallow with an almond inside, if there was such a thing; and that Tina was more like a hard chocolate with a soft centre. It was a satisfactory description, he thought, and a satisfactory contrast.

'Phew,' said Tina at last. 'Lovely.'

'And now I have to go,' said Alexander, 'if I can.' They laughed.

After Alexander had left, taking the iron steps from the basement two at a time, she noticed, as though glad to be leaving her, she sat for a while on the bed, holding the handkerchief they had used, his handkerchief, against her cheek. She sorted through her emotions as though they were rings in her jewellery-box, picking each one out to appreciate it slowly. She felt triumphant, glowing with victory. She felt delicious sorrow, a gnawing sweet pain behind her ribs, which wasn't indigestion, which she labelled as despair at a hopeless situation. It reminded her of the first time she had loved, sitting straight-backed in a church pew, black-gloved hands clasped on heavy-lisle knees, gazing with religious attention which veiled burning adoration at the new, smooth-cheeked curate who was feverishly reciting his first sermon and who, surely, was addressing it to her. Her love for the curate and her love for Alexander—if either were love—were equally hopeless, equally exquisite. Yet she knew, with detached clarity as she sat on the bed smelling Alexander sadly through the handkerchief, going through the motions of the lovelorn maiden, that this should not be called love. It was almost as though she were acting a part. Her feeling for Tim—regard, devotion, loyalty, friendship—that was love, though she was reluctant at the moment to call it so. Yet how dull! An everyday diet, valuable, nutritious, balanced. She saw her temporary defection as unlicensed gorging at the honeypot. She would take as many heaped and dripping, intoxicating sweet spoonfuls of it as she could. Before it was discovered, before it was taken away, she hoped she would be sick of it, have had her fill.

Meanwhile, what was she to do with the handkerchief? She should throw it away, destroy the stained piece of evidence with its embroidered A. Instead, she washed it through, folded it in a small polythene envelope, and tucked it in the bottom of her handbag, her keepsake, memento, adult version of the prayer-book the curate had used and she had kept, stolen property of St. Andrew's Church, Hill Place, Malvern, Worcestershire.

Tim, as he lay on the sofa at number Six, The Grove, held his hand in the air to see if his inner trembling was outward too. It was. This was no good. He must appear cool, calm, suave. After all, he was only going to borrow a little sugar from her. I've only come to borrow a little sugar, he would say to her, leaning against the front door casually. No, that wasn't right. It implied that she might think he'd come for something else. You think I've come for something else? Well, I have, he would say and clasp her round the waist, kicking the door shut deftly with his right heel. No, no, no, start again.

I wonder if I could possibly borrow a little sugar.

I say, I'm sorry to disturb you, but we seem to have run out of sugar.

What a strange expression, perhaps Helga wouldn't understand such a colloquialism. We are running out of sugar, we have run out of sugar, the sugar is running out.

Hello. We have no sugar. Have you any sugar? Could you give me some sugar.

Stilted. Progressive English for Foreign Students. Oh well, he would leave that to the inspiration of the moment.

They would go into the kitchen together. He might say something clever like, What a charming room. Absurd! But never mind, it would have to be something like that so that he could go on, but of course it would be.

Oh, why? Helga must say.

Because it's yours, he would reply, gilding the compliment with a winning smile.

In fact, Alexander chose the colours.

Oh.

Well, he would leave that to the inspiration of the moment, too.

He got up and went upstairs to the bathroom. How did he look today? He checked in the mirror. Feverish. He splashed his face with cold water, and mopped it with a towel, very gently to avoid yet more stimulation to the circulation. He dabbed a little After Shave lotion under his jaw. Far too much. He washed his face again, this time with soap. Now he smelt even more freshly and especially washed. He was only going to borrow a little sugar, for heaven's sake!

What he should do, of course, was to create the right, harried atmosphere of only going to borrow a little sugar. He must make himself a coffee, that was it. He went downstairs, as though in a hurry, and into the kitchen. The sugarbowl was full. He shook the sugar back into the bag, and washed out the bowl. Then he decided it would look better if there was a very little left in the bottom of the bowl, so he put in half a teaspoonful. This looked ridiculous. However, if he were to make it stick around the sides of the bowl, it would look right, perhaps. He added a drop of water and worked the sugar against the sides of the bowl with a spoon. The final touch was a dash of instant coffee which gave the appearance of agitated scraping away at not enough sugar.

Then, for great authenticity, he hid the full sugar bag at the back of the cupboard under the sink. 'There!' he said aloud, and clapped and rubbed his hands. 'All systems go.' He went out of the kitchen. 'Time for a quick coffee, I think,' he muttered to himself and looked at his watch. It was half past four! He was a stupid fool, only half an hour left in which to borrow sugar, seduce Helga, and be back at the office in time to leave the office. He must act fast.

He rushed back into the kitchen, switched on the electric kettle, put a spoon of coffee in a mug and said aloud, as though for the benefit of all-seeing God or Tina or neighbours, 'Oh damn, no sugar.'

He seized the sugar-bowl and made for the front door where he hesitated. It was all right if he was seen borrowing sugar; but far better for his purposes not to be seen at all. He went out the back door instead, switching off the kettle on his way. Once outside, the boldness of his plan struck him. There he was, bowl in hand, launched on the first stage of seduction. No turning back now. Or might he? No, it had taken him weeks to reach this position, standing outside the back door of his house, straining to hear communal sound as he clasped his excuse tightly to his chest. Voices! He sank to the ground.

A line of bushes stretched protectively from the corner of his house to the path leading to number Seven; behind these he would be out of sight of the rest of the houses and the central lawn. But the line of bushes was not unbroken. There were gaps of varying extents between each bush. Doing a kind of bunny-hop, he reached the protection of the first bush and from its cover, he peered through to the lawn beyond. There was Judith Toms and her wretched child. Surely not Red Indians again! Had she nothing better to do than infest the lawn with her child's play? She should be inside cooking an Elizabeth David meal for George.

Timothy waited in his agonisingly uncomfortable position. She was probably taking Bernard out for a walk, and would soon be gone. But no, she seemed to have no purpose but to stand outside her house, arms folded, looking down at her son who was looking down at his feet. Meanwhile, Timothy's time was running out. He dived for the next bush, and as he did so, he caught a glimpse of another door opening. Now Margaret Davies joined the scene. Tim watched her approach Judith, and from the way they arranged their arms and feet, he could tell this would be no quick exchange of words in passing. This was to be a chat. He was doomed.

Yet—he was only going to borrow a little sugar!

All he had to do was stand up and wander casually to Helga's front door, bearing his bowl aloft. Quickly, before he lost courage, he stood up and began wandering casually towards Helga's front door, bearing his bowl aloft. But before he reached the next bush, he realised he shouldn't be wandering casually; he should be *quickly* borrowing a little sugar. Another point, why from Helga? Why not ask Judith or Margaret? He panicked and sank, with palpitating heart, behind the third bush in the line and with twenty yards still to go.

He wasn't cut out for seduction, he really wasn't. Where was the candle-light? The murmured phrase? The jasmine? The bush he had crouched behind had thorns.

And time was running out.

He would walk fast, very fast and as silently as possible to Helga's front door. He would look straight ahead, as though unaware of the two on the lawn. They probably wouldn't notice him. If they did, well, it hardly mattered, did it? They wouldn't know he was going to seduce her. He heard Judith say to Tina, Oh, funny thing. I saw Tim here this afternoon. A day off? He was at Helga's. And Tina's casual reply, Oh, I expect he was only going to seduce her.

Holding his bowl as though he were in an egg-and-spoon race, Timothy made for the door of number Seven and leant on the bell. The door opened and he tumbled inside.

'I've only come to seduce you,' he panted and thrust the bowl into Helga's hands.

Tina sat on the tube, returning to Merrivale, her legs crossed over her secret. Beside her sat a young and dirty couple who, she gathered from their loud conversation, had been working on a fair-ground. They were dressed in much the same style, in mud-browns and greys, their hair cut shaggily to mid-neck length, both wearing jeans and plimsolls. The girl was stout and wore no brassière, her thighs stretched the cloth of her trousers. They were laughing and fighting, the boy tying a length of hairy string around her wrist and on to his belt, while she fought him off, biting his arms and flailing with her own.

Tina wasn't sure whether they were fooling loudly for the benefit of the others in the carriage; or whether they were so absorbed in each other that they were oblivious of their surroundings. Whichever was the case, she stared rigidly out of the window, determined not to pay them the compliment of her attention; but saw only the reflected scene of the couple beside her.

The girl lit a fag-end and with it in her mouth leant towards the boy. He closed his mouth over it.

That was love, too, thought Tina with conscious charity. But she was relieved when they got out at the next stop, the boy dragging the girl behind him, laughing, at the end of the string. They were followed by another young couple, both beautiful, beaded and fringed, with masses of flowing hair, who, beside them, appeared bastions of middle-class conventionality.

Helga stepped back. '*What* did you say?'

'SUGAR!' shouted Tim, and banged the door shut behind him. He cleared his throat. 'Hello, Helga.'

'Hello, Tim,' uncertainly.

He pointed at the bowl in her hands. 'We've run out of sugar. I'm just having a coffee. No sugar.'

'Ah. I will give you some.'

'Oh, thank you. Thanks very much. Just a little.'

'Or will you have coffee with me?'

This wasn't in his script. He hesitated, confused. Was there time? For coffee and for seduction? Would the one lead to the other? Or would it get in the way?

'It's no trouble,' said Helga, 'I will make some for myself. Please do. I am quite lonely here in the afternoons.'

Tim felt faint at this appeal. He should throw his arms around her, murmur something about how someone so beautiful should never be lonely . . . 'Well, thank you,' he said, 'if you're sure it's no trouble.'

He sat and waited while she went into the kitchen. Should he follow her? No, too sudden. There was time. He looked at his watch. A quarter to five! At five Tina would be home with Ricky. He jumped to his feet and made for the kitchen, just as Helga came to the doorway with a tray. They collided. Two cups fell to the floor and smashed.

'Again!' cried Helga, laughing. 'Oh, Tim, don't worry, I will get a dustpan.' He was grovelling on the floor, picking up the pieces, a tomato-soup flush on his face. 'Please don't worry, Tim,' she said again, and returned the tray to the kitchen. 'Lucky the coffee was not inside.' She came back with dustpan and brush, and pointed with the brush at a chair. 'You go and sit down, I will clear up. Please don't bother about it.'

Later, when Helga had sat down opposite him, placing two other cups like sentries on the table between them, he managed to speak. Helga cut into his apologies. 'Now don't say anything more about it. How is it you are at home this afternoon?'

To seduce you! 'Er,' he said.

'Do you get time away whenever you want?'

'Oh no! But I have an excellent second-in-command,' said Tim, thinking of Joyce, 'and she takes over when I have to go out. See a client or something.' In fact, this never happened, but it sounded important.

'Am I a client?' asked Helga, smiling. She suddenly had the idea that the sugar-bowl had been an excuse, that Tim was approaching her, and this roused her interest. She felt willing to help him along.

Tim smiled back. 'Well, you might almost be. Villa in Greece.'

'True,' said Helga, and got to her feet.

Tim reached for his cup of coffee in alarm. There had been a suggestive undercurrent in that exchange which had overloaded his bloodstream. Where was she going? No, no, she wasn't going anywhere, she was *coming towards him*. He watched her apprehensively, holding his coffee like a shield before his face. She stopped a little to the right of his chair, and leant over. She was wearing an open-necked blouse and the top button was strained, he saw, before he turned all his attention to his coffee. A skin was forming on the surface, and he concentrated on making it cling to the sides of the cup while he drank. When at last he dared look up, he saw Helga had only been reaching for a book from the shelf behind him, and she was now handing it to him.

'I have been doing my homework on our island,' she said.

'What's this?' asked Tim in the cracked tones of an ageing choirboy.

'The *Guide Bleu*.'

Tim took the book and Helga returned to her chair. He gripped the book tightly, feeling relieved as well as disappointed that the moment of danger had passed. Had she leant over him deliberately? It had seemed like it at the time. If so, then there would have been no resistance if he had reached up and pulled her down beside him . . . On the other hand, perhaps the thought of contact between them was so far from her mind that her leaning over him was as meaningless as her leaning over his chair. What a good thing he hadn't taken advantage of the moment. In any case, she hadn't exactly leant over him. She had wanted to get the book from the shelf, which meant she had to lean over, and as he was sitting in that particular chair, it meant she had to lean over *near* him. . . .

'It's in the section on islands of the Aegean.'

Tim opened the book guiltily in response, and began riffling hastily through the pages. Such a full and close-printed volume, he would never find the right section in his present state of mind. He couldn't even remember the name of the island they were going to. He tilted the book so that

Helga couldn't see which part he had reached, and gazed with an expression of rapt interest at a street plan of Salonika. 'Hmm,' he said. 'Ah-hmm.'

Helga got up.

She was coming for him again!

Yes, her slim and beautiful legs edged gracefully round the coffee table, positioned themselves by his chair, bent at the knees . . . God, she was going to sit on his *lap*! No, on the arm of his chair.

'Not there, Tim,' she said in a soft teasing voice, as though she could tell what he was thinking. This was agony. She didn't take the book from him, but with one hand flipped over the pages until she found the right page. 'There! It doesn't say much, but it gives you some idea of the place.'

He stared fixedly at the page, and saw not a thing. He determined to single out at least one word and understand it but, as in a nightmare, he was unable to focus. Then a giant finger appeared on the print before him and tapped at something. 'Here it is,' came her voice.

'Ah-ha,' came his own voice and, as though the sound had released his visual block, he managed to focus on a word. ' "Figure (b)," ' he read with relief.

It was the first time, he realised, that he had heard Helga really laugh. She had a delightful, musical laugh. Her head tilted back, her mouth opened, her tongue quivered behind white and even teeth; and, as he watched, he saw the beginnings of a gesture which would have ended in catastrophe, with her hand somewhere on his shoulder and probably nearer his hair line than his arm. But before her hand landed, he had shot to his feet. 'The time!' he yelped. 'What's the time!' The book had crashed to the floor, Helga had toppled from the arm of the chair, and Tim was half-way to the front door. Now safe, he returned to pick up the book, which he placed hastily on the table. 'Frightfully sorry,' he said, 'but I simply must get back.' His coherence broke down as Helga gathered herself together. 'Office, five, post, thanks so much, sugar-bowl.'

And he rushed from the house before she had recovered from her surprise.

She sat down thoughtfully to finish her coffee, and—as Tina had done elsewhere and earlier in the afternoon— sorted through her emotions. But unlike Tina's hers were more like the unpleasant symptoms of a nameless disease, than rings in a jewel-box. She felt embarrassed, irritated, puzzled, humiliated. She tried to fathom out what Tim had been after. Not sugar, certainly. Nor herself, it seemed. And, unable to diagnose the disease, she dismissed the symptoms, Timothy Blunden and the occasion, from her mind. 'Stupid man!' she said, washing up the cups vigorously, and this indictment, although she felt it was false, and her tone of voice almost fond, gave her a certain satisfaction. 'I won't help him along again.'

Tina took a deep breath as she turned from Beechley Avenue into The Grove and shook her mind, like a kaleidoscope, back into its everyday pattern. Help! She'd forgotten to collect Ricky. She turned swiftly and began hurrying back along the road. Luckily the mother, whose turn it had been that day to have the children, lived in Beechley Avenue. As she retraced her steps, she realised she had seen a curious sight in The Grove; the figure of a man suddenly disappearing behind a bush at the far end of the lawn. It reminded her of the Tuesday she had returned to find Tim behind a bush with Judith Toms, playing Red Indians or something. Moreover, the man she had just seen looked extraordinarily like Tim.

Without a pause, and perhaps helped along by her own infidelity, as though it would balance the scales, Tina suspected that Tim was after Judith Toms. What a pity! How much neater it would be if he were to choose Helga Frise.

Tim emerged from his cover, once Tina had unaccountably trotted back into Beechley Avenue. She must have forgotten to collect Ricky, that was it; but how unlike her, how weird. Still, it would give him time to return the sugar-bowl to the house, and decide where to be. He hadn't planned this stage of the operation, the post-seduction stage. Had he had coffee with Helga, or hadn't he? Had Judith seen him to be at home that afternoon, or hadn't she? Would Helga mention his having coffee with her, or wouldn't she? On balance, it seemed wiser to be quite open about it. He had got off work early, come home, run out of sugar, gone to borrow some from Helga, and stayed for a cup of coffee. That was, after all, what had happened.

'Oh?' said Tina, in a most disbelieving way when he told her. 'Didn't you look in the cupboard? I bought a 3lb bag this morning.'

'I couldn't find it,' said Tim. 'And did you have a good afternoon?' he asked quickly.

'Oh,' said Tina, briskly tying a bib round Ricky's neck, 'not too bad, really, I suppose.'

'Buy anything?'

'No. I tried on some hair.' And she had, rushing into Peter Robinson before catching the tube home, and making for the nearest counter, just in order to try something on, so that she could say she had. She didn't lie.

'Hare?' repeated Tim. Fur coats in the summer?

'A wig.'

'Oh,' said Tim, seeing the horrific image of Tina in a wig, a long blonde Danny La Rue. She didn't seem at all herself, what with forgetting to collect their son and trying on a wig.

Neither did Tina think it sounded like her, so she went on to describing an exhibition of paintings, without actually saying she had been to it. 'His spatial concepts are—' she began, and hesitated, deciding not to quote the *Evening Standard* critic, read specially for this purpose word for word. So instead of saying 'bold', she said, '—rather nice. Since you're home early, could you possibly do something about the coat-rack in the porch? It's about to come adrift from the wall.'

So Tim went and did something about the coat-rack in the porch, thinking how easy it was to get away with seduction. He had quite forgotten the reality of his afternoon with Helga.

Hmm, thought Tina as she gave Ricky his supper and listened to her husband's happy whistling. Next morning, when she found the sugar pushed to the back of the cupboard below the sink, her hmm changed to ho-ho. However improbable it was, it seemed as though he were up to something. But what a pity he wasn't up to something with Helga.

'What about Timothy and Helga? See that?' asked Paul of the head beside him.

'No, don't,' said Margaret.

'That's because—'

'*I* want Timothy, you're going to say. Perhaps.'

'Any case, you're heavily booked.'

'Don't you feel like a change?'

Paul leant over her, and did some growling and nuzzling

106

with his head between her slack, full breasts. This was much easier than answering.

'O.K.,' said Margaret, trying to hold his head still. 'So you do.'

He lifted his head a fraction. 'I didn't say—'

'You're tickling me.'

'—I did. I'm not.'

'Your beard is.'

'I'll shave it off.'

'You won't. You wouldn't. would you, in fact? If I said, shave off your beard, would you?'

'An interesting point. No, probably wouldn't.'

'You see! And if Polly did—'

'Shave off her beard?'

'Evasion.'

'Unfair question, Rule 12. In any case, I don't think I would. Not if she said: Shave off your beard! Then I wouldn't. If she said, your beard or your life, or your beard or your wife . . .' His voice lapsed into a mumble somewhere around her stomach.

Margaret pulled at the lobe of his ear. 'Don't go to sleep, for heaven's sake, I've got to go and fetch the children soon.'

Paul roused himself with a groan and a yawn, and lay back beside her. 'Timesit now, time you have to go?'

'It's half past now, and I must leave the house at five to.'

That was a relief. Hardly time enough. She always needed fifteen minutes to wash and dress.

'What were you saying?' he asked, folding his arms behind his head.

'Whether their marriages can stand it,' replied Margaret, and folded her arms behind her head. They lay side by side, in the same attitude, and considered the ceiling as though it were the ceiling that had to take the strain.

'Can ours?' asked Paul.

'Of course. That's been proved. How long has this been going on, three years, four years?'

'You know I'm no good at anniversaries.'

'Four years this Christmas, it must be.'

'Good lord,' said Paul and smiled, remembering.

It had been at a Christmas party that it had become clear that Paul was having an affair with Margaret, and Polly with Jake.

'Oh,' Paul had said, taken aback, 'we had been wondering

107

why it had been so easy to find opportunities.' The easy friendship between the two couples had lapsed temporarily into bashful politeness, each enquiring anxiously after the others' health, and making absolutely certain that a chosen time for swapping was quite convenient all around. This almost crippled the relationships; it certainly removed the quality of reckless and stimulating deception, proving yet again the adage of forbidden fruit. But, after a while, in much the same style that a couple adjusts to marriage, they settled down to the regime, and gradually formulated its unwritten rules and their own roles. The women, being in any case the organisers of their social lives, naturally took on the task of arranging the occasions, which after an initial stage of rather forced frequency had resolved over the years into a pattern which seemed to be governed by the moon. The rules of the association, as they called it in parody of The Grove, were few but strict. There must be no discussion between any couple of the other couple, in whatever permutation; any alterations to the form of the association must be discussed openly between all members; notice of resignation must be given in advance; no single member could resign, only as a couple; new members admitted in pairs, not singly; prospective candidates to be considered by the association as a whole, and admitted only after unanimous agreement; and finally, the association to be kept absolutely secret.

Now, with the proposed trip to Greece, the association was undertaking an experiment. They each felt the need to expand membership; to break away from the dull routine of their adultery, yet to do this within the rules of the association. When Paul asked, 'Can ours?' he was asking not only whether their individual marriages could survive the reshuffle, but whether the foursome could, too. He secretly felt that the best way to inject new life into the association and relieve the tedium was for each member, and himself in particular, to have a swift and secret affair, probably in his case with the girl in the Black Lion. Open discussion and agreement detracted from its potency.

'Not many couples,' he now said thoughtfully to the ceiling, 'could do what we're doing.'

'Key parties in Barnes,' said Margaret.

'Key parties in *Barnes*?' he repeated. 'What on earth are they?'

She laughed. 'Don't you know? Oh, heavens yes, we often go to parties in Barnes.'

'What happens?' he asked, turning anxiously on his side to look at her.

'Oh well, you know the sort of thing.'

'No-o?'

'Oh,' she said, very airily, 'all the men, when they arrive, throw their car keys on to a table or tray or something, and then, later on, after a decent amount of bolstering drink, the women go and pick up a key, choose a key, any key, sort of thing, and off they go with that car and the man who belongs to it.'

'Oh!' said Paul, irritable and critical with jealousy, 'what a strange way to handle it. I wouldn't drive off with just any female who happened to pick up my key.' He brooded at the ceiling. Fancy Jake and Margaret going to key parties in Barnes. And not telling them. And whose key had she been picking up? 'What happens if you go to the party on a bike? In any case,' he said crossly, 'it's against the rules.'

'Maybe it's the men who pick up the keys,' said Margaret, thinking it over.

He sat up. 'But I thought you said you often went.'

She laughed. 'No, of course not! I was just making it up.'

'Ha!' he said, and thumped back against the pillows.

'It may not even be Barnes.'

'Could be.' Did he know anyone who lived in Barnes?

'I was just saying it as the sort of thing that happens. You know, Christmas parties, suddenly you find yourself in a passionate kiss with the appropriate half of a couple you've exchanged chicken casserole with over the years . . .'

'You do?'

'One does. They do. What I'm saying is that there are various forms of our association, in varied degrees of er commitment. The chicken casserole Christmas clasp is one category, the key party in Barnes another, our association another. All are licensed safety valves for Happy Marriage. The couples that can allow, that can afford to license these skirmishes, are the ones that survive to Golden Wedding anniversaries.'

Paul pulled the sheet up to his chin. He scratched under his beard. 'Yes, maybe; but I think there must be quite a number of couples who don't need such safety valves.'

'You do? Perhaps there are quite a number who think

they don't need them. What happens?' Margaret asked the ceiling, but did not wait for an answer either from there or from Paul beside her. 'The man survives because he spends most of his life outside the home where the licensing laws, or rather non-licensing in this case, do not seem to apply. But the wife, at home with young children, lives in an all-female world, taking it in turns with other mothers to ferry children to school. She does meet males, the grocer, the milkman. Does she invite the milkman to receive his change in bed? Remember Camberley? Well, forget it, because I'm assuming the majority don't. So what happens?' she asked again and went on. 'At, say forty-five, she suddenly discovers the children are not watching, having left home, the career she has trained in and followed for twenty years is over. She comes, they say with shocked disapproval, unstuck—she gets a job and a lover. "*And they were such a happy couple.*" The drama she's wanted all her life in nicely small palatable doses, she gets in a fat wad, which rapidly turns to tragedy, because her astonished and outraged husband divorces her. He probably marries again, a rather younger girl. And she gets older alone, her lover having made a hasty exit early on in the proceedings.' Margaret shivered, as she had done as a child telling her brothers ghost stories in bed, to send them to sleep and to leave herself shaking with fright. She turned to Paul and found he, too, had been sent to sleep, having heard all this before.

And they hadn't even made love.

And she had now to rush off and collect the children from their party.

Polly sat up in bed, a rather grubby sheet draped around her for warmth, filing the nails of her left hand. Jake sat on the edge of the bed, surrounded by parts of a clock, the shell of which he held on his hairy lap.

The clocks ticked, Jake sighed every now and again and breathed heavily as he fiddled with the mechanism, Polly blew dust from her nails.

Jake began to fit the parts together again, and Polly started on her right hand.

There was a reverberating clang and ding and cuckoo as the pendulum fell to the floor, bouncing among other clocks. Jake swore.

'Don't bother about it,' said Polly, 'Leave it like that.'

'You asked me to mend it. I shall mend it.'

'Oh, *okay* then.'

'Bloody thing.'

Polly leant across and kissed the nearest ear. 'You're a magician,' she said to encourage him. 'Paul could never—'

'Rule.'

'Right,' Polly smiled and held out her hand to consider the length of her nails. She carried on filing carefully at her fourth finger-nail. 'And where will the children go?' she asked, carrying on with a conversation begun sometime before.

'When?'

'When we're away.'

'Oh. Summer camp. Same place as last year.'

'Do they mind?'

'Mind? They love it!'

Polly blew at her nails. 'You're rather remote parents, aren't you. What with Margaret working and summer camps.'

'Doesn't seem like it at seven in the morning.'

'I suppose they are at school in any case. But in the holidays—'

Jake had nearly assembled the clock, and was concentrating on screwing in the last few pieces. Then he attached the pendulum and gave it a tap. 'There, let's see if it works,' he said, closing its glass door, and looking for a place to put it down. 'Would you like them to come with us?'

Polly laughed. 'You're right,' she said.

The clock in Jake's hands suddenly struck four.

'Heavens, six o'clock,' said Polly, reaching for her clothes at the foot of the bed.

'Hell, four! I haven't mended it.'

'Get up,' said Polly.

'I can't understand it,' said Jake, opening the glass door to peer at the face.

'For heaven's sake, don't take it to bits again. Time's up.'

'Sorry about it,' said Jake and put the clock on top of another on the floor.

'Never mind. We'll be in Greece soon.'

'Oh, yes, well,' He hadn't in fact been apologising for spending their time together mending the clock, but for failing to mend the clock. However, he left it at that. It was she, after all, who had asked him to look at it, though probably she hadn't imagined it would take so long. He pulled on his trousers, and buttoned his shirt.

When he got home, he found Paul asleep in his bed. 'Wake up, you lazy sod, the children will be home any minute.'

Paul stumbled out of the house, seconds before Margaret returned with the children. He had reached the dividing wall between The Grove and Beechley Avenue, as the Davies car turned into the car park. He paused the far side of the wall, suddenly wanting to overhear Margaret in her role of mother. The car crunched to a halt on the gravel, and doors opened.

'—and we didn't have *jelly*.'

'—and there wasn't any *booze*.'

'Darling!' Paul heard Margaret's deep soft rumble of amusement. She had been lying beside him naked not half an hour before. 'And did you expect booze?'

'I gave them booze at my party.'

'Fruit cocktail.'

'I was top in maths today.'

'Well *done*, my love, that's marvellous.'

And still she might have been addressing himself. Was he, to her, a child? Did each member of her circle, her husband, her three children, and himself, get equal parcels of her warmth and affection? And what about the newspaper and the people she worked with?

'—and we didn't have sausages. And we didn't have—' The voices faded up the path, and Paul walked home.

Later that evening, like dancers in some complicated Scottish reel, the couples had resolved to their original and decreed positions, lying side by side in their double beds. Timothy and Tina Blunden lay back to back in number Six The Grove, each dreaming their private dreams. Alexander and Helga Frise lay on their backs, each wishing they could confide in the other the events of their separate days. In number Four The Grove, Jake and Margaret Davies made sweet, tired and slow-motion love. Above the Antique Shop in Merrivale High Street, Paul and Polly amicably decided they were too tired to make even slow-motion love.

And in number Twelve The Grove, Judith Toms said to George Toms, 'Funny thing, Timothy Blunden was at home this afternoon and called on Helga Frise.'

'What's funny about that?'

'Tina was out.'

'Well,' said George, feeling jovial and pleased with himself, because he had succeeded in making love to Judith. This was no mean feat as he had spent two hours at a typist's flat before coming home. ('Sorry I'm late, got involved in a session at the pub.' None of this suspect pressure of work excusing from him.) 'He probably only went to seduce her.' He laughed happily in the dark bedroom, and fell promptly asleep.

It was full moon.

CHAPTER SEVEN

Timothy lay on the beach between Polly and Helga. His tanned (angry pink) and muscular (when flexed) arm supported his head. At the moment his face was turned towards his left and Polly. His eyes were shut as though he were asleep, but he occasionally flickered his eyelids and checked that she was still there. She had been there since ten o'clock. It was now half past eleven. Every fifteen minutes she changed position according to some private system, and applied another coat of a different cream or lotion to yet another part of her body. She was revolving round the sun like the earth; and looked, thought Timothy as he squinted at her over the pebbles, very like the earth, rather a mountainous region perhaps, her red bikini showing the urban patches in aerial infra-red photography. Beyond her sat Alexander, already bronzed—there was no other word for his True Romance colour—and wet from the sea. He was half-turned away from Timothy and facing Tina, who lay on her stomach, propped up on her elbows, chin in her hands, and who had pinned him with her gaze and some earnest conversation which Tim couldn't hear above the sound of the sea pulling at the shingle. Occasional words came across, like maladjusted and recidivist; enough to make Timothy sympathise with Alexander and, with a gradual movement not to frighten either girl, turn his head the other way.

And there was Helga. It was almost too much for Timothy, and he lay rigidly, trying to give the appearance of a relaxed and dozing sunbather, when in fact he was in a state of high tension, thoroughly awake and far too hot. He would

113

give anything for a swim but the forsaking of his position. He dare not move. The subtle engineering, the swift following-up of opportunties, the chain of movements that had led up to this position between Polly and Helga on the beach at 11.30 a.m. might never occur again. It had begun at breakfast. 'Anyone swimming this morning?' Tim. 'We need shopping,' Tina. 'I shall go later,' Helga. 'I'm going right away,' Polly, 'I'll join you,' Jake. 'Men should shop too,' Margaret. 'We need a rota,' Tina. It had really taxed Tim's strength and ingenuity to forecast the individual movements of the party and dovetail his own to fit, without drawing undue attention to his strange inconsistency. There had been an awkward moment when he had volunteered to help shop when he heard Helga offering; and then had backed out again when Jake and Margaret said they would do it, as they wanted to send an arrived-safely telegram to the children. Margaret had looked at him with suspicion, Tim thought—or maybe, disappointment? Apart from that, it had been a beautifully planned and executed strategy, which had culminated in this intoxicating position and he must stay in it, even in agony, with his face in the shingle, and the backs of his knees and his shoulder-blades getting painfully burnt.

Helga, on his right, was much more jumpy than Polly. Every so often she worried him by getting up and wandering off; but so far, each time she had left her towel not a yard from him and a smell of Ambre Solaire. She came back from her sorties with things; a handful of shells, a sea-urchin, even the odd stick or two, like a retriever. Admittedly the sticks were nicely whitened by sea and sun, and could be put on shelves to stand there in warped and interesting shapes, but they were sticks all the same and not worth getting up and leaving him for. He shut his eyes very tightly on her return trips. He had the impression she might lean over and show these things to him, if she thought he were awake. Which would be too much, and make the alarm ring at 7.35 a.m. in number Six The Grove.

They had arrived on the island at half past five the morning before, and they each still wore a faint, almost defensive, look of surprise. It hadn't been quite what they were expecting, though if they had been asked what exactly they had been expecting, they would have found it hard to answer. Something a little bigger, or something a little smaller;

something a little higher, or something a little lower.

As the steamer from Piraeus brought them into the bay, they had stood nervously on the deck for their first sight of the place; nervously, because they felt that maybe they should be standing near the luggage on the lower deck.

'Mm,' said Margaret, inhaling, 'can you smell the thyme?'

'No,' said Jake, looking down at the gutter by the railing. It had been rough.

'Oh, look!' cried Tina, pointing towards the distant quay. 'A windmill!'

Paul had binoculars. 'It's a crane,' he said.

The sun edged the hills around the bay and Timothy tried to remember the quotation. 'Talk about rosy-fingered,' he said eventually.

Suddenly, with a metallic rumbling, the steamer drifted to a standstill. 'What was that?' they asked each other, imagining headlines EIGHT BRITONS DROWNED AEGEAN.

'I think the anchors,' said Alexander.

'But we're in the middle of the bay.'

'We swim from here with our luggage on our heads,' said Paul.

Tina looked at him anxiously, almost believing him.

They hurried down to their luggage.

'I suppose this is the right island,' said Margaret, laughing gently in a detached way at the image of the party disembarking at the wrong place.

'There should be notice-boards all the way along the coast, like on platforms,' said Paul.

'That would spoil it!' said Tina indignantly, again taking him seriously.

'Pyros? Pyros?' Margaret asked a man who looked vaguely nautical. They all watched for his answer. He regarded the party in turn, and then bent his elbows, turned his hands outwards, palms uppermost; hunched his shoulders, tilted his chin, gathered his lower lip into an n below his top lip, closed his eyes, and held this contortion, while they thought about it.

'That's not a sailor, that's Marcel Marceau,' said Jake.

Paul said, 'Not pyros. Peeeeeros.' He pushed towards the man. 'Peeeeeeros.'

The man relaxed his position and smiled happily at Paul.

'Peeeeros?' asked Paul again. The man went on smiling happily.

'Oh dear,' said Tina, 'this is rather worrying.'

Tim saw a boat approaching the steamer. He turned to the others. 'Small boats ferry us to the quay,' he told them with authority. He was their travel agent.

Margaret tried again. 'Pahros?'

The nautical man wagged his finger and said in English, 'No, no, no, no, no.'

Someone else joined in, turning away from the rail to do so. 'Poros?' he asked.

'No!' said Tim. 'Not Poros. Pie-ros, pie, pie, pie.'

Polly had been rummaging in her bag to find some cream for her nose and had paid no attention to all this. Now she applied the cream, replaced her dark glasses, which were hardly necessary as the sun was barely over the hills, and turned to the others. 'Isn't it marvellous?' she beamed.

'No Poros,' said the man. He flung his arm in a wide sweep towards the back of the steamer, and then made movements with his hand as though he was patting the head of a tall man five yards away. 'Poros,' he said firmly.

Then a third man intervened. He was elderly, and looked as though he had just stepped into his crisply-pressed dry-cleaned suit, and out of a barber's. The villa party felt immediately dishevelled.

'Excuse me,' he said, 'may I help you?'

'Oh yes, please!' 'Oh yes, thank you!' They gathered round him with relief, like eager children.

'Is this Pyros?' asked Margaret.

'Is this Peeeros?' asked Paul.

'Pie-ros?' asked Tim.

The man listened to them intently, and then asked them where they wanted to go.

'Pyros, Peeros, Pah-ros, Pie-ros,' they repeated.

'This is Fee! ross!' he said, staccato.

'Fee! ross!' they echoed.

The whole crowd turned and nodded and smiled. 'Feeros,' they all confirmed, and began disappearing over the side of the steamer. Tim peered over the rail and saw the queue clambering down the swaying companion-way into the boat tied alongside. 'Quick!' he said to the others. 'We must get off!'

Tina and Margaret were deep in their handbags, and now emerged with pamphlets. They thrust these at their helper, pointing at the caption to one photograph.

'Don't worry about that now,' said Tim. 'Off we get!' He seized two suitcases.

'But it may not be—!' began Margaret.

'Oh dear, oh dear, oh dear,' said Tina, and picked up a duffle-bag and made for the companion-way.

'Oh, what the hell!' laughed Margaret, and followed her.

'Helga! Where's Helga?' asked Tim wildly. In a flurry of checking numbers of the party and the luggage, they got themselves into the boat. Here, they were split up among chickens, hampers, boxes, people and baskets. Paul found himself with his nose between the shoulder-blades of Alexander. 'Of course!' he shouted against the engine noise. 'It wasn't pee, it was fee.'

'You'll have to wait,' Alexander shouted over his shoulder.

Tina was not far from Margaret. 'We never thanked that nice man!'

Margaret bobbed her head behind a bouquet of lilies. 'Lovely!' she screamed back.

Once on the quay, they decided the first thing was breakfast. A fair-sized town straggled along the waterfront, where a number of fishing boats were moored, and made an attempt at climbing the hill behind, where houses petered out at a certain level with a small white church providing their full stop. From the church the hillside was scored by a zigzag line which led up to what was probably another church on the peak. This peak dominated the bay.

'I'll climb that,' said Helga.

I'll come too, thought Tim. 'Which one shall we go to?' he asked. There seemed to be a good choice of cafés.

'What shall we do with our things?' asked Tina. It was she, all the journey, who had been most concerned for their luggage, as though she would have preferred it bound to the party by some umbilical cord.

'Leave it here,' said Jake.

'Take it with us,' said Alexander.

'Er,' said Tim.

The party lacked a leader as yet, as the others held back from the position in deference to Timothy who, as instigator, they felt, should assume the role. So far he hadn't done very well. In Athens they had agreed that at least they must visit the Acropolis, and they would get a taxi. 'No, no,' Tim had said, asserting himself. 'Not a taxi. The best way

117

to see the Acropolis is by walking up through the old quarter. That's the *classic* way.' And they had meekly followed him for an hour and a half around the old quarter, and then got a taxi.

'I wonder where the villa is,' said Polly and she and Helga left the group to go and sit down in the shade of the nearest café.

The others were still arguing and didn't notice. Every so often they were approached by members of the crowd who were watching the unloading of the boat. They dealt politely enough with the barrage of Deutsch? Otel? Otel? Zimmer? until, finally irritated by the plaguing, they paid no attention.

'Well,' said Margaret, at last, 'let's at least sit down at the nearest place while we decide.'

They were surprised to find Helga at a table already, chatting happily with a waiter, in German. Polly's cardigan hung over the chair beside her.

'Oh!' said Alexander, rather crossly, 'you're here.'

'Yes,' said Helga smiling happily. 'He has worked in Germany, they have Nescafé, we can have Nescafé, and a deep-freeze, and lobster!'

'Where's Polly?' asked Paul.

'She went to find the er,' said Helga.

Just then Polly came out of the café with a tight expression on her face. She didn't sit down, but put her cardigan around her shoulders. 'Let's go to the one next door,' she said.

'Why? What's wrong?'

'Come on,' she said and moved away.

'But—' began Helga, looking anxiously towards the waiter who was still standing beside them.

'What's wrong with here?' Paul asked Polly in a loud voice.

Polly gave her chin a little shake between her shoulders.

Tina peered into the café. 'I think it looks very nice,' she said, 'very nice and clean.'

'I'm staying here,' said Helga. 'He speaks German.'

'Well,' said Polly, turning back to tell them in a low voice, 'I want to go to the loo desperately. I was shown into a yard at the back, where there's a three-sided shed thing and a hole in the ground, and the smell—' Her throat contracted and it seemed she might be sick.

'Oh well, let's try the next place,' said Paul hurriedly, and took her arm. Alexander, Jake and Margaret followed.

'I'm staying here,' said Helga firmly. 'I've already ordered Nescafé and bread and butter and marmalade. It is too embarrassing.'

Tim hovered, anxious to stay with Helga and with the certainty of getting Nescafé and bread and butter and marmalade; but at the same time apprehensive of sitting alone with her at a separate café. Tina solved it by choosing to stay, thus providing a chaperone.

The waiter had watched their movements with curiosity; now he came closer again and asked Helga how many they were. She told him three, and he disappeared in a disgruntled manner into the café. Then Alexander drifted back. 'Aren't you coming with us?' he asked.

'No,' said Helga. 'We have ordered our breakfasts.'

'Oh,' said Alexander and wavered. He supposed he had better stay with his wife. And mistress. Though it would be more fun, he thought, with the others. He sat down, with a dissatisfied expression on his face. He felt a foot rubbed against his ankle under the table.

'What is it?' he asked Helga crossly.

'What?' she said, and he looked at Tina who was staring straight out to sea.

The foot withdrew.

There was silence. Tina broke in. She leant her elbows on the table, and rested her chin on her hands. 'Ah,' she said brightly, 'isn't it lovely?'

'You'd better order,' Helga told Alexander.

The waiter brought three breakfasts. 'And one for me, please,' said Alexander.

'Endaxi,' said the waiter and went.

'Endaxi,' repeated Tina, and got her phrase book from her bag. 'That means all right, a very useful word.' She had memorised the first three pages of the book already.

Just then the others straggled back to join them led by Polly who thumped herself down in her original chair, took a newspaper out of her bag and disappeared behind it. The three at the table looked from her to the others for the explanation. Paul whispered to Tim, 'It was the same loo!'

'Ha!' Tim gave a burst of laughter which he cut short for Polly's sake. Paul tried to cover his laughter by finding enough chairs for them all. But soon—except for Tina, who was sympathetically saying how revolting it was—they were all in a fit of suppressed giggles, exaggerated by the expression on the waiter's face when he returned with the fourth breakfast to find they were now eight. Polly remained behind her paper.

After eating, Tim went off in search of the man who would have the key to the villa. He returned an hour later, with what seemed to be a well-stocked family. Beside him waddled a stout woman with a broad grin of gold, who was treating Timothy as a long-lost son; laughing and talking and slamming him forcefully on the back. On his other side and a step or two behind came the husband, looking irritable. He led a mule. Children in various sizes embroidered the group, lean brown legs in slip-slopping plastic sandals. Timothy, looking bashfully proud, led them to the café.

'I've found it,' he said.

'*It*?' repeated Paul, looking at the family.

'Do they come complete with the villa?' asked Margaret.

'Shake hands,' hissed Timothy and nodded and smiled.

The group nodded and smiled dutifully, and shook hands with the woman, who was chattering away to them, most of it punctuated by question marks.

'Oreo, oreo,' said Tina from her phrase book.

'Poop, poop,' went the woman with her hands funnelling her mouth. Then she shook one hand at the wrist, palm downwards.

'How was the journey, that's what she's asking,' said Paul. 'Poop, poop,' he said to her, 'very rough.' He made huge wave movements with his hand.

She clutched her stomach, another question.

They shook their heads, smiling. 'Endaxi,' said Tina. The woman embraced her, much to her discomfort; and then threw her spare arm around Paul. Tina and Paul vanished. The woman laughed enormously, gold teeth flashing. The others quickly gathered their bags and moved out of range.

The husband had already strapped their suitcases on to the mule and was waiting to go.

'How romantic,' said Polly, 'going by mule.'

They paid the bill. 'How wicked,' said Polly. 'That's . . . heavens above, that's over £2!'

'Danke schön,' said Helga to the waiter.

'Aufwiedersehen,' he said.

'Not bloody likely,' said Paul.

They set off, the husband leading with the mule and an

increased number of children, the woman with the party, acting as guide, her chatter not checked in the slightest by the incomprehension of her audience. They were led along the water-front, and then into the back of the town by an alleyway.

'I hope it's not far from the sea,' said Polly.

'Just look at those flowers,' said Tina, pointing up at a balcony.

'Watch it,' said Tim, but she had already stepped into a pile of rubble.

They mounted steps, and soon they were all panting, except for Alexander who kept his mouth firmly shut to prove his fitness, and was breathing heavily through his nose.

'Heavens!' gasped Polly. 'I hate walking. I thought you said it was near the sea, Tim.'

'I thought it was near the sea,' he replied and rolled up his sleeves.

Then, to their relief, they turned off the steps, along a path which led them behind the houses which jumbled down to the promontory that sheltered the harbour.

'Oh, I know,' said Tim. 'It must be in that bay.'

'What bay?'

'I noticed a beach, this side of the harbour, from the steamer.'

'There looked as though there was a lovely beach the *other* side of the town,' said Polly, not feeling at all optimistic about the villa.

The path turned inland and sloped downwards. There were now spaces between the houses on either side of the path; some of the houses were in ruins, others were newly-built, with crisply cemented corners and brightly painted iron railings. All the way they had been watched by women leaning from windows and by old men seated in positions of permanence in doorways. Now, ahead of them, the mule stopped at what seemed to be the last house in the town. An old man was sitting in the small courtyard, watching them approach.

'Oh dear,' said Tina looking in dismay at the house. It looked cramped and very occupied.

Their guide, beaming happily, pointed at it, and touched her generous bosom.

'Her house,' said Paul.

'Her father,' said Jake.

The old man got up with difficulty and came to the gate. Tina said smartly, 'Kalimera', pleased with her homework.

'Hi,' said the old man.

'Hi,' replied Tina faintly.

'Hi, honey,' he said to Paul.

'Hi, honey,' Paul answered.

To their relief, the procession continued past the house. The old man took Paul's arm and followed. 'American?' he asked.

'No, English,'

'In America,' he said, 'fifty year.'

'Fifty years?' repeated Paul.

'Fifty year,' said the old man firmly. He held up one hand, fingers outstretched and beat it three times. 'Yer know,' he said to Paul, as though he was about to entrust him with a cherished secret. 'I am an old man. Yerknow how old?'

'No,' said Paul. 'How old are you?'

'Nineteen!'

'That's marvellous,' said Paul. 'You don't look it.'

The woman turned and smiled proudly. 'Speak American,' she said.

'No, no, no,' said the old man. He tapped his head. 'Forget, forget. Long time,' he said sadly. 'Old now.'

'You remember very well,' said Paul. 'We'll talk English together.'

'Yes, yes,' he said eagerly and then lapsed into thought. Then he asked, 'Was your name?'

Paul told him, and the man slapped his back with surprising vigour and joy. 'Good! Pavlos. Greek name, very good.' He patted his chest. 'Tony.'

'Right, Tony,' said Paul, 'we'll talk English together.'

They turned a corner past a ruined building, and saw the path lead faintly down a small cliff to a long, gently curving beach. The beach was edged with tall thick clumps of bamboo, and behind this belt were a few stone-walled, dry earthed fields in a small flat valley. Then terraced olive-groves and vineyards provided a band of silver-green and vivid green against brick-red earth before the land reverted to hillside, shale-coloured, dotted with holly-green bushes and herbs.

The party came to a standstill to take in the view. 'Shingle!' said Margaret.

'Grapes,' said Helga.

'Where's the house?' asked Polly.

'There,' said Alexander and pointed. The white of a building could just be seen in the middle of the bay, set back from the beach, and partially hidden by olive trees. They hurried on down the slope to catch up the mule.

'Oreo,' said Tina to the old man. She had recovered from the 'hi'.

'You like?' he said, pleased. 'My house.'

'Oh.' She was taken aback. Were they really going to share it with this whole family?

'We should have brought food with us, I'm not going to do this walk again today,' said Polly.

'Oh, it's not so far,' said Paul. 'The mule goes slowly,'

'You do the shopping then.'

The children had now run on ahead, some along the beach, splashing in and out of the sea while the woman screamed disapproval at them, others leaping over the stone wall at the back of the beach and taking a diagonal path across the fields towards the house, while the man hurled disapproval after them; and the mule picking its way carefully along the middle of the beach, where the shingle was levelled into a path by use, and punctuated every foot by evidence of animal traffic. Half-way along the beach, the stone wall was knocked down, and the gap filled with a bunch of brush wood, kept in place by a rock. The man threw this to one side, and led the mule through. Then he gave the party a pantomime of replacing the barrier. 'Maaa, maaa,' he said.

'Sheep,' said Polly.

'Goats,' said Paul.

'Endaxi,' said Tina.

'Ha! Endaxi!' cried the woman joyfully, and made as though to embrace Tina again, but she had swiftly nipped through the gap in the wall.

They crossed two fields and, over the third wall, they came into the olive trees and suddenly there was the house. Facing them was a small door and a barred and glassless window in the wall, which they looked at with misgiving. 'Store,' said the old man. 'Here, this way.' He led them to the side, while the husband unlashed the rope that held the suitcases to the mule and began unloading. Steps took

123

them up to a terrace and the house built on two sides of it. The old man banged his stick on the terrace. 'Water,' he said. 'Good, water from rain.' The woman unlocked a door in the wing of the house at the back of the terrace. They could hear her clattering around, and then shutters opened. The party stayed outside for the moment, taking in the position of the house, moving around the terrace, sitting on its surrounding wall or under the shade of a vine which covered the angle between the two blocks. Behind the house and to the left rose the hill, showing a rounder shape from this side than it had when seen from the harbour. Around them stood the olives and through the trees before the house gleamed a narrow line of sea. They could just hear it pulling at the shingle between the thumps and bangs of the woman in the house, and the dumping of the luggage. And now they noticed the insistent machine roar of the cicadas.

'*That's* going to get on my nerves,' said Polly and put more cream on her nose.

'I wonder if the two parts are connected,' said Paul and followed the woman indoors. He found himself in what he took to be the main room of the house. It had an air of faded glory, imparted perhaps by its proportions which were generous. The ceiling was high and wooden, painted at one time blue, then yellow and more recently eau-de-nil. On each side of the entrance, and set deeply into the thick stone wall was a tall window with an elaborately carved wooden pelmet and curtain rails, though no curtains hung from them. Facing the door was a cumbersome chest of drawers and over this, a heavy, gilt-framed mirror, its glass black and mottled. There was a table in the middle of the room with a lace cloth on it and a bowl of plastic flowers, once red and yellow, now grime-brown. The walls looked freshly white-washed, but there was dust, too, and peeling paint-work. In one corner he saw a bed, a narrow double or a generous single, its frame white painted iron, its mattress bowl-shaped. On either side of the chest was a door. Both were open, and through the one on the left, he could see the woman fighting a pillow.

Margaret came in behind him. He said, 'I get the impression they weren't expecting us.'

'Oh,' said Margaret cheerfully, 'I'm convinced we're on the wrong island.'

'I wonder how the geography will work out,' he said. 'Shall we investigate?'

'What's the competition for that bed there?' asked Margaret.

'Very little, but let's wait till we've seen the others.'

They peered into the room where the woman was thumping, and she unleashed a stream of Greek. They nodded and smiled at her and took in the room. It had two low and narrow single beds and a chair, and a window on to the hill behind. They went to look at the other room. It had two low and narrow single beds and two chairs, and a window on to a slightly different part of the hill behind.

'Bags the one with two chairs,' said Paul.

They went out on to the terrace again, as Alexander and Helga were about to go in. Alexander asked what it was like.

'Fabulous,' said Paul, and he and Margaret went over to the door in the other wing. It was open, and they found Tim and Tina in a corner with their heads up a chimney. Tina turned round. 'It's a sweet little kitchen,' she said with a determined expression on her face. 'And we can light a fire here if it's chilly.'

'It's August,' said Paul, 'and that's for cooking over.' Another door led into the last room. It was small but it had a mirror-fronted wardrobe and a double bed, and by squeezing past the wardrobe and climbing on to the bed, Paul managed to get to the window and open the shutters. A latch fell off in his hands. There was a view over the olives to the sea. 'This is the best room,' he said.

Tina behind him repeated, 'This is the best room?' her voice covering an octave during the short sentence.

'We'll have to toss,' said Margaret.

'Toss and turn,' said Paul.

'None of the beds are made up. Do you think there are sheets?'

This sent Tina hurrying off with her phrase book to find the woman.

'And where is the loo? And the shower that Tim talked about?'

They began laughing, and kissed each other quickly, their cheeks touching lightly.

'Shall we go and swim?'

'Yes!'

'We'll have to find our things—' began Margaret.

'No,' said Paul, 'we'll get bogged down in unpacking. Come on.' And they sneaked away, and ran across the fields to the sea, like escaping children.

'We'll have to be speedy,' said Margaret on the beach, 'and be out and dressed before the family starts returning.' She stepped out of her dress and folded it with the speed and neatness of long years' laundry experience. 'I think I'll keep my bra and pants on.'

'Coward,' said Paul. 'There's not a soul in sight. Fantastic to find a beach in the Mediterranean in August quite deserted.'

'Could be because it's only eight o'clock in the morning.'

'Seems like midday to me.'

'And it's one of the nastiest beaches I've ever come across.'

'Tar, shit and shingle and sea-urchins. Later on we might look round the point, there may be a better beach the other side of those rocks.'

'You have the whitest bottom in Pyros.'

'No. In Fee! ross!'

'Youch, it's cold,' She stood in the shallows, the water coming to her knees. 'Oh, I hope I get brown soon. I hate to feel white and fat.'

Paul staggered in beside her. 'Watch out for the urchins.' He threw himself into the water in a shallow dive, and swam out under the surface. Coming up panting and spluttering a short distance from Margaret, he called back, 'Do you know, there's sand out here. Walk out a bit.'

By the time she reached him, the water came up to her shoulders. He put his arms round her, as though to hug her, and she relaxed against him, to find he had unfastened her brassière and was pulling down her pants. 'Hey!' she screamed, and looked quickly back at the beach. It was still deserted. She put up a slight struggle, but rather than go under the water, she let him take them off. He swam ashore and threw the clothes on the beach.

'Hee, hee,' he said and dived back towards her.

'Aaa,' she said and splashed her arms around. 'What a curious sensation.'

Paul surfaced, and began making out to sea in a busy short-armed crawl. Margaret followed with a stately breaststroke.

'Heaven,' said Margaret after a while and turned and floated on her back. Paul trod water beside her. 'It's possible,' he said, 'to make love in water. Shall we try?'

'No,' said Margaret, nervously. 'We'd drown.'

Back at the house, Tina had been communicating success-fully with the woman with the aid of her phrase book and mime.

'Who is this Mistair Boooshlee she keeps on about?' asked Polly. They were sitting round the table in the main room.

'Mr. Bushley,' said Tim, 'he's a sort of agent for houses to rent in Greece. I think he lived here at one time.'

'Oh, and you arranged this through him?'

'Not exactly. An agency 'in London did it, through him in Athens. Medivilla. It wasn't too straightforward,' he said, hoping to excuse himself from any responsibility for the villa's shortcomings. 'My original client kept changing her mind, you see.'

'Ask her where the loo is,' said Polly.

'I've asked her,' said Tina. 'I'll tell you what I've found out.' She had made a list. 'The loo and shower are at the back of the house somewhere—'

'I'm off to see,' said Polly.

'—she will bring the sheets. They were expecting us on Saturday, not today. Her husband is bringing us something to cook on, bottled gas, as far as I could make out. Her name is Ourania. She has three children, Maria, George and—'

'—and Fred?' put in Jake.

'George and John—'

'Does she clean?' asked Helga.

'Oh, I haven't asked her that. Shall I?' She began turn-ing the pages of her book. 'Oh yes, and she will bring us flowers.'

'Frightfully important,' said Jake. 'We simply must have flowers.'

'What should I look under?' asked Tina. 'Ah, here's "clean".' She turned to Ourania, who had been watching them benignly, her arms folded on the table. 'Katharo?' she asked her. 'You,' she pointed at her, 'katharo?'

Ourania looked affronted and talked a lot back.

'No, no,' said Jake. He got up and began making vigorous dusting and sweeping movements round the room; then he turned and held out his hand to Ourania, with his eyebrows raised. 'Or,' he murmured, and dusted a chair and then indicated himself with both hands to his chest, 'us?'

Ourania shrieked with laughter. She shook a finger at him, raised both palms outwards, and threw back her head, chin

127

thrust out, eyes closed. Then she laughed again.

'Well, whatever that may mean, she enjoyed my act,' he said and sat down.

Ourania got to her feet, and with a long dissertation and much arm movement and golden grinning, went to the door. They watched and told each other their interpretations, as though they were explaining the plots of a variety of silent films. Then she said, 'Adio.'

'Oh,' said Tina, surprised, 'she was just saying good-bye. *Adio*,' she said to Ourania.

'Adio, adio,' they all repeated, and followed her on to the terrace. The other members of the family had disappeared.

Ourania went down the steps and off among the trees, her haunches pushing up alternate sides of her dress with brisk precision. Then Polly came up the steps, her face full of news.

'Do you know?' she began.

'What?' they asked eagerly. Polly's trips to the lavatory seemed full of incident.

'There was an old woman there. There's an old woman here!'

'Where?'

'In the loo.'

'In the *loo*?'

'An old woman?'

'Attached to the house. I mean, she seems to live here.'

'Where?'

'At the back.' Polly sat down on the wall, and gathered herself together to tell them. 'It's a small separate building. I found the door and went in. Quite clean and nice, looks newish, tile floor, and a proper sit-down affair and a shower and a basin. Well, I pulled the plug and nothing happened, went out and there was this old woman, I nearly fell down with shock. She was waiting outside the door with a jug of water. Then she went in, poured the water down the loo, and came out. She held my arm and said something, she hasn't any teeth, and then she disappeared round the corner. I didn't like to follow her.'

There was silence while they thought about this.

'Well I never,' said Tina, first as always to break a silence. Jake went to the steps. 'I shall go and see,' he said.

Paul and Margaret decided it was time they went back.

They were getting cold. They swam towards the shore on their backs, pedalling and splashing with their feet.

'Heaven!' said Margaret.

'Splendid!' panted Paul.

He turned to see how near they were to the beach and saw the old man standing by their clothes, leaning on his stick and watching their approach.

'Hi!' called the old man. 'Is good?'

'Christ!' said Paul. 'Stop!'

Margaret stopped splashing. 'Cramp?' she asked anxiously.

'No, Grandpa! Grandpa's watching us!'

They began treading water, now facing the beach.

'Hi!' the old man called to Margaret.

'Hello,' she called back, with strained joviality.

'Cold?' he asked.

'Yes,' she answered.

'No, no!' said Paul. 'It's lovely.' They would have to stay in the water till he left.

To their dismay, they saw the old man carefully lower himself into a sitting position on the beach.

'Oh God,' said Paul under his breath.

'What are we to do?' hissed Margaret.

'Hi, Paul, we talk English together, yes?'

'Sure, Tony,' said Paul, 'ohgodalmighty.'

'I shall freeze,' said Margaret.

'Keep swimming,' said Paul.

They swam.

When Jake came out of the lavatory, there was the old woman, waiting outside the door, with a jug of water.

Alexander went next. 'See her too?' they asked him when he returned.

'Yes,' he said, in a surprised tone of voice as though he had suspected the others of visions.

'Let's call her the True Niagara,' said Jake.

'Do you think she works for showers, too?' asked Polly.

'I'm not going to let her pour water over *me*,' said Alexander firmly.

'I'll go now,' said Tina.

'Oh no,' said Tim. 'Give her a rest.'

'But I want to go. I have to go.'

'There must be a better system.'

Alexander and Jake and Tim discussed other ways of flushing a lavatory.

'Where's Paul?' asked Tina, suddenly realising that one man was missing.

'And Margaret?' asked Helga.

'Oh,' said Jake. 'Swimming probably.'

'I can't keep going much longer,' said Margaret. 'I must get into my depth.' She swam towards the shore until she could touch the bottom and then, facing out to sea, moved her arms as though she were swimming.

'Here comes the whole family,' said Paul. 'Get back! They can probably see you.'

Margaret swam weakly out again.

Then, to their intense relief, Grandpa got to his feet and followed the family back along the beach towards the town.

'Thank the Lord,' said Margaret and swam inshore.

'Don't get out yet,' called Paul after her. 'They're all waving. Wave to them.'

They waved energetically, their teeth chattering. At last the family reached the path up the cliff.

'Surely they can't see us now,' said Margaret and staggered on to the beach, where she flopped down, heedless of shingle and tar. Paul joined her and rubbed her back with his shirt.

'Well,' she said when she had recovered her breath, 'that's the last time I try nude swimming.' And then they began laughing.

When they told the others about it, Polly and Jake laughed too, Helga smiled, Alexander tried not to look at the places where Margaret's wet dress clung to her, and Tina looked stunned. Timothy's expression was thoughtful.

What an extraordinary thing, he was thinking. Paul and Margaret swimming together, in the nude. This exactly tallied with the arrangement he had dreamt up at number Six. He and Helga; Alexander and Polly; Paul and Margaret. Things looked almost frighteningly promising. He lit his pipe, to cover his excitement.

They fell to discussing the arrangement of the rooms, urged on by Margaret, who was anxious to unpack and change her clothes. After a great deal of subtle engineering from conflicting positions, the final plan they all agreed to was for the Blundens to have the front room in one block,

Jake and Margaret to have the main room in the other block—

'The saloni,' put in Tina, 'that's what it's called,'

—Paul and Polly the left-hand back bedroom, and the Frises the right-hand bedroom.

'Community living,' said Jake. 'Shades of The Grove.'

'Well,' said Tina, thinking he was being critical of the villa her husband had organised, 'we'll have to make the best of it.'

'You have,' he replied.

'If you think ours is the best room,' she said tartly, 'you are welcome to it.'

'No, no, no,' he said, not wanting at all to be marooned in the separate wing. 'It's all arranged.'

'Let's look into the water system,' said Alexander, 'while the girls unpack.' He made it sound like a male versus female football match.

They investigated the building at the back of the house, and by climbing on to its roof from a side wall that gave on to a vineyard, discovered that the section of the roof over the lavatory held a storage tank for water. 'How do we fill it?'

'Buckets from the well?'

'And where's this old woman you're talking about?' asked Paul. He went to the far side of the roof and looked down. 'Ah, here she is.'

She was sitting right below him, spinning.

'Hello,' he said. But she seemed not to hear. 'What's hello in Greek?' he asked.

'What about good day? I know good day,' said Alexander.

'Try good day then.'

Alexander came to the edge of the roof, and bent down, his hands on his knees. 'Kalimera,' he said. The old woman below went on spinning.

'Let's go down and be friendly, she's probably deaf.'

They jumped down and went round the building to the back. The woman wasn't there, nor was there any sign of a chair or a stool. There was a door half-closed and a window with shutters closed save for an inch.

'What an extraordinary thing.'

They hung around, wondering whether to knock on the door.

131

'Better leave her,' said Paul. 'She would have stayed out-side if she wanted to see us.'

'But if she's deaf, then she can't have heard us.'

'But if she's deaf, how did she know when we went to the lavatory?'

'How odd.'

They went back to the house.

The rest of the first day they felt, at the end, they had wasted. They went to the town for lunch, returned for a rest; sheets and the gas stove were brought in the late after-noon by the husband; and then they had supper in the town at the same restaurant where they had eaten lunch. They went to bed early.

So, on their second day, they were all determinedly getting brown on the beach, except for Jake and Margaret who were shopping. They had decided they would have picnic sort of lunches at the house, and evening meals in the town. 'One good meal a day is quite enough,' Margaret had said firmly. Alexander had looked concerned.

Now, to Timothy's alarm, Polly, who had been lying quietly beside him for so long, began moving. One arm was flung sideways so it narrowly missed his chest; her legs were drawn up, then relaxed again. She twisted over on to her hip, so that she was now facing him. Her eyes opened, then shut again quickly. 'Er, ah, oo,' she said. 'Ouch.' She heaved her weight on to one elbow, while the other arm felt around for her sun-glasses. Finding them, she got them on to her nose and sat up. 'Phew!' she said.

Timothy lay quite still and shut his eyes tight.

And then he was conscious of movement on his other side. He heard pebbles scrunching, and felt a shadow on his face. Both of them were moving, getting up, leaving him. Well at least he would be able to cool down in the water.

'I'm going for a swim,' he heard Helga say.

I'll come too, he thought.

'Good, wake up then,' said Helga.

Had he said it?

'And so will I,' said Polly.

No! He in the blue Aegean with the two girls; they watch him as he plunges in to join them, a perfect swallow dive from the pinnacle of rock. He surfaces beside them, and they cling admiringly to either arm. He drowns.

'Tim darling!' That was Tina. 'Your *back*!'

132

Where had he been?

'I'll find my calamine.'

With difficulty, he turned over and sat up, twisting his neck to look at his shoulders. They did look pink. 'That'll be brown tomorrow.'

'Let me put calamine on it. You're going to peel dreadfully.'

'I don't peel.'

'Don't be too sure,' said Tina, and she came over with her tube, and began rubbing the ointment on his back.

'Ouch, gently,' he said, and watched Polly and Helga go to the edge of the water. Helga looked bony beside the larger girl. And Polly looked fat beside Helga. They detracted from the virtues of each other.

He wished Tina would hurry up. 'That's enough,' he told her twice.

'Just a little more down here,' she said.

Polly and Helga were in to their waists now. Helga began swimming. She had marvellous style, and soon was some distance from the beach. Tim wasn't sure if he would get out that far. Polly, on the other hand, stayed where she was, with the water to her waist. Well, he'd stay with Polly.

'There,' he said, 'thank you.'

'Just a moment,' said Tina, 'the backs of your legs.'

'Leave them, it'll come off in the water in any case.'

'No, it won't. It's water soluble.'

'Water soluble? What *do* you mean?'

'Or do I mean insoluble?'

'Probably.'

By the time she had done his legs, Helga was, it seemed, half-way to Athens. He gave her up, and concentrated on Polly. He walked carefully into the water, watching out for urchins.

'Ah,' he said loudly to Polly's back. 'Lovely.'

He reached her and stood at a distance of three yards from her, water coming to his waist. 'Ah,' he said again. 'It's sand here.'

'Yes, isn't it strange,' said Polly. She was moving her hands idly on the surface of the water. He noticed she was still wearing her glasses. Was she going to swim in them, too?

He curled his toes in the sand, longing to immerse himself in the water, but wanting at the same time to wait until Polly did.

Then, after a while, Polly said, 'Aren't you going in?'

'Oh yes,' he said. 'I'm just getting used to it.'

They stood and looked out to sea. Helga's head could just be seen bobbing in the distance.

'She shouldn't go out too far,' said Polly. 'There are sharks.'

Sharks! Tim's toes retracted, and his legs felt vulnerable. He peered into the water around him for shadows. And what about Helga? Would she have time to scream? Would he be able to reach her before she was quite eaten up? Would his fast crawl be fast enough? Might not the sharks eat him too? The pictures this conjured up were not heroic, merely messy. 'I don't think there are sharks in the Mediterranean,' he said.

'Oh yes there are,' said Polly cheerfully. She bent her knees and slipped under the water to her shoulders, holding her hair in its pony-tail well out of the water. After a moment she straightened again.

Of course, thought Tim, suddenly remembering Paul and Margaret's nude swim of the previous day, he should really be trying to encourage Alexander and Polly, according to his scheme; not himself and Polly. He would call to Alexander to come in and join them, and then swim out himself (a little way) and wait for Helga to return. He turned towards the beach and saw only Paul, who was sitting with his knees bent under his chin and covered in towels, reading a book under the shade of a wide-brimmed straw hat. Walking towards the far promontory were Tina and Alexander. He felt thoroughly irritated by this foiling of his plans by his wife. And how stupid of Alexander to be persuaded to go for a walk in the hot sun, rather than go for a cooling swim with Polly.

'You're taking a long time to go in,' Polly was saying.

'Oh, I—' began Tim. 'You've taken longer than I have!'

'But I'm not going to swim. I can't swim.'

'Well, that was easy,' said Tina, when they were out of ear-shot. 'I love you!' They walked along the beach not too close together. 'How are you?'

'How am I?' repeated Alexander, surprised. 'Very well, thank you.'

Tina laughed. 'I mean, how *are* you? Oh, I don't know

134

what I mean, but I just feel I don't, I'm not really in touch with you unless it's just us two together.'

'Oh, I see,' said Alexander who didn't at all. 'I've been missing you,' he said, to make amends for what he gathered was some omission on his part.

'Have you?' said Tina, gratified. 'Isn't it odd. We're seeing so much of each other, and yet less of each other, it seems, than in London.'

Alexander looked ahead. He hoped that round the cliff he would see much more of Tina. 'I wonder if we can climb round,' he said. They reached the end of the beach. The flattened path on the shingle led to the back of the beach, and then disappeared into the valley. 'That might lead round behind the point,' he said.

'Or should we climb along the rocks, and round the point that way?' suggested Tina.

'Or straight up and over?' He looked at the cliff before them. It didn't look too steep or difficult.

'Oo, no,' said Tina hastily, 'this way.' She began clambering along the rocks. 'We can pretend we're looking for crabs or something.'

So for the benefit of anyone who might be watching the progress of their walk, they stopped every so often and peered at their feet. Soon they were out of sight of Paul on the beach, but could still see Polly and Tim.

'Come on,' said Alexander, 'we mustn't be away long, or it will look suspicious.'

'Why are they standing there?' asked Tina. 'They've been there ages.'

'Polly doesn't swim.'

'But Tim does.'

They carried on, jumping from rock to rock. 'There must be another beach just round the corner.' said Tina after a while. They paused to look where they were. Now Polly and Tim were out of sight. The cliff rose more steeply beside them, rocks stretched ahead, and beyond sea and in the distance, another point. 'It *must* be a bay.'

'Let's reach that last big boulder, and then we'll be able to see.'

The rocks were bigger here, lying jumbled at the foot of the cliff, as though paralysed in the act of falling. Scrambling from one to another became more strenuous. Tina was out of breath, and beginning to sweat. She longed for a swim.

Alexander urged her on. At last they reached the boulder which had provided their horizon.

'I think the only way round it is over,' said Alexander after considering it for a while.

'Oh dear,' said Tina, looking up at it. Their walk, which she had imagined would be a short stroll to a secluded nook and a pleasant session of kissing, had deteriorated into an Outward Bound exercise.

'I'll just nip up it and see,' said Alexander. He nipped up it, in a fit and agile manner, and Tina determined not to be persuaded to follow.

'I see,' he called down to her. 'This stuff goes on a bit further—' In fact, he saw it would take them as long again. '—and then it looks as though there's a sandy beach. And pine trees. Shall we try it?'

Tina sat down. 'How long would it take us to reach the beach?'

Alexander hesitated, torn between his desire to get Tina to the beach, and concern for the time. She was getting tired and irritable; by the time they reached the beach, they would have to hurry back again. 'I think maybe too long.' He scrambled down to sit beside her, and put his arm around her shoulders. They searched the sea for observers. There was no one in sight.

'What a pity,' said Tina.

'Never mind,' said Alexander and kissed her.

'Mmmm,' said Tina. Alexander drew away and looked around for a flat surface. They were sitting on a relatively smooth rock, but it was small; certainly not big enough to lie on. Around them, the rocks lay at every angle but horizontal. Well, there were other positions, he thought, and kissed Tina again, more aggressively. She was wearing a sober navy-blue swimsuit, which he detached from her freckled shoulders and pulled down to her waist.

'Oh, you—' murmured Tina with a smile.

'You're beautiful,' said Alexander and Tina's smile deepened. Sitting beside her, he couldn't get his face down to kiss her bosom, so he got up and pulled her to her feet.

'Must we go?' she asked, with surprise.

'No, no,' he muttered and began work on one bosom. Tina, now she was standing, began to feel ridiculous and conspicuous. She gazed out to sea, and suddenly spotted a swimmer. She grew rigid, and fumbled for her swimsuit.

136

Alexander's head came up abruptly. 'What it is?' he asked. and turned to look. 'Helga!' he said.

'Crumbs!' said Tina, reverting to schooldays in her shock. She struggled her arms into the shoulder straps of her swimsuit.

They peered anxiously out at the swimmer, whose arms appeared rhythmically above the sea about a hundred yards from them, and travelling parallel with the shore.

'*Is* it Helga?' asked Tina.

'Looks like her.'

'But such a long way from the beach!'

'She's a fantastic swimmer.'

'Better be going back, in any case,' said Tina, and they set off. After some clambering, they paused on a high rock to look out again.

'It *is* Helga,' said Alexander. 'She's swimming back now.'

'Do you think she saw us?'

'No,' said Alexander. But he wasn't sure; and probably never would be.

'Oh dear, oh dear,' said Tina, 'wouldn't it be awful if she *had*.'

At last they were nearing the beach. 'Jake and Margaret must be back from the town,' he said, gazing at the group in the distance.

'If only we could find a crab—' said Tina, looking hurriedly into a rock pool they were passing. She would feel happier returning with something in her hands, an excuse for the walk. 'Let's say we nearly caught one, spent a long time chasing one or something.'

'You don't chase crabs. Anyway, far better not to say anything.'

This was beyond Tina. When they drew near the group on the beach, she called out, 'Hello! We tried to get round to the other bay. It looks lovely, sand and pine trees—'

But the others hardly looked up; they were listening to Jake's account of their morning in the town.

'Hello, darling,' Tina said to Tim, 'did you have a nice swim?'

Her tone of voice reminded him of Ricky. He wondered how he was getting on with Tina's parents. He hoped he wasn't unhappy.

'I was wondering,' he said, 'if we should phone Rick up.'

Tina looked surprised. 'But he hardly speaks yet! It might

137

upset him.' She thought Tim probably hadn't even noticed she had gone for a walk. 'I simply must swim now, I got so hot,' she said and went into the water. Paddling out on her back, she bumped into Helga. They both splashed and spluttered.

'Sorry!' said Tina.

Helga trod water and smiled at her. Tina couldn't quite diagnose her expression. 'You swam a long way,' she said, her voice almost trailing a question mark.

'I wanted to reach the next bay,' said Helga. 'But it is far. Did you?'

Tina wished to sink. Helga had seen them. But had she seen them kissing? 'No,' she said, 'it was difficult.'

'Yes, it looked difficult,' said Helga. 'I think the best way must be inland. Next time try an inland path.' She turned and swam ashore, leaving Tina still uncertain as to what she had seen.

And, because Tina was not yet ready to end her affair with Alexander, she totally if temporarily forgot this exchange, so pliable is memory.

CHAPTER EIGHT

The days passed lazily, the group drawing a triangle between the house and the beach, the beach and the town, the town and the house; sleeping late into the heat of the morning, lying long on the beach, sitting over evening meals well into the night, moving with the introverted care and slowness of convalescents. Ourania came daily, in the late afternoons, when they were recovering from their midday siesta, and banged around with a broom and chatter. She had taken a fancy to Paul and called him Papas.

'I don't look that old, do I?' he said, examining himself in Polly's powder-compact.

'Maybe she means like sugar-daddy.'

'No, it's because of your beard,' said Tina, the linguist. 'Papas is priest. All the priests have beards.'

So Paul always held up two fingers in benediction over Ourania after this, and she loved him more and laughed more, and shook a finger at him to excuse her own irreverence. She brought him sticky cakes, and removed from the

138

floor of his room any discarded clothes, which would be returned the next day smelling of soap and sun and herbs.

'I love Ourania,' said Polly, and the other wives were jealous.

Towards the end of the first week, Ourania arrived earlier than usual. Thump, thump, thump up the steps and the door opened into the saloni. Paul sat up sharply in Margaret's bed, and watched for her reaction, Ourania looked at him in surprise, and then came nearer the bed to see who was lying beside him. 'Ha!' she said.

Paul raised two fingers in benediction. Ourania's expression wavered, and then she burst into an earthquake of laughter, pulled out from her apron pocket a handful of red-wrapped sweets and scattered them over the two in the bed. Then she went over to the door of Paul and Polly's room and opened it a crack. 'Ha!' she cried again, and closed it with more laughter, mingled with head shaking, which soon gave way to a great deal of talk, as she began to tidy the room.

'Is she going to stay in here, do you think?' asked Margaret, her voice muffled by the sheet. 'I want to get up.'

'You'll have to wait,' said Paul.

'But before they—' She jerked her head towards the door of the Frises' room.

'Oh, they must know. This house is hardly soundproof.'

'Oh!' Margaret sank back on the pillow.

After a while, with Ourania still busy in the room, Margaret sat up clutching the sheet to her body. 'I've got to get up,' she said, and began arranging the sheet around her.

'Hey,' said Paul before it was quite pulled away.

'You have the bottom sheet.'

They scuffled around on the bed, and then, clothed in sheets, got up. 'Let's have a shower,' suggested Margaret, and they left the room, Margaret carrying her sponge-bag.

'I hope there's water in the tank.'

'Should be, we filled it yesterday.'

When they came out of the lavatory-shower room, there was the old woman with the jug in her hands. When she saw the two white-draped figures, she dropped the jug, shrieked toothlessly, crossed herself a number of times, and backed away fast.

'I wish she'd get the idea that there's no need for the water-jug,' said Paul, and he began miming the water-supply to her, one hand holding his sheet in position, the other above his head. Then he brought his hand down, sprinkling with his fingers. This obviously had the effect of some primeval curse, because the woman shrieked again, her hand on her heart, and disappeared round the corner of the building at a speed amazing for her years.

'I think she's mad,' said Paul.

'She thinks we're mad,' said Margaret, and they went back to the house.

Ourania had the broom now and was sweeping. They sat on the bed and waited for her to finish.

'Isn't it odd, she's not in the least perturbed to be in our bedroom while we are in a state of undress. In fact, I don't think she would be put out if we began dressing.'

'Try and see,' said Paul.

'No. I would be *very* put out.'

'Odd,' said Paul. 'In one way they seem much more modest than we are, with our mini-skirts, legs and bosoms on display.'

'What it is,' said Margaret, 'is that we reserve our modesty for the house, and they for the street. They live in extended families in small houses, so in the house they don't have room for modesty—'

'Yes, it is we who have it the wrong way round, I suppose.'

Ourania swept towards the door of the Frise room, opened it and then closed it again; she swept towards the door of the other room, and knocked.

'At least, she knocked.'

She went in.

'Before entering.'

They laughed. After a moment or two, Jake and Polly came out, also dressed in sheets.

'She's doing it very thoroughly today, isn't she?' said Margaret.

'It's Saturday,' said Jake. 'She won't come tomorrow.'

They sat round the central table and smoked. Margaret went to the kitchen to make them coffee. Then Ourania flushed the Frises out of their room, and they joined the group, Helga also in a sheet, but Alexander, looking Tarzan-like, in a diminutive green towel.

'We could dress in your room now,' said Jake to Paul.

'Coffee first,' said Margaret, bringing in a tray.

The Blundens now joined them, both dressed in their

evening town clothes, Tim in beige-coloured denims and a
light buff jacket over a white polo-neck sweater. Contrary
to Tina's Job-like warnings, he had tanned a dark mahogany,
and looked, thought Margaret, delicious. She resolved to
start work that evening. Tina was wearing a dress that might
have sunk without trace in Juan-les-Pins, but in this setting
reverberated.

The Blundens regarded the group with some amazement.
'You look like a Victorian engraving of a pastoral classical
scene,' said Tim laughing, and went to get his camera. He
lined them up on the terrace, where they arranged themselves in various classical poses and Tina stood on the edge
of the group with her arms folded and a bright smile on her
face. Ourania rushed out at the last minute, and joined them,
patting her dress into shape and composing her face sternly
for the camera.

'Relax, Tina,' said Tim, and she shuffled around. 'Do
something with your arms.'

She did something, but they kept refolding themselves at
her waist as though drawn there by elastic.

'Put an arm round Paul.'

She looked at Paul uncertainly, and then gingerly placed
a hand on his shoulder as though it were a hot-plate.

'Relax!'

'Oh, leave me alone,' she said. But she put her weight
on one foot, in an attempt at relaxation.

'Hurry up,' said Jake.

'Ready?' asked Tim.

'Yes, for God's sake, take it!' they shouted.

Click.

The Blundens were to show this photograph in later years
to friends. 'Our Greek orgy,' Tim would say, forgetting the
details of reality. The friends would look at them with awe,
and Tina would lower her eyes at the memories it stirred.

Later as the sun was setting, they started the walk into the
town. Till now, they had walked along the path in a kind of
crocodile, two by two, in married pairs. This evening, Tim
noticed, by the time they reached the beach, the order had
somehow changed during the course of crossing the stone
walls. He had set off, somewhere in the middle of the file, with
Tina. Now he was at the end of the procession with Helga.
He congratulated himself, and began to plot.

He would get a stone in his shoe, that was a good idea.

She would stay behind to help him get it out. No, no, *she* would get a stone in *her* shoe, and he would help her get it out. She would lose her balance, he would catch her, the others would be out of sight. 'At last,' he would murmur sexily, and . . .

'You're quiet,' said Helga. She was glad to find herself walking beside Tim. Now that she knew that Alexander was with Tina, she thought she understood the purpose of Tim's sugar-borrowing visit to her in London. He must have known then, and had come to find out if she knew, to be consoled, perhaps, to share the hurt. She would have liked to talk to him now, to discover what exactly he was feeling. It was possible he felt in honour bound to make an overture to her; maybe this was what was expected of them, to tidy up the arrangement in the same way as the Paul, Polly, Jake, Margaret foursome. She wasn't sure. Sometimes she felt Timothy must want her, by his behaviour; at other times, she was certain he didn't want her at all. And, until she was certain, she would wait for him to clarify the situation. She was conscious now of being so much younger than the others, and not English.

Tim suddenly spoke. 'Have you got a stone in your shoe?' he blurted out.

'No,' she said. 'No, I don't think so.' She looked down at her thong sandals, and shook a foot in turn. 'No.'

'Sorry,' said Tim. 'I mean, I thought you were limping a bit.'

'Was I?' Helga straightened her back and walked on a little ahead of him. 'It's a horrid beach, isn't it,' she said.

'Tomorrow I want to get to the other one.'

'What other one?'

'Round the point,' She turned to wave in the direction of the promontory behind them, so that she could glance at Tim's face. 'Alexander and Tina went there today.' It seemed to her as though her voice had lifted the sentence and hung it in the evening air, pulsating with query and significance. She waited for Tim's reaction, which should tell her so much.

He didn't reply. Tina hadn't told him she had gone off for a swim. It had been their turn to shop and he had gone to the town on his own as Tina had complained of a headache. He felt it was rather rotten of Tina to get out of shopping because of a headache and then to go off for swim

142

instead. No wonder she hadn't told him. 'Mm,' he said, a quiet all-purpose, non-committal sound that told Helga nothing.

'There's a path to it from the back of our house,' said Helga, 'through the trees.'

They walked on, stepping carefully over patches of tar.

'It's sandy, I believe,' said Helga.

She *was* going on about this beach; it was almost as though she were inviting him to come with her tomorrow. Dare he pursue this? How should he do it? How about 'It sounds nice; I'll come with you, if I may?' Or, 'Let's go together tomorrow.' That was too bold. More subtle would be, 'We might go tomorrow.' That was safe. She could interpret the 'we' as a number of people, or, if she really wanted him and only him to join her, then she could interpret the 'we' as the two of them. Very clever.

Helga, in front of him, suddenly stopped and turned to look at him. He stumbled to an alarmed halt. 'Oh look!' she said, and he saw she wasn't looking at him but beyond him. 'Isn't it beautiful!'

He turned and saw the sun sliding down behind the point. It was *sunset*! One of his standard fantasy backcloths! Sunset over the sea, the girl beside him, evening quiet, gentle lapping of waves at his feet. Everything was in position, even the girl. He listened intently for the sounds of the others. He and Helga had reached the end of the beach, and the others had climbed up the path, and must be nearing the ruined building. In a moment or two, they would be out of sight. Pretending to ease his neck in the collar of his sweater, he moved his head to check. Yes, they were almost out of sight. With mounting excitement, he settled down to gaze unseeingly at the sun. Now, how did it go? Usually there was a swift transition from this position of gazing with the girl towards the sunset to the position of the clasp. But how was he to work that transition in practice? Perhaps, with the arm nearest Helga, he could make a general sweep in admiration of the scene, the colour of the water and so on, and, at the end of the sweep, bring in Helga, like a mechanical shovel. He had another, better idea. As a boy, he had often looked at things with his head on one side, even upside-down. This had given views a new perspective and added to their charm. He might tell Helga this and demonstrate it. Then, with his head bent over towards her, he could bring it up suddenly, and there he would be right beside her. No, too eccentric. What was needed at a moment like this was something suave on the lines of 'Yes, like you,' in murmured enraptured tones, as he moved in on her. That was it.

Now. *Action*. He drew in his breath sharply, barked 'YESLIKEYOU!' and began the moving in. She wasn't there! She'd gone! He looked all around, baffled. There was no sign of her. The sun had gone too. What an extraordinary thing. He checked all around him again, at all levels and in all directions, but there was no one on the beach, and no one on the path up the cliff. Had he really spent so long in the planning stages? Incredible. He rebuked himself for his lack of speed, but mildly, because in fact he was very pleased with himself for getting so far—and another time he would be ready.

He dusted and straightened his jacket, as though it were dissarrayed, and hurried after the others.

At the top of the cliff, a voice made him jump. But it wasn't Helga, it was Margaret, sitting on a wall of the ruin, waiting for him. Suddenly he was reminded of the Dictionary evening at her house, which his protracted pursuit of Helga had quite put out of his mind.

'It was a marvellous sunset, wasn't it?' she was saying as he came up beside her, and she held out her hand. Working it out later, he thought he had probably taken her hand and helped her down from the wall. And there they were, kissing. Easily, naturally. No trouble at all.

After a moment, they drew apart and smiled at each other.

'Margaret,' Tim said her name softly, with wonder.

'Tim,' she said, gently mimicking his tone of voice and laughing. They smiled at each other again in new recognition, and then kissed again, harder.

'Not enough,' he said eventually.

'Oh no, not nearly enough,' she agreed and taking his hand they began walking along the path into the town. 'Come and see me tomorrow at siesta time,' she said, in such a matter-of-fact tone of voice that Tim was doubtful as to what she meant. 'Wouldn't you like that?' she asked, made doubtful, too, by his hesitation.

'Yes,' he said, 'but how? What about—the others?'

'Don't worry,' she said. 'I'll arrange it.'

'But Tina? What can I say? And the house, it's so small—where can we go?'

'Don't worry,' she repeated. 'I'll arrange it. Just come to my room at about half past two.'

They walked on in silence, till they came to the steps leading down to the quay. 'You will, won't you?' she asked.

'Well, yes, but I really don't know how we'll manage it.'

'We will. You'll see.'

And then they joined the others, who were waiting for them at the bottom of the steps. They decided to find a new restaurant that evening.

'I've noticed,' said Jake, 'other foreigners going off into the back of the town somewhere; maybe they've found somewhere good.'

So, after a couple of glasses of ouzo and grilled octopus on the waterfront, they followed a group of young Germans into the back of the town, who, after meandering awhile in the twisting alleyways, led them to a pile of rubble and disappeared.

'This isn't a restaurant.'

'Yes, it is. They just haven't finished building it.'

'On the contrary,' said Paul. 'They haven't finished pulling it down.'

At last, finding a door, they went in and passed the most pleasant evening of their holiday so far. The menu was varied and they discovered a Samos wine that suited them better than the retsina they had tussled with previously. A tape-recorder was playing English and American pop-tunes continuously, and later on there was demented shrugging on the dance-floor. Only Tina was reluctant to be pleased with the place.

'It's not very *Greek*,' she said. 'I think the only people who are Greek are the waiters.'

'Come and dance,' said Jake, and led her to the floor where she stood battling with her rigidity, and valiantly shrugging alternate shoulders in time to the music. Much later, the Samos wine permeated down her body and her hips started to move too, though her smile grew more and more rigid.

They all danced, except Tim, who hated dancing; so he sat out, with a different girl each time, and drank more than the rest of them.

Consequently next morning he woke late with a monstrous hangover. He thought at first he was back at The Grove,

145

and from force of habit moved on waking into his fantasy world. He was on the bus with Helga. He was dancing with Polly. He was kissing—now *who* was this he was kissing? Margaret! This brought him wide awake. Hadn't this happened sometime? His head felt as though it were laid between a road and a pneumatic drill. With caution, he turned over on to his back, trying to avoid the drill, and lay there suffering. He hoped very much he wouldn't be sick. He would never be able to walk again. He would spend the rest of his life lying here in bed. He sank again into an uneasy sleep.

The next time he woke, the sun was full on his face. Did he feel a little better? It must be late. Tina was up. He didn't feel a little better. There were no noises in the house. Cicadas outside aggravated his headache. He knew something momentous had happened, but as yet he couldn't think what it was.

And then he remembered, and the memory astounded him. How had he managed it? Had it really happened? Yes, and she had asked him to go to her room that afternoon. Incredible, unlikely, absurd. He must have imagined it. Yet he knew he hadn't.

But it wasn't what he had planned at all. He wanted Helga, and had got Margaret. He lay in bed with his head aching, trying to get used to the idea that in the afternoon he would be lying in bed with Margaret. His imagination, which had produced for him so many occasions for infidelity, balked at this. He didn't think he could carry it through. Nor did he think they would have the opportunity to carry it through. It was too unreal. And he would be saved by Tina.

Feeling a little more confident and equipped to face the day, he gingerly got himself into a sitting position and focused on the room. It circled him for a while and then settled down into a gentle rocking. There was something small and white on the wardrobe door, going up and down. He wished it were evening, and cool, and time to go to bed again. He'd feel better by the evening. Perhaps he should stay in bed all day; there was no reason to get up. If he didn't appear, perhaps Margaret would forget their arrangement. But, on the other hand, if he stayed in bed, she might come for him. It would be better if he could get up, and spend the day in the shade of the olive trees somewhere, and then creep back at dark.

He stood up. Then sat down again. What was that on the wardrobe door? A large cabbage white? A pair of Tina's pants? A note? She had discovered all! She was leaving him.

Timothy—that would be how she'd begin—Timothy. It has now become clear that you are playing fast and loose not only with Helga but with Margaret too. I will not stay and be made a figure of ridicule, and have taken the boat back to Athens and my toothbrush. I have left you the tooth-paste and the equivalent of five shillings. Do not follow me. My mind is made up. I will remember the good times, and try to forget the bad. Your once-loving wife, Antonia.

Tears of sympathy for them both came to Tim's eyes. How sad it was. He would follow her at once, and try to make her understand that his affairs with the two women had been purely imaginative—it *was* a note! He got to his feet quickly, and tore it off the wardrobe door, to which it had been stuck with a small piece of Elastoplast. His heart thudded and his head swam. He sat down sharply, and tried to read the pencilled words which fluttered before his eyes.

'Timothy'. It did begin Timothy. 'Gone for a walk with J, P and A. Didn't wake you, you were sleeping so well. Hope you don't mind, didn't think you would. We're going up the mountain to the monastery. Don't think we'll be back for lunch. I've washed yr. shirt, pants, socks. Clean ones in suitcase. Luv, T. XXX.'

Gone for a walk with J, P and A. Who did that leave behind? M, H and Polly. Or Paul. Which P had gone? He hoped it was Polly, for his Alexander-Polly, Paul-Margaret, Helga-himself scheme. Perhaps Polly was willing to undergo a walk for the sake of being alone with Alexander; and Jake and Tina, too, of course, but they would be talking and perhaps get left behind.

Tim, with renewed interest in the day, got up and dressed in trunks and a shirt. He went through the kitchen and on to the terrace. The blinding sun sent him back for his dark glasses and a hat. Now, shielded against the sun, he looked into the saloni; it was deserted. He went round the house to the lavatory, and on his way out, met as usual the old woman and her jug. He grunted an approximation of Kalimera to her but as he moved away, she caught his arm and led him round to her front door, where she sat him down in a chair, and then disappeared inside. He sat dutifully where he was, hoping she wasn't dangerously mad. There was no one around to hear his cries for help; if she were to come at him with a knife . . . . but he was twice her size, he reminded himself. More likely, she would bring him a poisoned drink, she looked a little witch-like. Or perhaps, she didn't exist at all. This thought had crossed their minds before. When trying to find out who she was from Ourania and old Tony, they had met with shrugs, or long explanations which of course they couldn't understand; and Tony's English wasn't extensive enough to cope with what was obviously an involved explanation of the old woman's existence.

He decided it would be wise to get away now, before she emerged from the house. But, before he had time to do this, there she was at his side, holding out to him the *poisoned drink*. It was a tiny glass of evil green liquid, handed to him on a tray with an innocent glass of water. When he hung back, she urged him to take it, nodding vigorously at him.

What an unreal situation this was. Here he was, being poisoned by a witch, in the middle of an olive grove, miles from anywhere. He thought desperately of Joyce and Dolphin-headed notepaper, Merrivale High Street, Boots and Woolworths and Tesco.

Smiling sickeningly in the witch's direction, Tim raised the glass to his lips and pretended to sip. She grinned toothlessly and then looked concerned when she saw the glass was as full as ever. Obviously encouraging him to drink, she worked her mouth and sounds came out. He tried a smile again and a nod, holding the glass to his lips. She was now almost leaning over him in her anxiety for him to drink the stuff. He took a modest sip, resolved to hold it in his mouth until she looked away, when he would spit it out. She watched. He smiled at her with clenched lips. She patted his shoulder, and went on watching. He felt an ever-mounting urgency to swallow. The liquid was sticky and cloying and smelt sweetly threatening. Perhaps if he were to fall off his chair now, clutching his throat, she would assume the poision had had immediate effect, and then—what? Out with the knife to cut him up and put him in the pot?

With sick horror, he now saw her reach into her apron pocket. Out came the knife. With a shriek and a splutter and a choke, he was out of his chair and running, running for his life, past the house, through the trees, over walls, across fields, his head hammering with his heart.

Meanwhile, the old woman had bent to cut a sprig of louisa from the pot by her door. With difficulty she straightened and turned to see the fallen and abandoned chair and glass. She looked at them with mild wonder and shook her head. It only proved once more the madness of foreigners. The money was very nice, but she didn't think she would agree again to the letting of the house.

Tim didn't slow down till he came to the beach, where he saw Margaret, Paul and Helga. He flung himself down beside them and held his head, his lungs going like bellows.

'Heavens above,' said Margaret. 'And I thought you'd have a hang-over!'

'Magnificent,' said Paul. 'What an athlete. In the heat of the sun, too.'

'Hunh, hunh, hunh, hunh, hunh,' went Timothy. He waited till he had some breath, but when at last he could talk, he suddenly thought he might have been mistaken. On the beach, in the sane company of the others, witches and poison sounded improbable. 'I wanted a little exercise,' he said and then quickly got to his feet, and luckily reached the back of the beach before he was noisily sick.

A third of the way up the hill, Polly paused and looked longingly at a small shut-up and deserted-seeming cottage off the path to their right. An almond tree shaded its tiny courtyard. 'Shall we have a rest?' she suggested.

'A *rest*?' repeated Alexander, with derision. 'We've hardly started yet.'

'We've been walking for ages.'

'Thirty-five minutes actually,' said Alexander.

'Ages,' agreed Polly.

'Let's just go and see, it looks a dear little place,' said Tina and led the way. The others followed, all willingly except Alexander.

'This is the place,' said Jake. 'This is where I'd like to live.'

'And walk down to the town and up again for food?' asked Polly.

'No, I'd send my woman down for that.'

'Just look at that view. You can see other islands from here.'

'So you can.'

'That must be Naxos.'

'No, Syros.'

'Heavens no, we couldn't see that far. It's probably Anti-phyros,' said Tina.

'No, that's Antiphyros, over there.'

'I've opened the door,' said Polly behind them. They went to look in the house. It was just one small dark room and in one corner was a trestle bed and on the bed there was a mattress. Each one of them looked at it, immediately calculating how to get rid of the unwanted couple.

'Oh!' exclaimed Tina. 'A bed!' She blushed.

'Do you think someone lives here?' said Polly. They poked around for evidence of recent occupation, but there was none.

'Maybe whoever owns it comes for a rest when he's working on the hill. Or something,' suggested Jake.

'It wasn't locked, was it.'

'No, because there's no lock,' said Polly. 'There was this bamboo through the rings on each side of the door.'

'I don't think anyone has been here for ages. Look at the cobwebs.'

'The mattress feels damp.'

They wandered outside again and sat on the wall round the courtyard, silently plotting. Jake and Polly had been instructed by Margaret to be absent for as long as possible with Alexander and Tina. She had hoped that Helga and Paul would join them too but when it had become clear at breakfast that Helga was resolutely against the idea of a walk, Paul had been detailed to decoy Helga, Jake had suggested they should go up to look at the church or whatever it was on the top of the hill, and have lunch in the town for a change; and Alexander and Tina had fallen in with this idea happily enough. But now the hill seemed more like a mountain, Polly was wilting, here was a house and a bed. Jake wondered how he could arrange to stay here with Polly, making sure at the same time that Alexander and Tina went on up the hill and did not return to the house.

'I don't know,' he tried, I'd be quite happy to stay here and sketch or something—'

'On what? A thumb-nail sketch?' put in Polly. He frowned at her non-co-operation, and carried on. 'You go on up,' he said, looking at Alexander and Tina. 'I'll meet you in the town at the place where we ate last night.'

Neither Alexander nor Tina answered immediately. Alexander knew that Jake wanted to stay there with Polly. He had heard enough through the walls of the house to understand this. But, on the other hand, this was an ideal place for himself and Tina. How he could arrange this without drawing attention to them as a couple was beyond his powers of invention. However, to his relief, he saw that Tina was going into action. Rubbing her leg, she said, 'Ouch.'

'What is it?' he asked promptly.

'Oh, nothing. I think I've pulled a muscle or something.'

'Perhaps you'd better not walk much more,' he said. Now it was his turn. He went and sat under the almond tree. 'Funnily enough,' he said, before thinking it out fully, 'I've got a bit of an ache in the back of my—' He had been going to say leg, but thinking this was imitative, hesitated and said instead, 'head. Too much wine last night.'

Polly began laughing and lay down on the wall. 'Let's all stay here then. None of us want to go to the top.'

'I want to go!' protested Tina. 'I'd love to see the monastery. The French girls we talked to last night said it was terribly interesting. Very graphic, they said, *graphique*. It's just that I don't think I could make it.'

'Better not to strain your leg any more,' said Alexander.

Jake stood up decisively. 'Well, having got this far, I shall go on.' He subtly moved alongside Polly, and with one hand behind his back and hidden from the others, he prodded her. 'Who's coming?' he asked. Prod.

'Yes,' said Tina. 'You lot go on. I'll be quite happy here, rest it a bit, and then meet you in the town.'

'Er,' said Alexander. 'I think one of us had better stay with you. Just in case it seizes up or something. Muscles seize up sometimes. You might not be able to walk.'

Jake prodded Polly again and, groaning slightly, she heaved herself into sitting position and then off the wall. Her face a blank mask of innocence, she said, 'Quite right. I'll stay with Tina, and you two go on.'

Horrid girl, thought Jake, to tease them so. Or did she not realise they wanted to stay together?

They all waited for Alexander to say his bit, Jake in sympathy for him, Tina in agony lest he were unable to follow it through. At last he said, 'I think it had better be a man. Just in case. I'll stay.' His voice sounded despairing under the strain.

'Well,' said Jake, relieved that Alexander had managed it, 'all right then. We'll meet at the restaurant, in a couple of hours I should imagine.' He moved off towards the path, and Polly followed. She turned to wave. 'Hope you'll be all right,' she called to Tina.

'Oh yes,' Tina called back, and then quickly began to massage her leg again. 'Don't worry. Have a good time.'

'Same to you,' said Polly.

When they were out of earshot, Jake said, 'You were cruel. Didn't you realise?'

'Of course. I've suspected as much since we arrived. But I thought they ought to work for it.'

'What convolutions! We all wanted the house—we should have tossed for it.'

'Certainly. And now, out of your charity, here we are, out in the midday sun, walking. Exiles. You don't seriously imagine I'm going to the top, do you?'

'What time are we allowed back?' asked Jake.

'Margaret said four, if we can drag it out that long.'

'Four! And all for the sake of expansion.'

'In any case, it's all gone wrong now.'

'Has it?' Jake looked surprised. 'How?'

Polly paused and looked back. 'Have we come far enough? Let's sit down here.'

'No. Come on. We may find another deserted cottage, you never know. How has it gone wrong?'

'With Alexander and Tina, of course, don't you see? They are obviously having an affair.'

'An affair?' Jake sounded like an outraged father.

Polly laughed. 'Well, what do you imagine they're doing down there? Playing noughts and crosses?'

'Don't be absurd!'

'What I mean is that they are together in quite the wrong way, from our point of view. At least Tina is, by the look of her. She is really involved with Alexander, I should imagine, and I felt sorry for her; because I don't suppose Alexander is approaching it in quite the same manner. In any case, their approach is not at all suitable for us.'

'Oh. Isn't it?'

'Then, another thing. Margaret's plan was that we should bring in the Blundens first. She is doing Tim, and you were supposed to be doing Tina.'

'I wasn't supposed to be doing Tina!' He sounded cross.

'What were your instructions then?'

'Well.' Jake hesitated. 'she just said that she had done stage one with Tim, and that she would appreciate it if we

152

could all be out of the house for as long as possible today. She said we could leave the permutation until discussion at breakfast-time with the others.'

'And then Paul and Helga didn't come with us, so it was obvious you had to do Tina. Can't we stop here?' Polly stopped.

'No,' said Jake, carrying on up the path which was growing steeper. 'I don't want to do Tina. I'd much rather Alexander did her. I'm quite happy with you. Lazy, I suppose. Laissez-faire, status quo. Helga now . . . that would be different. I would rather like—'

'Thank you!' said Polly, panting behind him. 'Thank you so much.' She was suddenly sickened by their bartering approach to sex, envious of Alexander's and Tina's romantic liaison, jealous of the way Jake was talking of Helga. 'You go on,' she said, her voice cold in contrast to her flushed face. 'I shall spend the day here.' She looked around for a suitably flat and shady place. But the hillside here was barren and precipitous. They had climbed higher than she had planned, and were out of protective trees. She wiped her face with her handkerchief, cleaned her sunglasses which kept slipping down her nose. 'This is torture,' she said. 'I didn't even bring my hat!' She eased her feet out of her canvas shoes. '*Look*! Just look at this.' On the back of each ankle puffed an angry-red blister. '*Oh*!' It was all Jake's fault. Rage suddenly welled in her against the sun, the stones, the thistles; against Paul who was having a lazy day with Helga, against Margaret who was in the cool of the house with Tim, against Alexander and Tina who were in *love*; against Jake who had dragged her up a mountain and given her blisters. She cursed and hated them all, the whole sordid lot of them. 'Leave me alone!' she shrieked at Jake, who had come to sit beside her. 'Leave me ALONE!'

Jake looked at her, astounded. He had never heard her raise her voice before. He made to put an arm around her shoulders and ask what was the matter, but she had sprung to her feet. Her body rigid, she bent with her hands on her knees, her fingers outstretched, her face contorted, in an attitude of wild defence. 'Don't touch me!' she screamed.

They listened with wonder as the cry reverberated from the crags above them. Neither of them moved for a moment; both were astonished by the force of anger which had burst from Polly. Then, with an indrawn sob, she turned and began stumbling hurriedly down the path. Jake watched her go. He didn't attempt to follow. He always left his children alone when they had tantrums—there was nothing one could do. After a while, he got to his feet, and continued the climb. At least he might as well reach the monastery.

On the beach, Timothy was being sick; and Margaret, Paul and Helga hovered behind him, being solicitous. When it seemed to be over, he straightened and took stock of himself, looking unseeingly ahead while he checked his internal feelings.

'Better?' asked Margaret.

'Have my hat,' said Paul. 'Lie in the shade.'

'There is no shade,' said Helga. 'He'd feel better if he went in the water.'

'He shouldn't go in the water in this state. He would do better going back to the house to lie down,' said Margaret. She was concerned about the chances for the afternoon. It would be unfortunate, having made such elaborate arrangements, if Tim was going to be ill.

Tim shuddered and then apologised. 'I must sit down,' he said and Margaret spread a towel for him, Paul gave him his hat, and Helga asked, 'It was the wine?'

'It was the running,' said Paul.

'How do you feel now?' Margaret asked, sitting beside him and lightly touching his arm.

'Better, I think,' he said.

'I am relieved,' she said softly and smiled at him.

'At least,' he said quickly and swallowed, 'a little better at the moment, but I don't know if it will last.'

'Oh *dear*,' said Margaret.

'I have Entro-Vioform at the house. Shall I get you some?' asked Helga.

'Ah,' said Tim. Maybe he shouldn't take anything and stay safely ill all day. 'Thank you. But don't bother to get it. I think I'll go back in a moment and lie down.'

'All right,' said Helga. 'I'll come back with you and find it.'

Margaret stepped in quickly. 'Don't bother. I was going back in any case in a moment. I'll give Tim something.'

Helga looked at Margaret with a slight and quizzical smile.

Paul gazed out to sea.

Tim said, 'I don't take pills much actually. I think I'd prefer to sleep it off.'

'We have Eno's,' said Margaret. 'Eno's would do you the world of good.'

'Yes,' said Paul turning now to Tim. 'Let Margaret give you a dose of Eno's.'

'No, really, really,' said Tim and clambered to his feet. 'I don't need anything, just a good sleep.' He would get away quickly, reach the safety of his room and lock the door. He staggered off.

Margaret got swiftly to her feet. 'I think I'd better go with him.'

'Maybe you had,' said Paul.

'You two,' said Margaret, 'will be having lunch in the town I expect.'

'Oh,' said Helga, 'I thought you said there was enough in the house for us four.'

'Yes, but I checked again and we've only one tin of sardines and no bread. You have lunch in town. I'd better stay with Tim.' She glared at Paul.

'All right,' he said dutifully, 'we'll see you after lunch.'

Margaret followed Tim.

There was silence on the beach. Helga sat with her knees drawn up under her chin and brooded thoughtfully at the sea. Paul lay down, turned slightly towards her, his legs crossed and his weight propped on one elbow. He watched her. After some time, he said, 'Odd how this beach is always deserted.'

She turned to look at him, and began laughing. He felt suddenly foolish, as though she had seen through the plan and understood the subtle arrangements. Impossible!

Then she stopped laughing and said, quite solemnly, 'Yes, everyone goes to the beach the other side of the town. It's much nicer. Sandy, like the one over there.' She pointed beyond the promontory.

'Oh,' said Paul. 'I didn't know there was another beach that side.' He looked at her, a little disturbed by the way her mouth twitched as though against a smile. 'Shall we go and look at it?' he suggested.

Now she did smile. '*Look* at it?' she repeated and paused. 'I think perhaps we mustn't.'

'Mustn't?' He really didn't know where he was with Helga. Did she know what he had in mind? Might she mean mustn't morally?

'That is where Alexander and Tina go,' said Helga.

'Alexander and Tina?' repeated Paul. He sat up to cope with this.

'Yes,' said Helga. 'Of course they may not be there today, as they said they would climb the hill. But they may have left Jake and Polly to climb the hill, and have gone to the sandy beach—as usual.'

'But . . . but . . .' began Paul, floundering. What was all this? Jake was meant to be having Tina today, what was Alexander up to? And how was it that Alexander's wife was calmly telling him this? '*Alexander* and Tina?' he asked.

'Oh yes. Didn't you know?'

Paul shook his head, amazed. After a pause, he said, 'You mean, Tina and—?' Her expression placidly confirmed this. 'Oh,' he said, adjusting. Then, 'But—don't you *mind*?'

'Oh yes, I do. I mind,' said Helga. 'But it's better to wait. It will be over soon.' She ran her hand over the shingle, and began picking out small shells. 'And luckily, I am very happy to be on my own. So please,' she said slowly, choosing her words carefully now, 'don't feel obliged to look after me today. It has been arranged so well, and I will be good and stay out of the way. In fact,' she went on, getting to her feet and taking a dress out of her bag, 'I shall go for a walk. I am certain none of the others will reach the monastery—especially as this was not the purpose of the expedition—so I think I will go there myself.' She pulled the dress over her head.

Paul sat and watched, dazed.

She emerged from the dress and tugged it down over her bikini. 'If you would please do the zip,' she asked and knelt down beside him with her back towards him. As he fumbled, she said, 'You asked if I mind. I can ask you the same. Do you mind about Jake and Polly?'

Paul's hands fell from their task. She knew this too! 'Christ!' he exclaimed.

'I suppose that yours is a little different. But you must feel jealous when you know they are together, even if you do have Margaret. Have you done it?' she asked, her hand feeling her back.

He carried on zipping.

'Thank you,' she said and stood up, 'What is the time?'

'Oh, er,' said Paul and looked at his watch. 'Eleven-thirty.'

'Well, I may be down again by lunchtime. In which case, I'll see you in the restaurant.'

She shook her hair, and slipped into her shoes. Picking up

her bag, she stood for a moment swinging it. 'Well,' she said, turning to leave, 'have a nice morning.'

Paul suddenly came to life, after his shock. He stretched out a hand to stay her. 'Don't go,' he said. There was so much he wanted to ask her now, but she was walking away, her footsteps on the shingle drowning his voice. 'Helga!' he called. She half-turned to wave, and then walked on. He watched her beautiful legs picking their way carefully over the pebbles. What he had missed! He wanted to know all about her, how old was she? How was she so composed and shrewd? How did she know all about them? Why had she married Alexander? What sort of life had she had to produce such a cool tolerance? Did she love Alexander? Could she love *him*? What would she be like in bed? How old was she, for heaven's sake? Did she like him? He desired her enormously now. But he wouldn't follow her. He knew it would be no good.

He lay back on the beach, feeling disgruntled, curious, hot and abandoned. Tim had taken his hat. Crossly, he arranged towels over his head and legs. On his own! Not allowed back to the house. Margaret with Tim, Jake with Polly, Alexander with *Tina*! Helga walking, and he roasting. What a mess.

Margaret, in fact, was not with Timothy. There was a barred door between them. She had knocked and called, 'May I come in?' and there had been no answer. She had listened and heard exaggeratedly heavy breathing. Later she had gone to the lengths of mixing a glass of Eno's and bringing it to the door. 'I've brought you a glass of Eno's!' she called, and again she was answered by heavy breathing.

Giving up, she went and sat in the shade of the vine on the terrace with a book, on which she was unable to concentrate. She waited and listened.

Tim, lying not five yards from her, waited and listened too. He felt a good deal better now physically, but mentally he was if not ill then disturbed. What should he do? Did he want Margaret? Yes. Should he have Margaret? Why not? Just once wouldn't matter. He wouldn't get involved with her. What did he feel about being unfaithful to Tina? He had, after all, been unfaithful to her so often in his imagination, that to do it once without her knowledge in real life would be nothing. Perhaps it would be a good thing, he

157

thought; if he did it in reality, it might appease his imagination, and instead of indulging in fantasies in the future, he would be much more attentive to his wife. There; he had found a marvellous justification. He felt instantly resolved, happy and soothed. He settled his head more comfortably on the pillow, and fell into a deep, peaceful sleep.

By two o'clock, Margaret was hungry and irritable. She knocked again, loudly, on Tim's door. There was no answer. In the kitchen she found two tins of sardines but no keys. She picked up a tin opener, and then threw it down in disgust. Instead, she went into her room, pulled on a skirt and blouse over her swimsuit, and left the house, banging the door shut behind her.

Polly sat in the restaurant, feeling cool and calm. When Jake came in, she smiled at him. 'Sorry, my love, about that,' she said. 'I don't know what got into me.' And then she saw Helga behind him. 'Oh, hello,' she said, surprised.

Jake added more chairs to Polly's table, and they sat down. 'Helga decided to see the monastery too.'

'It's beautiful,' said Helga, leaning her elbows on the table. 'There are no monks, though.'

'How was it I didn't see you then?' asked Polly.

'I went by the path from the back of the town. It's quicker.'

'Oh God, the way we went was ghastly,' said Polly. 'I gave up.'

'A pity,' said Helga. 'It's worth seeing. The view is marvellous.'

'And there are some fantastic ikons—'

'Where's Paul then?' asked Polly, cutting in.

'Oh, he stayed on the beach, he'll be here soon,' said Helga.

'I see,' said Polly.

'In fact, here he is,' said Jake. They turned to look at the entrance as Paul came in. He exuded heat.

'Whew!' he said, collapsing in a chair at their table. 'Water.' Polly handed him her glass. 'Tim took my hat.' He scratched his beard. 'I'll have to shave this off. It's unbearable.'

Jake asked Polly if she had ordered any food.

'No,' replied Polly. 'I thought I'd wait for you.'

'Well, let's order now, shall we. What have they got?'

'Shouldn't we wait for the others?' asked Paul.

They looked at each other, working out who was missing; and then when they had worked this out, they all said in a

158

different way that they didn't think it was worth waiting.

A waiter brought them a menu, and they were studying its translated oddities when Margaret walked in. Polly, sitting opposite the door, saw her first. 'Margaret!' she exclaimed.

'Margaret?' repeated Jake, turning in amazement.

'Yes, it is Margaret,' said Helga. They all watched her approach and then sit down with a thump.

Their hellos trailed questions. Margaret's hello was brusque. 'What's to eat?' she asked and took the menu. While they talked about the choice of food, Paul leant across to Margaret and asked in a low voice if she'd had a good morning. The others immediately stopped talking to hear her reply.

'No, rather dull,' she said. 'What about yours?'

Paul cleared his throat, embarrassed by Helga's expression as she waited for his answer. Then he said, 'It could have been better,' and looked at Helga; but she was now turned to the doorway.

'And here come the others,' she said. They watched Alexander and Tina come in. Tina was carrying a bunch of thistles, all she could find on the hillside.

'Oh, are we late?' Tina asked, sitting down flushed and breathless. 'I simply had no idea of the time.'

'One doesn't,' said Helga.

There was some shuffling of chairs as they settled down. Then Margaret turned to Alexander and asked conversationally, 'How was the monastery?'

He was unable to reply at once; but Jake said for him, 'Tina twisted her ankle—'

Polly said, 'Pulled a muscle.'

Tina said, 'Strained my leg.'

'—and,' went on Jake, 'Alexander stayed behind with her.'

'I didn't think it would be wise to go on up,' said Tina.

'Very wise,' said Margaret. 'I mean, it wouldn't have been wise. . . . Pretty thistles.'

'Aren't they,' said Tina, and hid them under her chair. 'Where's Tim?'

'Asleep,' said Margaret.

'Still asleep?' Tina looked at her watch. 'Well I never.'

'He came to the beach, but was sick,' said Paul.

'A terrible hang-over, poor lad,' said Margaret.

'Very fortunate,' said Jake.

'Oh dear,' said Tina and helped herself to some bread. As she tore a piece off, she saw Alexander put his hand on Helga's arm and rub it gently while he said something to her in a low voice. She felt an unpleasant twinge of jealousy. He had obviously asked Helga about her morning, because now Helga replied in a clear voice, looking straight at Tina, 'Yes, I had a very good time. What about you?'

Alexander managed to mumble, 'Quite nice,' but Tina choked on her bread.

CHAPTER NINE

After this, the foursome gave up all thoughts of expansion. In fact, with a tact that approached distant politeness, they chose to spend more time in their appointed pairs. Jake began sketching, and Margaret sat beside him with a book, on the quay, in the town's small streets, or among the olive trees, Paul and Polly spent a lot of time hunting for objects which they could sell for double the price in their shop.

Timothy took to his bed. After his hang-over and his long sleep, he had woken with a hammering headache and a slight temperature. They suspected sunstroke, gave him aspirin, and advised rest and shade. Although the following day he hadn't felt too ill, he had come to the conclusion that this was as pleasant a way to spend a holiday as any. The others brought him books and sympathy and fresh lemonade; and then left him in peace. By the evening he felt capable of joining them for the evening meal, and Tina would hold his arm and help him into town. It was very pleasant and undemanding.

On the third day of his illness, Margaret brought him his lemonade about eleven in the morning. She sat on the edge of his bed, and asked him how he felt.

'I'm sorry about the other afternoon,' he said to her.

She smiled at him. 'So am I.' She smoothed down his sheet in an absent-minded and maternal way. 'But maybe it was just as well.'

Tim felt relieved.

'Is there enough sugar in it?' she asked.

'It's delicious. Thank you,' he said.

'Like the window open more?' she asked.

'It bangs. It seems very windy today.'

'Yes. It's a horrid north-west wind. Everything's blowing around.'

'Where is everyone?' asked Tim.

'In the town, I think. Jake's sketching at the back here—True Niagara is posing for him.'

'Tina was going shopping.'

'Yes,' said Margaret.

'I suppose it's rather rotten for her—' began Timothy. 'My being ill. I hope she's not too fed up, bored.'

'I shouldn't worry,' said Margaret. 'It's not as if she's on her own . . .'

'No,' said Tim and began to feel excited by Margaret's proximity.

'I should think you are the one who's bored,' said Margaret. 'Have you enough to read? Shall I find you a magazine or something?'

Her hand rested close to his shoulder.

'No, I've got masses to read. You're looking after me very well.' He moved and caught her hand. As he pulled her down towards him, he thought with wonder how easy it was with Margaret.

'Oh, Tim,' she said before they kissed. But she was withholding from him and, after a moment, he let her go.

'No?' he asked.

She shook her head with a regretful smile. 'No,' she said. 'Better not, in lots of ways.' She got up, and made a business of arranging a chair near the bed as a bedside table. 'You know, you'd do better elsewhere.'

Tim looked startled. What *did* she mean?

'Can I get you anything else? Water? Aspirin?'

'No, no. I'm fine, thank you,' said Tim.

'Well, then I'll leave you in peace. I'll join Helga—she's alone a lot . . .' She glanced at Tim's face, pursed her lips in a kiss, and closed the door behind her.

Helga. Back to Helga. If only he could manage Helga as easily as he could Margaret. Tomorrow he would get up and try.

The following day Tina climbed out of bed, not to disturb Tim. It was early. It was her turn to leave the house first. Alexander would join her at the cottage on the hill later in the morning, whenever he could slip away. She took her things to dress in the kitchen, and tiptoed out of the room. Tim watched her through his eyelashes.

Ten minutes later, in she came again, very quietly, and put a note on the chair by the bed. She glanced at herself in the wardrobe mirror, twisting to see her back view; then, with a wet finger, she smoothed her eyebrows, stepped back, sighed, and left the room again, as quietly as she had entered. Tim waited till he heard her go across the terrace and down the steps, and then stretched for the note.

'*Darling Tim*,' this time. She seemed almost enthusiastic in her sympathy for his illness, she who never believed other people were really ill. 'Do hope you feel a bit better. I'm going for a long walk today, want to see a bit of the island (getting a wee bit bored!). Only got 3 aspirin left, so only take them if you really need them. I know you said you felt better last night, but I should stay in bed till you are absolutely O.K. The sun is vicious, luv, T.'

What luck! Tim sprang out of bed, full of energy and good health. He dressed with care and went to shave. This took a long time as, for the appearance of his illness, he hadn't shaved for the last few days. He was sitting in the shade on the terrace when the others appeared by degrees.

'Well! Timothy!' they exclaimed. 'What a surprise.'

'You're better!'

'Want a coffee?'

'Or lemonade?'

'Bread and marmalade? We've found a proper orange marmalade, quite bitter and nice.'

Tim said he might be able to manage coffee and a little bread; and in the end got through a good deal. They fell to discussing plans for the day, to which Tim listened intently. Paul and Polly were going to the town in search of old lamps; Jake was going to carry on with his drawing of the old woman; Margaret said she would be pottering around; Alexander was non-committal. Helga ws going to the sandy beach.

'Won't you come?' she asked Alexander.

He took a sip of his coffee. 'I might,' he said. 'I'd prefer a walk actually. Like to come for a walk?'

She looked at him, without replying; and then went into their room.

Tim was in suspense; everything looked so promising. He must encourage Alexander to go for a long walk. 'Tina,' he said, swallowing hard on his bread, 'has gone for a long walk, she wants to see something of the island. She didn't leave so long ago, you might catch her up.'

The silence of the others seemed to convey a shared suspense.

'Oh, er, has she?' said Alexander to his cup of coffee.

'Yes, I saw her setting off,' said Margaret. 'She went that way.' She pointed in the general direction of the hill behind the house.

'Oh well, er, I might—' mumbled Alexander.

Tim took a deep breath and said boldly, 'If you went now, you'd catch her up.'

Alexander glanced quickly and curiously at Tim, but Tim had turned all his attention to scraping the last of his marmalade on to bread.

The others seemed to be waiting for Alexander to get up and leave. He got up. 'Well, then, I'll be off.' He tucked his shirt into his trousers, and adjusted the belt. He glanced into his room and called to Helga, 'Sure you won't come?' There was no answer to this hypocrisy, and he turned and made for the door, hesitantly.

'Have a good time,' said Polly.

'Er, thanks,' said Alexander. 'Same to you.'

'Will you be back for lunch?' asked Margaret. 'We've eggs and cheese and grapes.'

'Oh yes, I think we, I'll be back by then.' He lifted a hand in a vague salute, and went out on to the terrace. He paused and sniffed. 'It's a lovely day.'

'Good,' said Margaret, after him. 'Bye.'

'Bye,' He went away down the steps at last.

The others leant back against their chairs, exchanging smiles and glances. Tim sensed a definite relaxation of tension, though he thought he was probably attributing to the general atmosphere his own internal feelings.

Paul and Polly made movements to leave now. But they took even longer about it. Polly had to find her hat, her dark glasses, and change in and out of several pairs of shoes. Paul was hunting in their suitcase for their money which seemed lost. Jake left the table to get his drawing things ready.

'Hey,' said Margaret, left alone at the table with Tim, 'it's not my turn to wash up. I did it yesterday and the day before.'

'Leave it till after lunch,' said Jake.

'Then we get flies and ants after it, and I end up doing it in any case.'

163

'*I'll* do it,' said Tim, with the nobility of unaccustomed servitude.

'Yes,' said Margaret promptly. 'It's certainly your turn.'

Helga now appeared and began piling up plates. 'I'll help,' she said. She and Tim set to work, carrying the things out to the kitchen. 'Now don't break anything!' she told him, laughing.

'I'll try not to,' he said and laughed as well.

What bliss this was, he thought, as Helga handed him soapy plates to dry. When they had finished, the house was deserted. He was alone with Helga, alone with Helga, alone with Helga—he clung to the drying-up cloth, as though to a pillar for support.

'Well,' said Helga briskly. 'I think I am going now.'

Tim watched with alarm as she began unbuttoning her short and frilly housecoat. He tried to turn away, but couldn't. However, underneath she wore a white bikini. He was relieved, far more relieved than disappointed.

'Do you feel all right?' she asked, in concern.

'Oh yes,' he said abruptly. 'Quite all right. I think I might. I think a swim. I think I could.'

'Come too? Please do. Take a hat,' said Helga. 'There is shade at that beach, pine trees. I think you'll be all right.'

Alexander joined Tina in the deserted cottage.

'Well done,' said Tina. 'You're early.'

'Tim's up,' said Alexander.

'Heavens!' said Tina, looking towards the door in alarm. 'Are we safe?'

'Oh yes. I think so. He won't be going out of the house, I shouldn't think.' He sat down on the bed beside her. 'Do you know, it was rather funny. He actually sent me to find you!'

'Sent you? How do you mean?'

'Encouraged me to join you. Said you'd gone for a walk, and why didn't I catch you up!' Alexander was laughing, but Tina looked worried.

'So,' said Alexander, turning to her, 'let me follow your husband's instructions. Let me catch you up.'

He put his hands on her shoulders, still laughing, and she recoiled. The day before the touch of his hands had excited her; now, as he laughed at her husband his hands were a stranger's, heavy and insensitive. She gazed at his face with incredulous distaste as he described the scene at breakfast, Tim's innocent encouragement of their affair —'Fancy!' he said with renewed laughter, 'fancy sending me to find you!' He kissed her neck and didn't notice her skin cringe. And, because he didn't notice, and because she was paralysed by shock at the reversal in her feelings, she allowed him to undress her and lie down with her on the damp mattress. As he made love, her feeling of revulsion towards this stranger grew. She longed for Tim. The enormity of her offence struck her for the first time, its daring, careless boldness. It was as though she had been pedalling a bike happily along with her eyes fixed ahead. Now she had looked down and seen that it was not a road beneath her but a tightrope. Her desire for Alexander had provided a convenient obstacle to rational thought. Now that this desire had dissolved, she could see her situation and behaviour objectively.

And Helga knew.

Of course Helga knew. 'Next time try an inland path,' she heard Helga say; 'and did *you* have a nice time?' Tina now realised that she had been aware of this for some days, but until now it hadn't suited her to admit so much to herself. She felt sickened, burning with shame. How *could* she have done it? At last she put her hands on Alexander's shoulders and pressed him away, and at last he realised. 'What's wrong? he asked, lifting his head.

She began to cry. All she could say was, 'I'm sorry, I'm sorry,' and she struggled to roll away.

'Tina! What's wrong?'

'I can't, I'm sorry, I'm sorry.' She got away from him, and began hunting for her clothes. Alexander sat up and watched her, irritation and incomprehension crossing his face.

'What's happened?' he kept repeating. 'What have I done?'

But Tina could only say, 'I'm sorry,' and fight her way into her clothes, to get away down the hill, and back to Timothy. She wouldn't be able to face Helga again. Could she get Tim to leave? They must get away, back to England, back to Ricky, to The Grove. Home. How could she persuade Tim without telling him anything? Could she perhaps use Ricky as an excuse? How would she manage it?

She was dressed now and shuffling into her shoes. She didn't turn to look at Alexander. She couldn't bear to face his injured and baffled expression which demanded an

165

explanation she couldn't give. She hardly knew herself yet what had happened. All she knew was she must get away from him, from them all, and back to safe normality. Then she was out of the house, and stumbling down the hill in the burning sun.

Tim and Helga lay in the shade of a pine tree on the sand. A light breeze moved through the tree above them every so often and they smelt the pine. They could hear the occasional goat-bell. The beach was so perfect, it seemed unreal. Perhaps because of this, Tim didn't find it at all hard to lean quietly over Helga and kiss her.

They kissed for a long time, exploringly, gently, almost sadly; and then slowly they undressed and made love. Later, they lay back and saw the sky through the pine tree, and they heard more goat-bells.

They were silent.

For Tim, the situation and setting which had seemed so unreal, had come alive. His senses were sharpened to unaccustomed awareness. It was as though a layer of membrane had been gently pulled away from each of his senses, to give him his first experience of reality. He felt the sand packed firm beneath his body, pushing at each bone; the rough texture of his maroon-coloured towel separated his back from the sand, but his legs were on the sand, forming channels down the sides of which rivulets of glitter eddied when he stirred, its substance powdered crystal. He lay on his side, propped on one elbow which dug through the towel, through the sand to connect with the centre of the earth. He heard silence that was not silence; a heavy humming in the dome of air under which they lay, a bell-jar that preserved time, in which insects distantly flew, on which silver spoons distantly struck. He smelt pine and Helga. He saw Helga. But not the Helga of his imagination. The girl that lay beside him was a stranger, a friend of many years, a sister, someone he had loved in another age, someone he had just met. She lay on her back, her hair framing her face, her face turned towards him. Her hair was corn-coloured on the blue towel beneath her. The tanned skin of her face was covered by a down of minute fair hairs. The plane of her forehead sloped back under her hair and depressed in two pennies either side of her eyes, which were connected by the long loop of her cheeks and chin, creating a pure oval. Her mouth looked upside-down, the longer being the upper lip, an impression exaggerated when she smiled, as she did now, a half-formed, pleased smile, which pulled the skin of her nose into pleats towards the bridge and puckered the nostrils, and gave her round chin a tuck in the centre. She had spots and an incipient moustache.

'Don't look at me so,' she said, 'I know I've got spots.'

To obliterate this prosaic announcement from her upside-down lips, Tim leant over her and kissed her. Then they got up and went into the water. It was cold; refreshing but cold.

'I hope,' said Helga, 'you didn't do that because you felt you had to.'

Her words were more shocking than the temperature of the water.

'*Had* to?' repeated Tim, incredulous.

His expression reassured her, but the damage was done, because he now insisted on knowing what she had meant.

'To be tidy,' she said at last.

'Tidy?'

'Because of the others, of course.' She couldn't believe that Tim didn't know.

'The others?' he asked, as though by repetition he could extract the meaning.

'You mean,' said Helga, amazed, 'you don't know?' She turned to look at his face. 'No, you don't know,' she said in wonder, and resolved to say no more. But Timothy was persistent and eventually she gave in. 'Well, there is the Paul and Polly, Jake and Margaret, how would you say, arrangement—'

'Oh yes,' said Timothy. 'I know they are always together. They're very old friends.'

'Swapping, that's the word,' said Helga, remembering an article she had read—North Country Judge says Wife-Swapping in South Led Wife to Prostitution.

'Swapping!' repeated Tim, astounded. The word, with its boyhood association of marbles and conkers, shocked Timothy as much as its implications with the four he thought he knew quite well. And Margaret was involved! And Polly. And had Margaret planned to bring in himself? Had it been like that? He hardly noticed that Helga was continuing.

'—and so that leaves us four, Alexander and Tina, you and me.'

Not comprehending the significance of the way she had linked the names, Tim said, 'Well. Let them do what they like . . .' The hardest part was to reconcile this news about Margaret with the brief and unfulfilled rapport between them. 'Even if I had known about them, I wouldn't have felt I *had* to—' He glanced back at the beach.

'I am very glad,' said Helga, smiling at him, and holding out a hand to him. He took it and rubbed the palm with his thumb. 'I am glad. Because I thought perhaps you might have done it out of jealousy.'

'No. Why on earth? Why should I be jealous?' Did she know about Margaret? 'Let them do what they like, why should it worry me?'

Helga was astounded by his tolerance. 'It worries *me*,' she said. 'I hate to think of Alexander and Tina together.'

Tim went white. *Alexander and Tina.* He felt sick from shock. He gripped Helga's hand, but she receded. The image of Tina with Alexander filled his vision. Tina, his wife, and Alexander, so polite. 'If you go now, you may catch her up.' He had sent Alexander after her this morning. Where were they? He began pushing his way through the sea back to the shore, his mind a hot, confused jumble of thoughts. Tina in London, Tuesday afternoon shopping, had she been with Alexander then? How had he not noticed? How could he have been so blind? He would find them together, he would shock them to their senses, he would hurl Alexander down the mountain-side. How would he face Tina; he didn't want to see her. But he would punch Alexander in the guts, punch him till he crumpled.

Timothy reached the shore, and now free of the restraining sea, calmed down. He saw himself doing it much more subtly. He would fling open the door—which door? where were they?—and there they were in bed, horror on their faces. He would pause a second, and then say with icy restraint, 'Oh, excuse me,' and shut the door quietly. That would make them squirm in their guilt.

He stumbled up the beach to the shade of the pine, and bent to pick up his towel. It smelt of Helga's sun lotion. He sat down suddenly and resting his arms on his knees, laid his forehead on the backs of his hands, Guilt! He was guilty too. Not just because of this morning with Helga, but guilty of neglect, guilty of too fertile an imagination. If he hadn't spent so much time imagining his own infidelity, he would have been able to see his wife's; even perhaps to have prevented his wife's. But—Tina and Alexander; the thought sickened him with jealousy yet again. His reason fought with his emotion and he banged his head against his knuckles.

Helga swam, gazing back at the beach, leaving Tim alone in his misery. She felt sorry for him and regretted, selfishly too, her inadvertent question that had caused it.

Tina hurried down the hillside, but the difficulty of the path which demanded concentration composed her mind. She felt her sudden withdrawal from Alexander had been needlessly abrupt. She wished she had been able to end it more gently, explain to him the reasons for the swift reversal of her feelings. But as yet she hardly knew herself what she was feeling, let alone the causes. All she was certain of was revulsion; against herself, against Alexander. She wanted to become again the person she was six months beforehand, Tina Blunden, mother of Ricky, wife of Timothy, her parents' daughter. She longed suddenly to be sitting before her dressing-table with its china roses of childhood. She wanted to get home, above all.

After a while, Timothy got to his feet, and picked up his towel. He didn't know what he was going to do. He stood for a moment, and looked out at Helga. He waved briefly, and she waved back. Then he turned, and began walking.

As he walked back along the sand and in among the olive trees, he felt a calm resolution. He would say nothing to Tina. He would wait until she came back to him of her own accord. He had no right to expect more. He was as guilty as she. And when she came back, he would give her all his attention. No longer would he dream. He would keep his mind fixed on reality. He would concentrate more on his work, too. He would get a rise. They would move to a bigger house, in the country perhaps. More children. They wouldn't want to stay at The Grove with—the others. He felt almost happy as he walked along.

Near the house, where his path met the one from the hill, he paused and looked about him. The beauty of the place struck him for the first time, and he stretched to touch the twisted ancient trunk of an olive tree. To his left, he could see through to the distant line of bamboos which hid the sea. Ahead and hovering in the resounding blueness of the atmosphere rose the clear crags of the hill. What lay beyond? What of the rest of the island? He chided himself for his ignorance. All he had seen was the town and two beaches. It was typical of his life. How much he had lost.

Tina, coming down the path, saw him first and stopped. She wanted to run straight into his arms, but restrained the impulse, which, being unusual, might give her away. Tim looked up and she walked slowly towards him.

'Oh!' said Tim. 'Hello!'

'Hello,' she said and joined him on the path to the house. They might have been two acquaintances bumping into each other in Merrivale High Street. 'Are you better?' asked Tina.

'Yes,' said Tim, wanting to feel her hand in his, yet at the same time shrinking from her as though from contamination. He loathed her and he loved her. He wanted her comfort. 'I am much better.'

They walked on slowly through the trees. Why was she alone? Where was Alexander? Might it not be true?

'Tim—' she said and stopped. They stood among the trees, Tina looking at the bark of one, Tim looking at her feet which showed grubbily through her sandals, and were scratched and bleeding.

'Tim—'

A lizard darted by Tina's feet.

'I want to go home,' she said it in a rush. 'Let's go home.' She turned to him to see his expression.

'Go home? Now?'

'Yes, I'm worried about Rick. I want to see Rick. We've been away two weeks, can't we—'

Tim stopped her talking by joyfully hugging her to him.

There were no explanations. Neither wanted to risk excavation into the other's motives. Merely they accepted with relief that they both wanted the same things—home and normality.

'There's a boat at four today,' said Tina.

'We'll catch it,' said Tim, and they hurried on towards the house. 'What about the others?'

'We'll say we had an urgent telegram. Measles, Rick.'

'Darling, I don't say it often enough. I love you.'

'I love you too.'

They began laughing, and ran to the house. There was no one there.

'Let's pack now and get to the town in good time,' said Tina and Tim agreed. They were both anxious to get away without seeing the rest of the party.

'We'll leave them a note.'

Tina began flinging clothes into their suitcase, with feverish haste and excitement. Tim found paper and pencil. 'What shall I say? Won't they think it odd?'

'And what about the tickets? The plane tickets. Don't we have a group ticket?'

'I can fix that in Athens with the agent.'

'And our bills here? We haven't settled up.'

'We'll do that in London.'

The thought of meeting the others again in London made them both silent. Tina had nearly finished packing, when Tim on the terrace caught sight of figures climbing over the stone wall from the beach. 'Hurry!' he called to Tina. 'They're coming.'

He thrust the note on the table in the main room, and went to help Tina shut the case. In desperate silence, without conferring. they got the case shut, picked up odd belongings, and rushed out of the house, crouched low not to be seen; down the steps and into the trees to the right of the house. They were only just in time. They managed to reach the cover of a particularly wide-trunked olive, before Paul and Margaret appeared at the foot of the steps. Paul had his arm around Margaret, and they were laughing and talking quietly, bumping against each other. Tim and Tina watched. Halfway up the steps Paul turned and kissed Margaret.

Tina drew in her breath sharply.

They now went into the house and after a moment Paul appeared on the terrace again and went into the kitchen. He came out, and called down towards the beach, 'No one here. O.K. if we—?'

Jake and Polly now appeared. 'Fine!' called Jake. He waited for Polly at the foot of the steps, and they began kissing. As Jake unhitched the strap of Polly's bikini, Tim and Tina turned away, and studied the bark of the tree before them. At last the two went on up the steps and into the house. Tim took Tina's hand and led her quietly away.

They didn't talk about what they had seen. They got to the town in silence, and went to the restaurant where they

171

had eaten breakfast their first morning. Tina couldn't eat any lunch; nor could she speak. Tim managed to eat his own large plate of spaghetti and mincemeat and hers as well.

Back at the house, they didn't discover the note until the evening.

'Oh heavens, look here!' cried Margaret, who had found it. 'The Blundens have left!'

'Good lord,' said Jake. 'Why? What's happened?'

'Measles. Ricky has measles.'

Paul, Polly and Jake gathered round the table to see the note, Alexander scratched a bite on his hand and Helga combed her hair in front of the heavy gilt-framed mirror.

'What a shame,' said Polly, when she'd read the note.

'I hope it's not serious,' said Helga.

'Oh no,' said Margaret, 'measles isn't serious.'

Alexander felt at last he was expected to comment. 'Oh,' he said glancing unseeingly at the note in Tim's writing. 'Oh dear.'

They settled down to enjoy the last week of their holiday.

Tim and Tina were back in Athens later that evening. The weight of the city, its traffic, crowds and cement, exerted pressure on their brief confederacy and they drifted apart again. This would have been the moment for re-establishing their marriage on the firmer basis of communication. If they had talked of their experiences, confessed, shouted, defended, burnt a little their relationship, perhaps they would have created something stronger. As it was, with pleasantly blank expressions on their faces, they booked into a hotel, and ate a meal, and undressed and went to bed, talking lightly of planes and tickets; and with concern of Rick, transferring the responsibility for their dramatic return to their son, as though he really had developed measles. It was as though nothing had happened whatsoever, the island and the Frises didn't exist, and again they were the Blundens of The Grove. And perhaps again, this was all to the good. Their marriage worked well enough, and would no doubt go on working at an even tempo; it had, after all, been proved strong enough, within its limitations.

Tim in bed, drew Tina towards him.

172

'I'm sorry, darling,' said Tina, withdrawing. In the dark-ness she patted his arm. 'It was—the others,' she said in explanation.

'Never mind,' said Tim. 'We'll be home soon.'

He was full of good resolutions. The next morning, he contacted the agent, and arranged the transfer of tickets quickly and efficiently, so that they were able to catch the midday flight back to London.

As the plane rose over the sea, Tina looked out towards the distant, invisible island, and thought of Alexander, with only slight revulsion and some guilt. Much later, she would trim and cut and elaborate the memory of her affair, and use it as a stiff drink in moments of depression.

As for Tim, he gazed straight ahead, intent on taking in the reality of his surroundings. The Olympic air hostess smiled down the aisle reassuringly, and began walking to-wards him. He noticed her legs; they were almost as slim and beautiful as Helga's. She paused at his seat, and said something to him in attractively Greek English.

Hello, he said sexily. . . .

A Selection of Popular Fiction from Sphere